Praise for Lori A. May's *The Profiler*

"Lori A. May writes a psychological thriller that
will have you turning pages even while chills chase
up your spine…. If you love a good mystery with
an action-packed plot and more twists and turns
than a roller coaster, pick this one up today."
—Cathy Cody, *Romance Junkies*

"…action, mystery, deception and growth….
The story will keep you glued to the pages as you
turn them to find out what will happen next…."
—Pam Clifton, *A Romance Review*

* * *

"Severo, what the hell are you doing? Didn't I tell you not to follow me?"

But as his shadow moves from the backdrop of the
sun, clarifying his silhouette, his shoulder width is
different from what I expect. This is not Severo.

He raises a hand, revealing a container of
kerosene. He angles the container downward and
fuel drizzles into the room. "Revenge. I'm sure
you can understand that, Angie."

He pulls a lighter from his pocket. As I scramble
to grasp hold of my fallen gun, a blow finds its
way to my head, and the shadows stop.

Dear Reader,

What's in *your* beach bag this season? August is heating up, and here at Bombshell we've got four must-read stories to make your summer special.

Rising-star Rachel Caine brings you the first book in her RED LETTER DAYS miniseries, *Devil's Bargain*. An ex-cop makes a deal with an anonymous benefactor to start her own detective agency, but there's a catch—any case that arrives via red envelope must take priority. If it doesn't, bad things happen....

Summer heats up in Africa when a park ranger intent on stopping poachers runs into a suspicious Texan with an attitude to match her own, in *Rare Breed* by Connie Hall. Wynne Sperling wants to protect the animals under her watch—will teaming up with this secretive stranger help her, or play into the hands of her enemies?

A hunt for missing oil assets puts crime-fighting CPA Whitney "Pink" Pearl in the line of fire when the money trail leads to a top secret CIA case, in *She's on the Money* by Stephanie Feagan. With an assassin on her tail and two men vying for her attention, Pink had better get her accounts in order....

It takes true grit to make it in the elite world of FBI criminal profilers, and Angie David has what it takes. But with her mentor looking over her shoulder and a serial killer intent on luring her to the dark side, she'll need a little something extra to make her case. Don't miss *The Profiler* by Lori A. May!

Please send your comments to me c/o Silhouette Books, 233 Broadway, Suite 1001, New York, NY 10279.

Best wishes,

Natashya Wilson

Natashya Wilson
Associate Senior Editor, Silhouette Bombshell

Please address questions and book requests to:
Silhouette Reader Service
U.S.: 3010 Walden Ave., P.O. Box 1325, Buffalo, NY 14269
Canadian: P.O. Box 609, Fort Erie, Ont. L2A 5X3

the profiler

LORI A. MAY

Silhouette®
BOMBSHELL™
Published by Silhouette Books
America's Publisher of Contemporary Romance

SILHOUETTE BOOKS

ISBN 0-373-51370-4

THE PROFILER

www.SilhouetteBombshell.com

Printed in U.S.A.

LORI A. MAY

began her writing career as a freelancer until one day she decided to aim for a higher word count. While creating thrilling dramas is her primary focus, she continues to pursue other literary interests, and her short fiction and poetry has been published in Canada and abroad by periodicals such as *The Claremont Review, Zygote* and *Coffee Press Journal*. Lori lives in Southwestern Ontario and more information about her writing may be found at her home on the Web: www.loriamay.com.

Thanks must first be given to Lynda Curnyn who offered encouragement and the first editorial eye in my Bombshell journey. Your kindness and support has never gone unnoticed, and I wish you the best of success forevermore.

To Natashya Wilson, who is not only a wonderful and attentive editor, but also shows such tremendous support in developing new authors. You are a gem, and I am honored to be working with you.

Without the support of my agent, Jay Poynor, who knows where I'd be? Jay, you are perhaps the most kind and generous person I have ever met. Many thanks for your hard work, luv.

To the countless Red Dress Ink authors who have provided words of wisdom and encouragement along the way, I must offer sincere thanks for your willingness to cheer on emerging authors. You ladies—and you know who you are—have my utmost respect and gratitude.

Exceptional thanks must go to Erica Orloff for friendship and professional guidance. This road would not be the same without you in the front seat.

Without the knowledge of Sandra De Salvo, I would have spent much more time researching the hard way. Thank you for your insight, suggestions and willingness to pick up the phone.

Much love to my family for your support and applause throughout the years. And to Zaida, for reminding me to laugh.

Chapter 1

I lean my forearms into the open car window to get a better look at him. He's clean shaven, wearing a pricey suit, and looks as though he could be my bank branch manager. But he's not.

Smoothing down my black, vampy skirt, I look at him with eager eyes. *"Wie hätten Sie's denn gern?"*

He unlocks the passenger door and tilts his head. "Get in."

Sliding into the plush seat, I take in the scent of bleach and notice the immaculate state of the interior. When someone's car is this clean, they have to be hiding something.

I fasten my seat belt and face him. In stunted, slow-motion English I repeat my question. "How would you like it?"

His eyes remain on the road as he pulls away from the corner. "I don't much care for small talk."

I nod my head silently. Traffic on the streets is sparse and the neighborhood is fast asleep at this hour—4:00 a.m. I guess even New York can have its quiet times. There's the odd cabbie in sight, but little action. But action's exactly what this man's looking for, and I plan on giving it to him.

He pulls into a parking lot outside of an old warehouse. Everyone knows the general atmosphere of the meatpacking district. For crack dealers and runaways it's a haven amid the streets' reality, but for guys like my john it brings a whole new meaning to hanging meat.

The Hudson's proximity lingers in the air, reminding me of the uncomplimentary reputation this area has come to possess with its history of criminal activity, where strangers seek solace in an abandoned corner of the city. The only remote sign of humanity, in a very generous definition, is the flock of hookers hanging out along the docks. This is a world far removed from Lower Manhattan, yet for someone decked out in Wall Street gear this man sure feels at home.

When he turns off the ignition, I wait for his movements before exiting the car. He's taller than I first noticed, and his walk is swift and rigid. Out of sight from catcalling workers, busy on the end of the night shift, my john maintains his focus on getting me indoors and to himself. Just as I suspected he would.

I follow him closely and when I reach his side, he grabs the back of my neck, guiding me into an entrance. With one hand, I reach to my necklace and feel the pendant resting against my throat. It's safely in place.

Inside the deserted warehouse, the man pushes me against the concrete wall. His force is powerful, and I do as he says.

He gestures while demanding, "Take off your shirt."

Though his voice at first sounds soft and almost gentle, it has depth to it, as though he is hiding years of being held in subordinate corporate disrespect. It's as though only now, here in this dark place, he is able to reach beyond his station in that other world, where bottom lines and cocktail parties regulate his worth.

I slide my blouse over my head and toss it to the side, careful not to disturb my pendant. With an aggressive shove, he presses his face into my neck, biting at my skin. I feel little shots of pain, but remain calm.

This place smells like death and urine.

It's disgusting. Evidence of this man's previous engagements are sparsely scattered throughout, proving he is no ladies' man. The floors are caked in mud, blood and piss, and I have to breathe conservatively to keep focused.

Rapidly, he scrapes his teeth against my flesh, biting into my bra to access my nipples. He won't be getting away with more than that today.

He holds me against the hard surface of the stained,

worn wall. With his eyes intent on my body and one hand placed on my head, he pushes me down so that I am eye level with his crotch.

I've never wanted to chomp down on something so badly.

"Do it," he says, unzipping his slacks. His voice is threatening, yet defensive, as though part of him cannot believe the words coming from his own lips. "And no spitting."

My pulse is quickening. I can feel my own heartbeat as I try not to struggle against his restraints. When I see his trademark tattoo, I know I'm in the right place at the right time. However much he might vacillate, hot one moment and cold the next, this man's final actions speak volumes about his struggle for power.

This shouldn't be taking so long.

"Open your mouth, bitch!" As if to emphasize his words, he slams the back of his hand against my face.

I instinctively fight back, scrambling to my feet to elbow him in the stomach. As I grab hold of his head and knock it against the cement wall, he fumbles for my hair and, with it, pulls my face close to his. His inner contradiction is officially over.

"You gonna do what I say or do I have to make it easier on you?" His two hands are cradling my neck, and I know that, with one quick twist, he could garner some animalistic satisfaction.

My eyes speak for me as I contain myself, and he licks the creased corner of his lips with pleasure as one of his manicured hands reaches behind him, only to return to my face, revealing an unusual weapon. He playfully slides the edge of his knife, unique with its hook-like point, down past my cleavage, and I brace myself, knowing this is the moment I've been waiting for.

My nervous perspiration feeds into his needs and, content with my display of fear, he slides me back into position, all the while keeping the knife's edge within an inch of my flesh.

I feel the skin of my knees wear against the friction of my latex-enhanced boots as I dutifully kneel on the pavement. He shoves his hips into my face, and I am fragments of an inch away from the infamous inked image of Zeus.

His moaning begins even before I move toward him. Leaning in closer, I slowly slide one hand into the lining of my thigh-high boot and feel the trigger of my Bauer .25. The man moves his groin into my face and I prepare to pull out the pistol.

"Put your hands up!"

As I hear the familiar voice from a cluttered corner of the warehouse, my blood ignites. With a sweep, I grab hold of the john's legs, tripping him to the floor to unleash his grasp on the knife, and aim my gun at his dick.

"You foreign bitch! You set me up!" Although he wriggles in my grip, having his crotch as my target keeps him in place.

With one eyebrow raised, I coyly lean forward and say, "The only thing foreign to me, pal, is how you've been able to get away with your bullshit for so long.

You got a thing for raping and gutting immigrant prostitutes? Not anymore. Your last victim gave away your trademark, *Zeus.*"

As I wrestle the man into place, I look to my mentor. "It's about time, Cain."

Approaching with his casual slouch, the old pro winks at me. "You wanna work the big time? Then you do it my way, Angie. I run the schedule. No matter whose dick is in your mouth."

"Very funny."

"Hey," Cain says with innocence, as though he had little choice in the matter, "we couldn't make a move on Zeus until we saw that knife. You know that, right? We had to be sure."

I know he's right, but his candor doesn't rub me well. With drops of blood sticking my skin to the lining of my boots, I return my focus to the perp.

Once the man's wrists are cuffed, I lean into his body before standing him up. Baring my teeth, I bite close enough to his face to make him wince, but far enough to keep my safety. For fun, I ask in German if he understands me. *"Verstehen Sie?"*

He starts in on a foulmouthed protest, but I bring a finger to my lips and calmly say, "Shh. You really should work on your manners."

He spits in my face, and I don't wipe it off.

"That's no way to treat a lady," I say, settling my eyes on his. "Especially one who's a federal agent. Asshole."

Two arresting suits take the captive from me, and only now do I wipe off the man's saliva.

"Hey, that's evidence," Cain jokes as I turn to face him. "Angie, kiddo. Do you have to get so riled up? He wasn't going anywhere. Not with this entourage."

"Well, what the hell took you so long? This thing not working?" I pull the pendant from my neck. "Or do you just like to hear me suffer?"

"You really want an answer to that?"

I chuck my pendant at Cain, and he picks the small, clear piece from its backing. The temporary wire is good for forty-eight hours, but it didn't seem to bring me much benefit in these last few minutes of socializing with my first assigned infamous criminal.

"Relax, Angie. You did good. We've been tracking this Zeus freak for some time, but it took you and your interchangeable nationality to nab him. You'll do just fine here in New York."

Cain tosses me my recently earned, gold FBI identification badge and a paper bag containing more preferable work clothing. He leads the rest of the investigators to the main attraction, and I step back to watch the famed profiler live up to his reputation.

One criminal down, countless more to go.

Just six days back in my hometown and I'm already jaded. But for me, returning to New York City means more than a paycheck.

"You clean up good, kid."

I eyeball Cain and reach for my coffee, contemplating the remaining hours of my elective double shift. No one wants to work on holidays, and I've quickly learned Thanksgiving is generally "volunteered" by singles such as myself. It's as though the world assumes a person has nothing to do on a holiday if there's no one to go home to. Whatever. It's just another shift, and I'm indifferent to what the calendar has to say.

I settle into paperwork, trying to produce order in my new work environment, though it's not so easy with Cain's files scattered throughout the office. Now that he no longer has this ten-by-ten-foot box to himself, I suppose the both of us will have to get used to sharing the quaint space. I just want to get some of the clutter organized this morning so I can get home before the Macy's parade kicks in and holiday hell breaks out on the streets.

Cain tosses a balled-up scrap of paper at me and says, "Angie, look pretty."

When I meet his eyes to give a few words of wisdom, I see we are no longer alone in Cain's twenty-third-floor office at 26 Federal Plaza.

"This is Detective Carson Severo from the Fifth Precinct, down on Elizabeth. My darling protégée, you are looking at one of NYPD's finest."

The detective dons a humble frown, but it does little to affect his overall appearance. He looks as though he's been on the job all night, too, but it doesn't bring him below nine on a scale of one to ten. Ten would be too assuming. Though one thing I can assume with ease is this boy is homebred Italian.

Severo extends his hand to shake mine and asks, "How are ya?" in just enough of an accent. My observation is confirmed.

I study his dark brown eyes, focus and reply. *"Molto bene, grazie."* His head tilts a little, and I can see his analytical senses are sizing me up.

In a cautious voice, he asks, *"Parla italiano?"*

"Un po'," I say, before returning my focus to the stacks of paper.

"Ignore her." Cain hands the detective a mug of black coffee. "Or she'll start in on Russian or Japanese next and we'll both be screwed."

The detective's brow rises. "Impressive."

"Yeah, she's got her mind set on grandiose things, all right. Got in on that Foreign Language Proficiency jazz they're doing in Quantico nowadays," Cain explains, and I try to ignore that I'm being talked about within hearing distance. "Anyways, good to see you. What brings ya by?"

I let my peripheral vision remain aware as to Severo's presence, but return intent on getting these files caught up. As soon as this report is out the door, so am I.

"Heard you got Zeus tonight. Figured I should drop by and extend my congrats."

Cain sets his ass on top of his desk, gently relaxing his posture into that casual, confident slouch I have seen on a daily basis. I've been in this office six days, but the old guy's habits are as easy to read as a pop-up book.

"My, oh my, news travels fast," he says, slurping at his office brew. "Sure as shit we did. Couldn't have done it, though, without this one," he adds, poking a finger in my direction.

"Is that so?"

I meet the detective's glance to measure his comment, but he simply offers me a friendly nod.

"Hell if I could pass as a foreign hooker." Cain's crusty laugh sends a shiver up my spine. He's a skilled profiler, but the guy could use some social skills. "My girl Angie's got what it takes, if you know what I mean."

I toss a discarded wet tea bag at my mentor, but it lands in a corner bucket containing Cain's dying six-foot-tall, leafy plant.

"Now that I think of it," Cain says, as he watches me stuff my file folders into an internal mail envelope, "maybe you can be of some assistance to me."

"How so?"

"I need to grease her up for the field, show her what New York is all about, from the gritty perspective, you know? Seems to me, with you dealing with a variety of crap on a daily basis, you might come across something meaty to share."

"I'm more of the finders, keepers theory, Cain. Unless something comes up that's task force related…"

"Ah, come on. I'm not talking about running off with your caseload, Detective." I watch as Cain jabs Severo in the side, and I wonder what is it that makes guys display camaraderie through physical force. "I'm just asking for a hand, is all."

I feel the detective's eyes on me as I shoulder my bag and prepare to head home. "But Cain—" he leans in, whispering to my mentor "—it looks to me like you'll need more than that."

"What do you think—carrots or corn?"

I don't wait for a reply. My stomach is alerting me of my hunger, and all I want is to wolf down this Thanksgiving spread and get back out there before the sun goes down. The nap did me good, but too many hours at home can lead to too much thought. And my mind's no place to wander on a holiday—not without my father in my life.

"Since you're not arguing, it's corn." The two plates are dressed as though our dinner is formal, but right here—the apartment I grew up in—it's always been casual. "Dinner's on!"

I set the food down and light a few candles to make this evening's meal ambient. With a little jazz in the background, reminding me of my father's favorite choice of music, I almost feel at home again. Though I've been back in the city for nearly a week, I have yet to unpack most of my things from Virginia and transform my teenage-style bedroom into one that will represent who I am now.

I'm itching to rediscover the neighborhood and absorb all the changes Chelsea has been through over the years. It was more than four years ago when I ventured off to Michigan to pursue my degree, and then went to Quantico for training. But now that I'm back to my native grounds, I want to dig my heels in deep and feel at home again.

It'll be no small feat, considering that the last time I lived here my father was alive. Getting past the hurt and anger will not be easy, especially surrounded by constant reminders of his existence. But I know he would have wanted me to live my life to the fullest. I'm going to do all I can to live up to his reputation and make him proud. Wherever he is.

Taking my seat, I hear the familiar footsteps approach. Welcoming my dinner partner, I return focus to the holiday meal. "My, you're a mighty fine fella. Thanks for joining me."

Muddy lifts his heavy body to the two-seater dining room table and I smooth down his wrinkles. The drool starts from his bloodhound folds, but I don't mind. It's in his nature. And he's been the best damn friend I've ever had.

Maybe this isn't your typical family meal for a holiday, but I've never lived in a Norman Rockwell portrait. Since Dad… Well, the family's not a big unit where I come from, so I make do with what and who I have.

As soon as I get settled, I'll be insisting Grandma David pack her things and move home from Detroit. I know returning to NYC will be painful, with so many reminders of what happened to my father within a stone's throw. But if I can keep that extra connection to him in any way possible, I will. Reuniting her to the city, now that I'm back, has to help in the healing process.

Hopefully, for both of us.

* * *

"Bless me, Father, for I have sinned."

"How long has it been since your last confession?"

With time to spare before my next shift, I've detoured to Gramercy Park for a moment of family nostalgia. I peer through the mesh window and hold up a plate of leftovers, still warm from the oven. "Ah, hell if I know. You hungry?"

"Angie! I did not see you so well."

Uncle Simon lets himself out into the open, widening his arms to grasp me in a hug. Forget the confession; the months have drifted by quickly since I last saw my father's brother. He and my grandmother are my only living relatives and I intend to keep closer contact with my uncle, now that I'm back in New York.

"I brought you some turkey—slightly burned—and some fixings," I say, handing him the container. "I figured you'd be here all night, blessing this and that for the holiday, but heck, even us solos need to eat, right?"

"Ah well, that's very fine of you to think of an old man. I am so sorry I could not join you at the apartment, but you know duty calls." His hands wave about, gesturing to the leftover evidence of the Gramercy Park holiday Mass. Between offering blessings and sharing prayers, he would have had his hands full, I know.

"No, I understand. I'm not really settled in yet, so I'd only embarrass myself with the mess I've made. I'll have you over real soon, though, okay?"

Simon nods his head as he leads me to take a seat beside him on a pew, and I let him refamiliarize himself with his niece. I have to do the same with him, as it's been way too long. As far as I can tell, though, this man has changed very little. He's thin, lanky and slightly hunched. His skin is pale and his features show his age, but I know his heart is still large with love.

"Your hair has grown long, I see." Simon's hand extends along my cheek, brushing thin fingers through my unruly hair and tucking the strands behind my ear. My current shoulder-length locks are usually pulled back into some makeshift do, but tonight they hang loosely.

The last time Simon would have seen me, at my father's funeral in July, my hair would have been cropped a bit shorter, making it easier to take care of during long days of training in Quantico. If I hadn't been smack-dab in the middle of starting my career as an agent with the FBI—engulfed in the tenth week of training—I wouldn't have left my uncle's side so soon.

It still stings that I had to make that choice. With the Bureau being so competitive, I didn't have much option but to promptly return to Quantico. Had I dropped out of the sixteen-week training program, there would be slim chance I could get back in, despite my top-notch proficiency levels.

"Angie, tell me. What day is it?"

I know this game all too well. It started when I was barely able to speak English, let alone Latin. *"Dies Iovis,"* I say, pleasing the frail man.

"Yes! It is Thursday. Oh, good for you, for keeping it up. You study hard?"

"When I can."

Although I can't use Latin on an everyday basis, my language skills have come in handy from time to time. Especially since it was my exceptional scoring on the Foreign Language Proficiency tests that moved me into the Special Agent training program. It also proved beneficial in third year for my internship with the FBI's National Center for Analysis of Violent Crime.

NCAVC likes to see well-rounded agents in the field, and I'm willing to use any skill I have to help my goal of becoming a profiler, even if it takes ten years to get into their elite Violent Criminal Apprehension Program. After all, my father worked with NCAVC for a time, and he was so honored when I decided to follow in his career path. His death just makes me want it more.

Simon studies my features and places a finger under my chin, bringing my eyes up to meet his. "You work so hard, my sweet. I can see that."

A small smile forces its way across my lips. "You know how it is. Never a dull moment."

Simon rests a palm on my shoulder and he looks at me, his blue-gray eyes growing soft with love and encouragement. "I know it's difficult for you, Angela. Your father, he was a good man. Such a strong man. He didn't deserve it. But you cannot feel guilty about not being here, you understand? Your father would be so proud of you."

"I know," I say, but keep my eyes low while trying not to dwell on the pain. I hate that my father was killed in the line of duty, but I'm even more angered that his death happened during my training. I know my father would be proud of me, but sometimes I wonder whether, if I hadn't left the city, our lives would've been different. If maybe he would still be alive.

"You are a wonderful, caring, smart girl, Angie. And a Special Agent! You couldn't have made your father any happier."

"I just wish… I just wish I had more time with him, ya know? After leaving for college, stopping by for holidays and special occasions…it wasn't enough. I should have been here more. I should have been here when he died."

Simon wraps his arms around me, and I let my body relax into his hug. If anyone understood the relationship between me and my father, it was Simon. The two of them prodded me to excel through my youthful education, prepping me for my future. My father, though, was the backbone of my training. Growing up, I spent every single day with him, and not one of those days went by without me learning something from him. Without his intensity and skills as a profiler, I would not be the person I am today.

"Oh, that kid!"

I follow my uncle's concerned look and spot a thin young man dashing out of the church with the sparse contents of the donation box.

"All the time, this kid taking from us!" My uncle's voice trails into the background as I bolt after the offender.

Outside the church, the kid stumbles into the damp streets, and I chase him through an alleyway leading to a small neighborhood park. I can't tell what he looks like or how old he is, as his hooded pullover conceals his face and the evening light is fading into darkness.

He treks down a sloped path, but I veer along the upper side of the bank, hoping to nab him from above. Darting past bushes and weathered trees, I kick into high gear and, when the timing is right, pounce down on him.

"Drop the money!" I yell.

The thief resists me, anxiously trying to slide away, but I place my booted foot on his chest and pin him to the cold earth.

I lean closer and with the barrel of my gun push the hood back from his face and see that he is just a kid. A teenager—maybe thirteen or fourteen—and obviously homeless. His skin is scaly with dirt, and his hair, apparently once greasy, is now dry and brittle.

"You think stealing from a church is going to help you?"

His eyes flicker back to me with fear and shame, and I don't know if I want to cuff the kid or take him home and clean him up. "That's not the way to do it, man."

His silence is unnerving, so I reach out a hand and pull him up from the ground. When he stands, he is a few inches shorter than I am, and I see the wear his clothes have been through. This, at the start of a winter.

The boy holds his wrists out in front of him, but I

pause. The obvious thing to do is take him in, but all that will do is punish him for looking after his own welfare.

Don't get me wrong; stealing is anything but acceptable. But I know these kids. They're not the ones who rob banks or assault people. They steal bread and blankets for their own survival.

He stares at me as I reach into my back pocket and hand him a tattered card detailing the services of a nearby shelter.

When I give him five bucks, I say, "This is your warning. I catch you stealing from anyone—and I mean anyone—ever again, you're going in. Got it?"

He nods his head and a single tear rolls down his cheek. "Now get on over to the shelter and tell them Angie sent you."

The kid's sea-blue eyes barely make contact with mine as his timid voice speaks. "Is this a friend of yours?"

I pause, caught off guard by the personal question.

It wasn't my intention to think of Denise. Not yet. But I guess by sending a needy kid her way, I guarantee she'll be thinking of me.

"Friend of the family," I say firmly, and then add, "She'll look after you for tonight and give you something to eat. Go on, get out of here."

The kid hightails it out of my sight, and I collect the loose change from the earth. There wasn't more than twenty bucks in the box, yet the kid was willing to take his chances for such a small amount. Probably had little choice.

For a moment, I let the evening wind push fallen leaves against my feet, let my body and mind settle into New York soil. The constant sounds of city traffic, the mixed aromas of ethnic eateries…it all funnels into faded memories of my youth, enlivening the forgotten shadows within my heart.

Denise.

I haven't given much thought to visiting her, but now that I've let her name enter my consciousness, I have no choice but to acknowledge her existence. The last time I saw her was at my father's funeral, and even then I paid little attention to the proximity of this woman.

A buoyant plastic grocery bag slaps against my calf and alerts me to reality. As I unwrap the garbage from my leg, my cell phone rings and I focus on the present.

"David."

"Angie," Cain says in his age-worn voice. "Meet me at the men's mission by St. Augustine's. Have I got a body for you."

Chapter 2

When the cabbie drops me off at the scene, Cain is standing outside the mission building with Detective Severo, who's talking to a middle-aged woman. I wasn't expecting to see him, and now that I do I'm curious as to why he's here.

"Nice Thanksgiving?" he asks as I step up to the curb outside the mission.

I shrug my shoulders, not interested in small talk. "Fine," I say. "Burned the turkey." Regret for confessing my culinary taboo immediately follows. Severo doesn't need to learn one of my flaws so easily, but it doesn't seem to faze him much.

"How ironic," he says, then lifts his cardboard take-out box of stale-looking nachos, offering me a sample.

Shaking my head, I step closer to Cain to see what's going on.

"Angie, thanks for getting over here quick. This is the housekeeper for the mission." I note her fearful eyes, desperate for answers to which I myself have no idea of questions. "She was checking on one of the resident spiritual advisors when she found him…. Hell, I'll let you have a look for yourself."

As I offer a meek smile to the lady, trying to provide comfort for something I don't yet understand, I notice the many guests of the mission. People are lined up outside the building, food in their hands, protective of what is likely the best meal they've had all week— or longer.

The building itself is plain and camouflaged with its unassuming exterior, only now it looks like a disco with the strobe lights of emergency vehicles dancing across its concrete exterior in the darkening night.

We climb the narrow staircase to the upper level, and I take in the stink of kerosene mixed with something more potent.

Burned human flesh.

Inside the advisor's room, dim in this evening light, I see the corpse propped upright in a wooden rocking chair.

One thing doesn't make sense. The room has no fire damage.

"Matthias Killarney. Fifty-two. Caucasian. Dead."

The monotone of Cain's voice signals the beginning of a long shift and I step closer to the body, interested to understand. A few investigators are rounding up forensic evidence and I'm careful not to step across their boundaries.

"This is Severo's deal," Cain says to me as I lean closer to the man's body, covering my nose and mouth with some gauze. "The detective and I were enjoying our own holiday feast of wings and nachos down at Dooly's Pub when he got called on this one. He was kind enough to invite us over to check it out. You know, so you can get your feet good and stuck in the mud."

"How considerate," I mumble, wondering how much Cain had to argue to convince the detective to extend that invitation. But I keep my focus on the crime scene.

The man is sitting in a firm position, placed in the wooden chair as though he were a puppet. Rigor mortis has reached its full extent, making the victim's posture as static and flexible as a brick. This condition can last anywhere from twelve to forty-eight hours, and may provide an estimated time of death for the crime scene unit and medical examiner.

At first glance, the room appears calm and untouched by any intruder, but trace will undoubtedly disprove that naive impression.

I step back from the body and pull the cloth from my face. Despite the stench, I need to breathe freely. "What do we know?"

Detective Severo flips open his notepad and runs through the time of discovery and a few comments from resident workers. "But most important, albeit obvious, this guy was set up here on display. We don't know where the actual crime took place yet, just that he was brought back to his home and propped up for someone to find. Excuse me a moment," he says, and I watch as he meets up with some of his teammates for a discussion.

Cain leads me back outside, letting Severo's team do their job. "The medical examiner will provide clues as to the fire. Whether this guy died in a blaze or what."

"Why would someone go through all that trouble?" I lean on a tree and watch as the detective makes his way to meet us outside. I look from him to Cain, realizing in some ways the two men are complete opposites, yet by some arguments they are one and the same.

Cain's hunched body, beaten with years and the streets, is deceiving. His appearance may be worn, but the profiler is like wine, only getting better with age. His exterior belies the solid, analytical man inside. His reputation alone…well, it's enough to make a rookie agent like me drool with envy.

Though Severo is much younger, Cain obviously has respect for him, so there must be worlds of experience beyond his facade.

Cain lights up a cigarette and peers at me with narrowed eyes. "You'd be surprised, kid. And that's for you to figure out, my little profiler in training."

"But burning this man, and then bringing him back here—especially seeing how this is a busy place this time of year—it's like he wanted to make a point. Why not just leave him at the original scene?" As I speak aloud, I find myself running the events through my mind, trying to make sense of them.

"The housekeeper says the last time anyone saw Killarney was yesterday afternoon. Wednesday," Severo interjects. "But anything could have happened overnight, when only resident staff are around and likely asleep. But, yeah, seems risky."

Before much silence has passed, Cain turns toward his car and motions for me to join him. "Come on, Angie. We'll let the detective do his job here. And Severo—you know where to find us. If you don't mind, once your CSU team cleans the place I'd like to give Angie here a chance to mull over the findings."

I slide into Cain's passenger seat and look back at Severo, who peers at me suspiciously before walking back to the mission.

"You know Detective Severo well?"

As we drive along the dimly lit street, spotted with decorations in preparation for the holiday season, I try to look occupied with my seat belt so Cain doesn't get any funny ideas as to my inquiry.

"Severo? Shit, we've had our moments."

He pulls up to a street corner deli cart, hops out to retrieve two extra-large coffees, then shuffles back to his seat before starting out on the road. I hold the take-out cups as Cain slides his seat belt over his chest.

"Ah, he's a pain in the ass sometimes. His bark is worse than his growl, though, that's for sure." I hand Cain a steamy cup to balance while driving. "Thing is, kid, working in this city is like fighting for your corner of the playground, ya know? Everyone has their turf and no one likes sharing the dirt. You better get used to that, and quick, too. Best advice I can give you is don't piss anyone off unless you have good reason."

"Nice," I say, vowing to remember that bit of insider knowledge. Quantico was definitely competitive, but Cain is making NYC sound like a battlefield.

"Don't get me wrong, Angie. The guy knows his stuff and he's a pro on the job, no argument there. He's a good guy to let loose and sling back a few beers with, too." Cain leans his head in my direction and briefly lifts his brows, then returns his focus to the road. "But his noggin… He got messed up by a dame and I think it's got him all in a bunch, you know?"

I nod and sip my coffee. Almost a week in his presence and the guy can't remember that I take cream, so the black liquid is a little harsh to the palate. As I swish the beverage in my mouth, letting it cool before swallowing, I try to imagine Severo in a relationship. Just doesn't seem to suit him.

Maybe his hard-to-read exterior is just a front. Guess I won't be playing poker with him anytime soon.

"Yeah, he got dumped, all right," Cain says, barely containing a tainted laugh. "She did a job on him, boy. Just a few days before the wedding, too."

The information jolts me, and I look to Cain for more.

"Ah, hell, everyone knew it was over months before she ditched him. He was just too stubborn to give up that easy. She was a detective, too. A real good one, I might add."

Cain reacts momentarily as a bump in the road causes coffee to spill onto his sleeve. After he licks his wrist, he continues. "She was offered a promotion. Well, a transfer and a promotion. I guess it came down to choosing one or the other. No way in hell Severo was going to move his ass out of the city."

"So she took the job?"

Cain hands me his cup as he parks the car in his designated spot outside 26 Federal Plaza, then takes it back from me before getting out of his seat. "Yup. The dumb schmuck was scrambling the week before the wedding to tell a hundred guests not to bother showing. Gotta love drama. I doubt he's ever really gotten over it."

I slam the door shut with my butt, coffee in hand, and walk with Cain to the entrance. "He still loves her?" I'm smug to think he can retain feelings for someone who humiliated him days before saying "I don't."

"Nah. I mean, I doubt he's ever gotten over a dame leaving him for a job." Cain stops at the double doors and looks at me, sort of surprised, and asks, "You mean, you haven't noticed?"

I shrug.

"He's got a chip on his shoulder about the whole thing. But he's a dedicated sap, whether with women or on the job, so whatever makes him tick is apparently working. Unlucky in love, but a damn good detective. Schmuck."

I tail Cain's echoing laughter through the white-walled halls of the New York FBI Field Office, ready to start in on our night of business. Cain has much to familiarize me with yet in the office I'll be calling home for at least four years. It's good to get the formalities over and done with so I know what to expect of my work environment…and of my coworkers.

Though I still can't shake the concept. Carson Severo hurt by love? Anything's possible. I guess it explains his suspicious glances toward me. Maybe he thinks I'm one of the bad guys. Then again, I've never been all that skilled at being good.

"Me llamo Denise. Tome asiento."

I keep my presence unknown, outside the reception window of the shelter, and listen to Denise welcome a new intake on this Friday morning. With only a few hours of sleep to my credit, curiosity couldn't keep me away before heading into work for my next twelve-hour shift.

The young Hispanic man takes a seat, as instructed, and allows the social worker to touch his shoulder. Despite my attitude toward her, I have to give Denise credit where it's due. She's mild mannered and truly attentive, giving strays and misfits comfort they can't find on the streets. But just because I respect her doesn't mean I have to accept her as a friend.

Even though I've never really welcomed her into my life, I suppose I can understand why my father was so enamored of her. She's a smart dresser and always smells like vanilla. Not like the simulated scents you can find at the perfume counters. More like Grandma's kitchen vanilla.

More important, at least to my father, would be Denise's ability to find the good in almost anyone. Her motherly approach to dealing with strangers in need of help must have melted my father's heart. I wasn't so quick to embrace her, though.

The newcomer catches my eye from inside the window, and Denise's gaze naturally follows his. I've been made.

The door swings open as I push through, and Denise offers a meek smile as she approaches.

"*Pase.* Come in." Her slender hand flows in the direction of an empty chair across from the man. I nod at him as I take a seat, and he asks Denise if I understand his language.

A broad, almost proud smile crosses her lips as she says, "*Sí, y también habla francés y portugués,*" letting him know I also speak French and Portuguese. To name a few.

I study his scarred face and he lowers his head. I don't know this man's misery, but he wears it full frontal.

I wait until his eyes again meet mine and say, "*Hola.*" It seems to lessen his shyness.

When I shake his hand, which he offers reluctantly, his skin is rough with calluses, and I feel for whatever unfortunate circumstance has brought him to this place.

Denise suggests Miguel follow a shelter volunteer to the kitchen and get something to eat, and when he does, we are left alone in the pastel-painted room.

"It's nice to see you," she says, retrieving a bottle of juice from the vending machine. "I half expected you would drop by, but I didn't want to get my hopes up."

I remember the thief I sent her yesterday and am glad he took my advice. "Is he still here?"

She nods her head but doesn't elaborate. Maybe she thinks she needs to protect him from the law. It doesn't matter. That's not why I came.

Now that I think of it, I'm not sure exactly why I bothered to stop in. I'd been carrying the shelter's business card in my pocket since arriving back in NYC, but I can't honestly say I planned on visiting Denise. Not this soon, anyway.

At least I have to work later. I can use that as an excuse to leave anytime I want. But Denise senses my unease, and when she speaks it's as though she's encouraging one of her clients to open up hidden wounds. Her voice is coated with sweetness, but the concern is evident.

"I see you have your badge now. Your father would be so pleased, Angela." Her smiling eyes measure me for a response as she continues. "It's hard to believe July is so far behind us now, isn't it? That's enough time to start healing. Or fester in pain. Which has it been?"

I don't want to be treated like a street kid. Actually, I'm not sure what I want. There's too much connection between the two of us to talk as strangers, yet this woman hardly knows me. And vice versa.

My momentary lapse of nostalgia has faded. "Look, Denise. I just came here to… Well, I don't know exactly why I came. I guess I wanted to see you were doing okay. And you are, so—"

As I get up to leave, Denise rushes to my side and gently wraps a hand around my arm. My nose takes in a waft of her feminine fragrance as she softly begs, "Please don't."

Sadness fills her brown-sugar eyes, and though I can relate, I don't want to share my pain with her. Not yet. I need to allow my feelings to settle on their own, before I can open up to a woman I never really took to in the first place.

I don't sit, but I let my shoulders release some tension and I look her in the eyes. "I can't. I'm not ready for this."

Her hands slip to her stomach, and she presses her palms to the tiny belly hidden under her sheath dress, emphasizing her emotions. "I miss him, too, Angie. But you have to let it go. You have to let him go."

She steps back, out of my immediate space, and looks me up and down as a mother would. Only she's not my mother.

"It was his job. His life," she begins. "And he was shot during a terrible, terrible accident. It shouldn't have happened. He didn't deserve it. No one does. But you have to let him go, Angie. You saw the reports yourself. He died while out there doing what he loved best— fighting for justice. You have to accept it and get on with your life. It's what he would have wanted for you."

They all make it sound so easy. Just accept his death and move on. I'm trying. Really, I am. There is nothing worse, however, than growing up to be just like my father only to have him miss out on everything he wanted to see me do.

I face Denise and release the cold words. "I have to go."

"Wait!" she says desperately, grabbing hold of my hand. I pause, my patience running low, and stare blankly at her with little curiosity as to why she is dragging out my stay.

"Please, Angel," she begs, and I cringe when I hear the pet name. No one except my father called me Angel, and hearing it now, from Denise, is like being sucker-punched without warning.

"I know you haven't always accepted me as part of your father's life. I don't blame you. The two of you were inseparable, like twins who have their own language. Believe me, it was hard on me, too. The two of you had something most people could never understand, and I respected that. It's what made you both so special."

It's true. Growing up as I did in a single-parent home, the relationship I had with my father was unique and indescribable, the passions of both of us revolving around solving crimes and understanding the motives of those who commit them.

"But you cannot remain chained to the past. I know you feel regret and sorrow for having to go back to your work, just as you need to feel guilty for leaving the city after Joshua's death. You mustn't, Angela. You must look toward your future now. It's what your father would have wanted you to do. You must let your heart begin to heal."

She means well, I know. Every word she utters about my father, though, reminds me of all that I have lost. And I don't need any more reminders. There are enough at home, on every street, with every breath I take.

"Goodbye, Denise." Her eyes moisten as I turn away, but I can't stay here.

They were involved for years. Her attachment to him is still clear, and the fact that she put up with me— the protective daughter—every step of the way…. But I'm just not ready to make friends with Denise. Accepting her condolences would mean accepting my father's death, and I'm not yet ready to do that.

As I exit the shelter, my cell phone vibrates against my hip and I'm surprised at the feeling. I must have leaned on it at some point, causing it to switch to an unobtrusive vibe.

"Angie, I've been trying to reach you. Where ya at?"

I peer at my watch and note I still have several hours before my shift officially starts. But apparently Cain enjoys shuffling the schedule. "I had an errand to run. What's up?"

Through the earpiece, I hear Cain exhale from a cigarette before he speaks. "I got something you'll wanna see."

"All right, all right. Where are you?"

Through his cursing and spitting sounds, I decode my destination. "Riverside and 112th? Why?"

"Angie, you're going to church."

Chapter 3

I hail a cab to the curb, and just as I am about to open the back door, my hand meets that of a stranger.

"Oh, sorry," I say, looking at the man, whom I gather is also leaving the shelter where Denise works. His clothing, specifically a tattered bomber jacket with the hood pulled over his head, and old worker-style jeans, looks frumpy and worn, clearly aged from the streets.

He quickly steps back to allow my entrance to the cab, and his slumped, limping body begins to walk away from me, the fabric of his jacket pocketing air with the wind that recently picked up. With December just around the corner, the city streets are no place to wander, and I get the feeling this man spends more time in alleyways than indoors.

"Hey, mister?" I call after him, my hand keeping the cab door open. "You take this one. It's okay."

He pivots slightly, taking his time to evaluate my offer, and I think of Cain awaiting my arrival. "Or better yet, we can share it on my dime. I'm going to Riverside and 112th. Does that work for you?"

I watch as he stands there, obviously debating my offer, and then gradually accepting it by walking toward me. I know the city is no place to pick up strangers, and maybe I shouldn't have offered. But my father taught me to accept people regardless of their position in life, and to not hold prejudice against those who are less fortunate than others.

Over the years, I've developed a soft spot for the homeless, poor and needy. This city, despite its magnitude, can be lonely for most of us, even on a good day, with countless strange faces walking by and in and out of our lives. For those with little hope, it must be so much worse.

I give the driver my directions and twist in my seat to face my fellow passenger, who smells faintly of cheap cologne and musty newspapers.

"Just tell him where you need to stop," I say, and his hooded head nods, acknowledging me without meeting my glance. Peeking out from the fabric are loose curls, mousy-brown hair long and matted, the streaks of gray evidence of his tired age. Some mystery is concealed by his bundled clothing, but it's not my business to ask.

"I can't believe winter is just about here." My small

talk may not offer much to this man, but at least it's keeping the quiet between us from turning into discomfort. "I just got back to the city after spending some time in Virginia. I forgot how cold it gets." Only a few states away, it's amazing what difference a few degrees makes once winter kicks in.

Thankfully, the stranger's hands are covered with woolly gloves, keeping his fingers protected against the weather. Today is bitterly cold, and though the sun shines on deceivingly, it wouldn't take much to lose body heat out in the wind. I can't imagine spending my days without the shelter of a warm home or even the comforts of a café.

My thoughts prompt me to reach into my wallet and hand this man a voucher for a free beverage at a coffee shop in my neighborhood. I doubt he ever hangs out in Chelsea, but who am I to judge? Maybe it'll add some warmth to his life, even if just for a few minutes.

His gloved hands wrap around the voucher, his covered fingers momentarily grazing mine, and he nods again. I have to wonder if he's shy and reserved, mute, or simply doesn't want to speak with me. But he shoves the coupon into the ragged pocket of his jeans and I have to leave the rest up to him.

Dialing some digits into my cell phone, I spare this stranger from any more useless chatter as I wait for my next-door neighbor to answer the phone. "Hey, Mrs. Schaeffer, it's Angie," I say when the widow answers. "Looks like I'm starting work earlier than expected, so

I was wondering if you'd be able to check on Muddy later this afternoon?"

"Sure, sure. That's fine, Angela. He's about due for a visit with me."

Her friendly voice brings a smile to my face, and I'm glad I can depend on her, knowing Muddy has a friend to walk his old bones around the neighborhood block. After all, it was she who took care of Muddy during the months between my father's death and my return to New York. Said she liked the company in my father's absence.

"Thanks. I appreciate it."

We say goodbye and I tuck my cell phone back into its cradle against my hip.

"This is good here," I say to the cabbie, seeing our approach to the cathedral across the street. I hand the driver twice as much as I need to.

"Drop him wherever he wants to go," I say, trying to make eye contact with the stranger, to no avail. He modestly turns his head a little to the left, away from me, so I simply wish him well. "Stay warm."

Before I shut the door, however, the man leans across the back seat, reaching to give me something. His cupped hand contains a wooden rosary, but I shake my head at him. "Oh, no, thank you. But I'm not actually going to church."

He persists, shoving his cupped hand toward me, and I don't want to be rude so I take the beads from him. "Thank you."

I watch as the cab peels off from the corner with the

strange man sitting in the back seat, and I slip the wooden beads into my coat pocket, not knowing what I'll ever do with them. Hailing Mary just ain't my style.

As I cross the street, I spot Detective Severo standing tall atop a hill that acts as a gateway to the historic place of worship. Despite his angelic smile, he looks more like a devil with those dark tinted shades.

"This way, Agent."

I follow his lead across the brown grass of the cathedral yard, pushing thoughts of Denise out of my head. Maybe it was too soon to visit her, though I'm glad I at least got it out of the way. My duty, as the daughter of the man she loved, is now fulfilled. There will be no need to visit her again anytime soon.

With my focus returning to the task at hand, I shorten the distance between me and Severo, but maintain a six-foot separation. I notice the detective is not dressed formally, but has casual gear on—cargos and a light sports jacket. Not a bad rear view, either.

As we hike down the slope, I see Cain hanging out by a decaying water fountain, grumbling some sort of vulgarity about the scene, but I'm not yet sure what the issue is.

I can't see much of anything in the glaring sunshine streaming through the leafless trees and shrubbery of this landscaped yard. "I'm here. What's the deal?"

"Looks like this is it, Angie. The scene where our spiritual advisor guy got barbecued."

Detective Severo leans against a concrete statue of Christ and gives me more to work with. "The landscaper thought something smelled a little funky when he was taking care of the courtyard this morning. When he saw the lock on the tomb had been busted, I got called in to check it out. Since Cain wants you to see the forensic reports on Killarney, I figured I'd go one step further and invite you to the point of origin."

He gestures to the west and I follow his movement to see where the rest of his team is working. Beyond the footpath, there's a door propped open in the earthen bank, accessing an underground staircase.

"They used to use it for cremation, so it's fireproof down there. Now, though, it acts as a sightseeing highlight." Severo hands me a tattered brochure outlining the tourist attractions of this 120-year-old masterpiece. "Seems kind of grotesque, but hey, whadda I know?"

The promotional pamphlet describes the former methods of burial and gives detailed explanations of cremation history. Like I need to see the accompanying photos.

"Anyways," Severo adds, "the place has been used recently, and that's what set off Mr. Dunbar."

"The groundskeeper?"

"He prefers landscape technician," Cain says with a smug chuckle. "Gardener's more like it."

As Severo leads us along the path, Cain takes on a more serious tone, prepping me for the scene. "Now, Angie, you're going to see some pretty freaky shit out in the field, so go easy and take it one step at a time. It'll take some getting used to. But NCAVC doesn't accept just anybody, ya know. The only way to get quality field experience is to get tangled right up in its disgusting face, okay?"

Cain's got a point. Since I was placed at the Virginia field office for only a few months—until Cain agreed to work with me, allowing for my placement in New York—there was little opportunity to get anything solid accomplished. In order for NCAVC to take me on as a candidate for the profiling program, I need to do a lot more in these next few years with my mentor to attract their attention. That's why I agreed to work with the well-respected, though sometimes socially dysfunctional, Special Agent Marcus Cain.

"So is NYPD handing this one over?"

Severo looks at me as though I've just threatened his life. "I wouldn't get too excited, Agent. I'm just doing Cain a favor. Ran it by my captain, and he didn't have any problems with me bringing Cain along. Who knows, I might even learn a thing or two from the old master."

My gaze narrows on Severo's deep-set eyes. Amid the late autumn landscape and the increasingly cool breeze, this hotshot looks fearless. Which makes me very curious as to who he is.

"Why would you bother doing this for Cain?"

I notice my mentor has moved on down the path, and I don't feel my question will bring any immediate falsity.

"We have a history, having worked together on a multiunit task force. He's a good guy. He wants to find something juicy where you can get some field experience, so why should I argue? What the hell? Maybe he knows a thing or two about God."

"I highly doubt it." Cain just doesn't seem the type to know anything more than a few variations of blasphemy. "But what about you, Detective? Are you not a God-fearing man?"

Severo nearly spits when he says, "Phsts! Yeah, right. I go to church on Sundays and pray every night."

As he continues toward the scene, I follow at his side and offer a few words of advice. "Well, maybe you should. From what I can tell, you're no angel."

He turns his face to the side, and just the corner of his lips curl before he comes back at me. "And you are?"

"Hey!"

Detective Severo and I both turn our attention to Cain, who appears bored and bent with frustration.

"Can we please get on with this? I'd like to retire soon."

A genuine laugh escapes Severo for the first time and it surprises me a little. They say you can judge people by their laughter, and if that's the case, my guess is Severo has a softer side I haven't yet seen.

Yet? Hell, I doubt I ever will. Not with that chip on his shoulder protecting him from evil.

Cain's hollering about picking up the slack, and Severo shouts, *"Per l'amor di Dio!"*

I laugh. "So you do believe in God?" I ask, eyeing him playfully.

Severo seems almost disappointed when he looks at me. "Oh, right, I forgot you understand Italian."

"Among other things." In my delivery there is a little bit of flirtation even I wasn't expecting.

Cain mutters, "Christ almighty," as we reach his side, before venturing down to the pit of the tomb. Even though he is referring to me and Severo, when I enter the burial site I feel like whispering blasphemies of my own.

"What is that smell?"

"Eh, didn't I tell you?" Cain chuckles, handing me some gauze to cover my nose. "You should recognize it from the men's mission, only it's a bit more potent here. Burned human flesh, my dear. Ten times worse than animals, and all the more horrifying to look at." At least with the body placed at a different scene I don't have to deal with visuals and smell all in one take.

"The church once used this?" I can hardly believe it when I see the timeworn ruins. The place is like a catacomb, only scarier due to the knowledge of what this labyrinth of rooms was used for.

Inside the main chamber, there are countless burn marks on the broken concrete, and the stench seems more than a century old. A path winds on to smaller rooms under the earth, and even though this is New York City, I feel as though I've been transported through time to a more dark and sinister world. One that is consumed by death.

"Watch it. Ya don't wanna compromise the scene, Angie," Cain says, holding me behind the yellow tape. "You trying to make fast enemies with the CSU?"

I look on as the forensics team begins to separate

trace evidence from useless material, and am amazed how decisive they are in their actions. To tell one piece of dirt from another and know for certain it is a crucial piece of evidence takes skill and dedication. Not to mention a great deal of patience.

"So this is where Matthias Killarney was killed?" I ask, wanting to know what connects the two scenes.

"It seems so, but we'll find out for certain," Cain says, pointing to the forensics experts. "They'll take this stuff to the lab and once they're on to something, we'll have a look and see what we can do to get you some profiling experience, kiddo."

I hate that he calls me that. Especially in front of Severo. I realize Cain has taken me under his wing, and for that I'm eternally grateful. But the last thing I want is some detective thinking I'm inferior.

I bring my focus back to this case, though, as I am anxious to prove my interest in profiling. Forensics will lead us to scientific answers, but I'm interested in fingering any indication of what sort of person does this to another. It's not every day a person is burned up in a crematorium. At least not with criminal intent.

As I let my eyes drift along the walls, my attention is quickly diverted by a small carving in the concrete to my left. It's Latin.

"In nomine Dei."

Cain looks at me quizzically, shaking his head. "Angie, can't you stick to one freakin' language when you're around me?"

But when I point to my findings, the Cain I know

as a serious and effective profiler returns, and his badass, bad-attitude exterior leaves. "What is it?"

I scan the walls to see if there's more to decode, but finding nothing, I explain. "It's Latin, meaning 'In the name of God.'"

Severo steps closer to the wall, and thereby closer to me. I feel his breath cross my shoulder as he inspects the carving, and briefly, I am caught in his scent. Man. Masculine.

In just enough of a whisper to keep the detective close, I ask, "Now who knows a thing or two about God?"

"Looks fresh, too," he says, breaking eye contact and taking a step back from me. He signals to the photographer and leads us aside. "Well, folks, I think we may have ourselves a note. Let's say we get out of CSU's way and wait for the lab to fill us in on the findings."

As we exit the tomb, I begin to tail Cain back to the road, then I spot some movement in one of the ill-tended gardens. When I spy a man in his twenties looking perfectly suspicious, my hand slides down my side toward my holster.

The movement prompts him to flee.

"Stop! FBI!"

I pick up speed, hurtling over bushes and forensics gear, passing the groundskeeper and Severo. Tree branches bat against my cheeks as I snake in and out of the brush.

"FBI! Stop!"

The man continues on, hopping over stone carvings and winding along pathways. The garden is a maze and, clearly, this guy knows it well.

I race forward, gaining on the man, and vaguely hear Severo trailing behind me. His voice warps through the air but I ignore it.

When I see the man hop the fence separating the neighboring apartment building from the church property, I scramble under the wire to make time.

He turns back to check our distance, and with the twist in his body, loses ground and tumbles into a ditch.

"Lemme see your hands!" As I close in on the guy, he gets up and begins to bolt, but I make it to his side just in time.

He swats at me with fury and I duck my head, then hook a foot behind his knee to pull him down. When he hits the ground, he swings his leg and nearly knocks me on my face, but I quickly leap up and hop over it.

Still standing, I pull the man up by the collar of his jacket, and when I do, he uppercuts me and doesn't miss.

The hit doesn't slow me, but it does bring his body closer to mine. I don't miss a beat, wrapping my left arm around his neck in a choke hold while he writhes about, trying to get free.

I slam him against the fence and lean into him, ready to snag him with my cuffs, despite his slippery attempts to escape. One of his arms loosens as I reach to my side, and within a heartbeat I see the knife he has pulled from his pocket. I slide an inch to escape his swift swipe, but when the gunshot goes off it alarms me, and the guy wriggles from my grasp, dropping his weapon as he runs.

"What the hell d'ya do that for?" I yell at Severo, while speeding down the grassy slope.

Severo yells some explanation as to his tactics of protecting me from the knife, but I ignore his annoyance.

Beyond the apartment building's entrance, I see a tunnel leading to the underground garage. The hunted man darts in, and I run to the opposite side, where the garage roof meets the hill of the cathedral's garden.

Severo is yelling, "Angie!" He's trying to get me to follow him through the garage entrance, but I can see the fire escape exit protruding from the east side of the roof.

With my Bauer .25 in hand, safety off, I slow my pace as I walk along the garage roof. I listen closely, feeling the crisp late autumn air hitting my cheek.

As I expected, the man bolts up the fire escape ladder and onto the roof, facing me.

"Put your hands up!"

The guy is freaking out and shouting, "I didn't do shit, man! I didn't do nothing!" But no one innocent ever runs.

I go to his side, aiming my pistol, and cuff his wrists before walking him across the roof, back to the garden.

Severo meets up with me and I want to cuff him, too, but I just tilt my head and say, "You think I need you to protect me?"

The guy is read his rights, but it only takes a minute until the gardener runs up to Severo, who seems rather disgruntled at the moment.

"That's my boy! My boy don't do no wrong. Please!"

Severo wipes his brow—as if he worked up a sweat out there—and tells the old man, "That's for us to determine, Mr. Dunbar. Come on, you can ride with me and we'll get this sorted out."

"Eh, Severo," Cain says with a grimace, showing his smoke-stained teeth. "My girl Angie give you a run for your money out there, huh? Didn't I tell you…"

Severo smirks and turns away, while I yell at him, "Do you always shoot prematurely, Detective?"

He looks back to me, small beads of sweat trickling down his jawline. "Cute. Real cute."

"Where the hell did ya learn all that kung fu shit from?" Severo asks, handing me a foam cup with black coffee.

"Am I the only person in New York who uses cream?" I suck it up, though, and take in Severo's Fifth Precinct stomping grounds. I wouldn't say it's comparable to the Ritz, that's for sure. Especially in this contained interrogation room. You'd think we were the bad guys, being holed up in here, but Severo insisted it would provide the most quiet work space for now, instead of having us pile up around his desk in the open concept offices of the Elizabeth Street Detective Squad. I can't help but feel a little claustrophobic, though.

I find a can of no-name whitener and add a dose to my mug while I inform him, "That wasn't kung fu. Just common sense."

Severo drops into a plastic interrogation chair and eyes me. "Here I thought you were trained in some fancy-schmancy karate or something."

"I was." I take a seat opposite him and start peering through files I have yet to absorb. "Among other things."

"Like?"

I attempt to let my heavy sigh inform the detective I'm not particularly interested in swapping macho locker room talk, but he eggs me on.

"Krav Maga, hapkido, Jeet Kune Do. And a little Ninjitsu for good measure."

"Jesus. I don't even know what any of that is. Where'd you learn all that razzmatazz?"

My coffee is room temperature, but I'm getting heated. Especially after the gunshot stunt he pulled on the scene. I realize he suspected the guy was about to knife me, but I know what I'm doing, and I know what I'm capable of.

Hell, out of thousands of applicants for my term at Quantico, I was one of few to get accepted, and one of even less to earn a badge. I don't need a bodyguard or a babysitter. The detective will learn that soon enough on his own.

"My father. Mostly. Some in Quantico," I say, getting up to reheat my coffee. Severo rolled in a portable microwave cart and all we'd need to make us feel at home in this room, but frankly, I'd have preferred it if we ventured to the other side of Columbus Park to the Federal Plaza. I fare better on familiar ground. "I took a lot of classes, too, but my father's the one who got me interested in it. Knew his stuff."

"Does he kick ass, too?"

My eyes lower, but I'm quick to recover. It's not Severo's business and I don't want him—or anyone, for that matter—to see I'm still saddened by my father's death. My grief could be deemed as weakness, and I can't afford that interpretation.

"He's dead."

Severo starts to get up from his chair, but when my eyes focus on his, he realizes it's best to stay put. "Sorry. I didn't know. He wear a badge?"

For the sake of getting it out of the way, I provide enough information to satisfy his curiosity. "Fed. Damn good one, too." For a moment, I don't think of his death, but recall his living years. "Great one. Knew his shit. Not just martial arts, either. He was just so amazing. He could sniff out a killer like no one. Great instincts, great control. He was a profiler who knew how to hunt. He always got his way."

Severo snorts a chuckle and says, "Sounds like you."

"Well," I say, sipping at my now hot coffee, letting the stale taste distill my emotions. "He was a great mentor. I couldn't have asked for better training."

Before I take a seat across from the detective, I remove my Special Agent ID and wallet. Flopping into my seat, I give an annoyed sigh when Severo reaches across the table to inspect my credentials.

"Agent David?"

I lick my lips clean of the hot coffee. "What now?"

"Angela David?"

Severo's look is one of confusion, and I'm starting to relate to that emotion. "Yes." I speak slowly, making fun of the detective and his momentary lapse of sanity. "I am Angela David. Do you know who you are?"

"So your father—" as he ignores my sarcasm, the words come slowly from Severo "—was Joshua David?"

I stand up and grab my badge from the detective. "Did you know him?" My pulse increases as I watch for his reaction, but I have little patience left today. "Severo? Are you saying you knew my father?"

With his head shaking and a softer look on his face, the detective speaks in a calm voice. "Hey, cool down. I know of your father's reputation. I didn't know *him*. Not personally."

"But you knew enough to recognize his name."

Sitting back down, urged by Severo's hand wrapped around my arm, I look into his narrowed eyes to measure his sincerity.

"Of course I've heard of him, Angie. How could I not have? He had a reputation that could kick some serious ass around here. That's good to hear, right?"

"Yeah, no, of course that's good. It's just…strange, I guess."

I take a few deep breaths to put things into perspective. Of course he's heard of my father. He's a detective. Anyone on the job would have at least heard of Agent Joshua David. But any time a stranger mentions my dad, it's as though there is a piece of him left behind, for me to discover, and the feeling is bittersweet.

"Hey, it has to be hard. But bad shit happens to good people all the time. Part of the job. I know that doesn't make it any easier, but hey, my condolences. No wonder you're so feisty. You got some big shoes to fill."

Cain enters the room, so I pull my energy back to focusing on this case. I do have a lot to live up to, with my father's reputation, but it's Marcus Cain who's going to be there for me as I make the right moves to get into NCAVC.

Cain looks at each of us. "I guess we're up to our asses, uh?"

Severo nods his head knowingly, but I have to ask for clarification. My mind has too much new information to deal with to keep up with subtleties.

Cain leans on the table and explains. "The gardener's kid? Yeah, he was up to something, all right. But nothing to do with the case." He slides my files closer to him, glancing over the sparse paperwork. "Just a grower, is all. Planted pot in the garden where his pops wouldn't blow his cover, but he was all freaked out when he saw us. Too doped up to know we weren't DEA. Gotta feel bad for his pops, though. Didn't know what the hell to think of it. Poor sap."

"He's taken care of?" Severo asks, which I think is kind of sweet, being concerned for the unfortunate events the gardener had to go through today.

"He's gone. He's just relieved his kid's no murderer, ya know? Speaking of which, where we at?"

Severo straightens in his chair and spreads out the files before us. "It's all yours, Agent David." He lays the photos across the table for viewing. "Cain wants you assessing something scandalous, so I guess this is your lucky day."

I peer at the remains of the scene, captured on film, then look to Severo, knowing this is his case. Cain warned me to be mindful of the turf war, so I have to ask. "You really don't mind if I look?"

"Knock yourself out. Captain Delaney doesn't mind me sharing, and it's all right by me. I'm going to call the lab and see if any results have come in to verify these two scenes match up."

As I watch the detective pass through the door, Cain fills me in on the process. "Severo's got them looking at the bits of stone found on the body, to make sure it does come from the crematorium. It doesn't look like we'll get much other trace from that scene, which tells us what, kiddo?"

"The doer knew what he was doing."

"Right. Which doesn't always make it easy, but it most certainly makes it interesting," he says, before slurping coffee from his mug. Cain dabs at his chin with his cuffed sleeve and then glances at me. "You hurt?"

"Excuse me?"

"From that little chase out there with the gardener's kid. You got a bit of a bruise coming through," he says softly, placing the edge of his thumb against my chin, right where the kid landed an uppercut. "You know Severo was only trying to do right, out there. Don't be mad he tried to save your ass."

"Yeah, I know. I'm fine."

"Like I said, you can't be making enemies around here, so lighten up a little and try to warm up to the detective. He's a good guy with a good heart. He may seem like a horse's ass some days, but he's a team player. Give him a chance, Angie."

"I'll do my best," I say, taking in my first scolding.

"I hope so. Now, tell me what you see." Cain pushes aside his mug, making room to spread out the crime scene photos.

Inspecting them closely, I try to look beyond the obvious and open my mind to discovery. I realize Cain wants me to find my own way, which I appreciate. It's nice to have the opportunity to work with a reputable profiler, but it's even better when that person really accepts his position as mentor and doesn't incessantly impose his own theories. Guess I got lucky being matched up with Cain.

"Come on," he urges, tapping the photos. "What does Killarney's body tell you?"

I edge off of my seat to get closer to Cain as we review the black-and-whites. "He's burned."

"Look harder."

Cain slides a close-up of Matthias Killarney directly in front of me. I take in the details and am a little surprised. "His foot. It kind of looks like a stab wound."

"Now what would Killarney be doing with a stab wound?"

In the center of the victim's right foot is a delicate slice, easily made by a pocketknife or other small weapon. It's barely noticeable in the photo, but definitely strange.

"The killer messed up?"

"Are you asking me or telling me?" Cain retorts.

"I'm not sure," I say, which is true. It seems strange that the killer would make a superficial cut on the victim's foot. If he was burning the man to death, why bother?

As I get up to circle the table and walk through my thoughts, I see Severo outside the doorway, hanging up from his telephone conversation. He catches my stare when he enters the room, but Cain speaks before he does. "Well?"

The detective crosses his arms across his chest, looking to me first, then smiling at Cain. "They're still working on the bulk of things, but it looks like we'll have an ID."

"On the killer?" I ask, intrigued to peg our man.

"They pulled two sets of prints from the crematorium. My guess is when the killer was roasting our victim, he got caught in the flames and lost a little flesh of his own."

Cain gets up to stretch out his muscles. "Good job.

Did AFIS bring anything up?" I look to him, knowing I should recognize the acronym, but he quickly clarifies. "Automated Fingerprint Identification System."

"They're running the prints now," Severo says, topping up his stale office coffee. "If this guy's got priors, we'll get a name, address and anything else you want to know about him. Just one thing we need to figure out though… Why?"

Cain wraps an arm around my shoulders, grinning. "And that's where you come in, my dear protégée. Welcome to the land of profiling."

Chapter 4

Cain and Severo have gone to check on the AFIS results, so I take the opportunity to do what any self-respecting agent would do—spy on the competitor's turf.

Severo's desk is a mishmash of unruly paperwork, discarded fast-food containers and personal effects. I was hoping his work space would reveal more of his personality, and I can't say I'm disappointed.

A couple of coworkers nod at me, acknowledging my trespass into the apparent boys' club. I think one even puckers his lips in a chauvinistic display, but I just nod and say "How's it goin'?" before turning my back to their curiosity.

The beaten, old oak desk is layered with all the official stuff, but right now I'm more interested in the quirky photos, gadgets and stress relievers. As I lay a finger on the head of a windup toy chicken, it begins to peck with every stunted step of its mechanism. When its progress is halted by a glitter-trimmed picture frame, I lift the image to inspect it further.

The wooden square is decorated as though it's made for a child, but when I look into the young girl's eyes, I wonder if it was simply made by her, for Severo. A daughter? A friend? A friend's daughter? No identifying marks lead to an answer.

There's a stack of CDs on the corner of Severo's desk, yet I don't recognize any of the artists' names. Sea of Is. My Dad vs Yours. Mike O'Neill. Who are these bands? They're certainly not the tunes I was raised with.

My father found his passion with jazz and blues. Sunday breakfasts of sausage and eggs, when we would linger over the city stories found in newspapers, were accompanied by old records by Louis Armstrong, Thelonious Monk and Muddy Waters. Heck, Dad even named our dog after his favorite. It seemed to suit the bloodhound perfectly.

My memories are set aside as I inspect a group photo that undoubtedly provides pleasant memories for the detective. The group of men, all in casual attire, sit around a table with half-full glasses in what is apparently a neighborhood pub. Third from the left is Severo, giving a slightly inebriated grin to the camera.

They all seem a little happy and under the influence, if you ask me.

"You won't find a better group of guys," Severo says, startling me as he approaches, before eyeing the surrounding onlookers. "Unlike this crew. Don't you guys have work to do?"

Content with his boyish authority, Severo sidles up beside me, putting a finger to the glossy image as he begins to name the strangers. When his finger stops at the last man, he says, "And that there, well, that's our friend Cain."

I peer at the slightly younger version of my mentor and can't help but gawk. "Really? God, he's so… happy."

"It was a good day. We'd just cracked a very large case, and that night we all went out to celebrate. But I gather you figured out the celebration part."

Pushing a few unorganized stacks of files out of the way, I take a seat on the edge of his desk. "Now, this may seem like a dumb question, but I have to ask. How is it you and Cain work together so much? If I believed everything I saw on TV, I'd say the PD and the FBI don't always get along so well as the two of you. What gives?"

"The Violent Crime Task Force," he explains, flopping into a tattered chair identical to all others in this office. "The task force brings together some of the PD, a few feds, a sprinkle of DEA…a little bit of every law enforcement agency. It's the state's way of combating serious crime, in a very serious way. It's actually how I met Cain."

"So that explains why you feel so at home in the Plaza?"

"Yeah, you could say that. I get a few extra privileges, like being able to use the gym and some of the resources. Now how about you. Why'd you hook up with Cain?"

"He's the best," I state matter-of-factly. "He knows my history, my style. If it weren't for him, I might still be stuck in the Virginia office. But Cain agreed to be my mentor, and when the paperwork for my requested Hardship Transfer was approved, well, the rest is history."

"Hardship what?"

"The FBI has a bit more compassion than you might think, Detective. If an agent has a sick parent, or family emergency," I say, tapping the windup chicken for kicks, "they can transfer to an office closer to home, wherever that may be."

"So after your father died…"

"I wasn't officially an agent yet. But once I made it through training, I immediately asked to come to New York. No offense to Virginia, of course."

"Of course." Severo's breathy chuckle stirs the stale office air, and his intense eyes focus on mine for a moment. His irises are like liquid dark chocolate, glimmering, yet slowly cooling into an even darker center.

As Cain approaches us, Severo's warmth disappears as though a switch has been flicked. For the life of me, I can't put a finger on him. I wouldn't go so far as to say he's complex, but he certainly seems to have a few crossed wires. One minute he's mouthing off and shooting his gun at the sky, the next he's quiet and contemplative. I can't figure it out, but I guess we all have multiple dimensions to our personalities.

Standing in front of us now, Cain unpleasantly scratches his chest, letting an unruly hair or two peep through the cotton of his shirt. "It's for certain," he acknowledges, hands in his pockets as he teeters back and forth, rolling on the balls of his feet. "AFIS positively identified the mystery man from the crematorium. We got fingerprints, evidence, so now we go knock down our fire starter's door. Jean something or other."

"Forensics find anything else at the men's mission?"

"Nope. That place was clean as a baby's ass. We're dealing with someone who knows his stuff, gentlemen." My glance at Cain does little to shake him. I guess anyone with a badge is a man to him, so I let it slide.

The three of us gather our gear and head off to the identified address. I hop in with Cain, as usual, and I watch as the detective takes the lead in a sporty Jeep Liberty.

"What's the suspect's name? You said it was Jean?"

Keeping his left hand on the wheel, Cain slides some files to me and I sort through the findings. Jean La Roche.

"I gotta hand it to you, kiddo. Yeah, you got a long way to go for NCAVC, but you're doing all right. I imagine it's overwhelming to get back into the city and dive right in, but it's looking like I made a good choice."

"Thanks. I appreciate it, you know. Virginia was fine, and I'm sure I would have done okay there, but it was important that I come back here and be with my uncle."

"You all settled in?"

I grimace wryly as I look to my mentor. "Um, no? Let's just say there's lots to be done before I can have any company over. Between unpacking and figuring out what to do with some of my dad's old stuff, and me reuniting with Muddy…oh shit!"

"What?"

Fumbling for my cell phone, I gasp as I fiercely enter the digits. "Mrs. Schaeffer? Hi, it's Angie again," I say, and then cover the mouthpiece to explain to Cain, "I have to ask my neighbor to check on my dog."

Returning to Mrs. Schaeffer, I ask for the favor. "I'm real sorry to do this again, but it seems I'm going to be a while. Still. Again. I dunno. Would you mind—"

"Sure, sure, Angela. He's actually still with me, you know. Sleeping at the foot of my bed, if you can imagine," she says, happy to oblige.

"Yes, I can definitely imagine that. Thanks so much, again. I really do appreciate it."

Mrs. Schaeffer has been our neighbor for as long as I can remember, and she was all too pleased to find out I was moving back into the old apartment, instead of selling it off after my father died. We reside in a tiny, three apartment walk-up, with Mrs. Schaeffer living just below me on the second floor. It's quaint and small, and if you don't like your neighbor it can feel even smaller. But Mrs. Schaeffer, she's fantastic.

I didn't realize it at the time, growing up, but I'm so lucky she's always there. I love that dog about as much as my father did, and I hate that I am away from him so much. Once I get settled in, and between hot cases, it may not be so bad. In the meantime, though, she's really coming to the rescue for me. Well, for Muddy, too.

"You gave her a key?" Cain asks after I hang up.

"Actually, my father did years ago. It's tough being on the job and having a dog at home. But Mrs. Schaeffer loves Muddy and swears she looks forward to spending time with him."

Thoughts of my father push my gaze to the outside world passing us by. It's a crisp day, and the sun has faded behind a collection of dense clouds. The evening streets are occupied with New Yorkers bundled up in sweaters and jackets, oblivious to the crimes occurring around them just one day after eating their turkey and stuffing.

Sometimes I wish I felt how they do. Content to discover life through cafés and museums, rather than through corpses and trails of blood. But I'm like my father in more ways than one. I didn't just get his genes, I also inherited his passion for wanting to understand the motivations behind people's crimes.

For the first time in what seems like days, I notice my appearance in the reflection of the side-view mirror.

The sleepless hours have taken a toll and my skin has turned a muted color. Even my hazel eyes are looking a little foggy. I pull at my elastic hairpiece and tidy up the loose knot clinging low against my nape. With a few facial stretches, I try to bring some life back to my tired skin.

Cain lowers his foot to gain more speed, and I press back in the seat for stability. He takes corners as if the car's on rails. I know we're on our way to take someone down, but sometimes I have to question Cain's driving skills.

As we round a corner, the little keepsake picture frame dangling from Cain's rearview mirror sways violently. I hadn't really paid much attention to it before, but now that its swift movement has caught my eye, I have to ask.

"Who are they?"

"Ugh, well…they're my kids."

"What?" I take a good look at them, then twist in my seat to gaze at him full on as I analyze my mentor and this unexpected statement. "I didn't know you have kids."

Cain reaches a hand to steady the swaying photo, and clears his throat before smiling with pride. "Gregory is eleven and Gracie's nine. Good kids."

"Wow. I had no idea you were married."

"Were is right, kiddo. Got divorced nine years ago, one month after Gracie was born, in fact."

"I'm shocked." This is an understatement. I had no idea Cain had a family, as he hasn't brought them up in conversation this past week. During our telephone interview, Cain asked most of the questions, and though I had no reason to assume one way or the other, I just figured he must be a bachelor with the way he carries on. "What happened?"

Cain lights up a smoke and drags on it before rolling down his window a bit. "Shelley didn't like my job. Well, she did at first, mind you, 'cause she thought it was so damn exciting. Sure enough, though, she grew to hate it. Every bit of it. That included hating me, of course."

"I don't get it."

"Said it wasn't a suitable environment for raising kids. Maybe it was different in your home, what with you having an interest in it all, but Shelley hated me coming home to the kids after being out all night tracking down murderers and the like. Couldn't deal with it anymore, I guess."

"Sorry to hear that." Cain's right. It was different in my home, and I can't imagine growing up in any other environment. My father's livelihood was what drove him, pushed him to succeed in all other areas of his life, and I had utter respect for what he did out there on the streets. Though, from time to time, I do hear stories of how hard it is for some families. "That's sad. Do you see them? Your kids?"

"Every other weekend. I'm up for a visit this Sunday, in fact. It's not much, but I'll take it. They're off at some stuck-up preppy school learning how to be proper robots of society, and Shelley's shacked up with some theater snob or something. But I visit the kids when I'm allowed."

"She remarried?"

Cain's chuckle seems full of spite. "Hell, no. If she were to do that she wouldn't be able to rake in all this child support and alimony she gets from me. She's living it up on the Upper West Side with that hoity-toity director fellow, and I'm the one footing the bills. Must be nice. No one sure as hell is gonna do that for me, kiddo."

"Cain, I'm sorry. I had no idea. But your kids are lucky. It's good you make a point to visit them."

"Every kid needs a father," he says, extending a hand to briefly graze mine. "You know that. Damn shame, what happened to yours. Read all about it in your files. I mean, I didn't know the man personally, of course, but what a reputation."

"What did my file say?"

Smokers' cough lets loose before Cain clears his throat. "Ah, nothing I didn't already know. Just that your father was one of us and that he died working the streets. Good man. That's how I knew you'd be a good kid to take on. Hell if I want any newbie to deal with, ya know? I knew you were it the moment I saw Joshua David was your pops."

"Did it say much about…that day?"

"Just the formalities. Guess that wasn't any of my business to see. Course, it doesn't matter for picking a mentoring partner, now does it? I just needed to see what kind of person you were. What you were made of."

With Cain as my mentor, I'll get the proper guidance I need to pursue my career with NCAVC. My father spent most of his younger years working with NCAVC in the Behavioral Analysis Unit, until he and my mother returned to New York and he settled back into the NYC field office, years before I was born. Even though my intention is to work in a different division, with the Violent Criminal Apprehension Program at NCAVC, I aim to live up to his profiling reputation.

"I just hope it's not too much too soon," Cain says, and I listen to his well-meaning words. "It's tough to take, I bet, coming home without him here for you. You'll let me know, though, if you run into any personal troubles, right? You and I both know you're no good as an agent if your emotional health isn't centered."

I nod as Cain's eyes dart side to side. He tries to keep focused on the road ahead while offering support.

Though I smile, there's no way I can foretell what emotional baggage I bring to the table. Everywhere I look, every day that goes by, I think of my father. He's my blood. And it's not like I'm willing to forget him, or what happened to him. I suppose the trick will be finding the fine line between treasured memories and sanity.

Learning more about my mentor, though, finding out that he's a father and a former husband, makes me even more certain of my time with him. Cain has his own baggage in his personal life, but perhaps the two of us will somehow find a way for me to get past mine. And maybe, somehow, I can help him out, too.

We slam up against a curb and I spot Severo's black Jeep across the street. It looks like a Hollywood take-down with the sirens and lights flashing, but the neon dance is not coming from the detective's unmarked vehicle.

"What's all this?" Cain forces his rugged body out of the car and meets Detective Severo on the opposite sidewalk. The handful of emergency vehicles keeps my attention momentarily, but I am careful to bring my focus back to the team.

Severo looks as bewildered as we are. "I guess there's only one way to find out."

The three of us slide into the historic-looking elevator, complete with a wrought-iron gate, before its doors close and, unified, we stare at the illuminated numbers, counting along until we reach the sixth floor. When the doors open, we are welcomed into the foyer of a penthouse suite.

The building did look a little posh from the outset, but I had no idea what to expect once inside. I may be a born and bred New Yorker, but never have I visited such a pristine upper-class dwelling. My upbringing in Chelsea has seen an average-rated artsy neighborhood transform into a popular and stylish retreat, and though I have fond memories of my life there, its esthetics are still quite the opposite of this East Village suite.

Despite my immediate notice of the decor, it's the

commotion inside of the penthouse that maintains my interest.

"Lord almighty, what do we have here?" Cain grumbles. "Looks like a retirement party. I hope it's not in my honor."

My mentor's snicker is matched with a distasteful smirk from an approaching officer. "Cain." His eyes scan the three of us and then he begins to walk us in, but out of the way of the traffic. Two ambulance workers and a handful of cops are busying themselves in the apartment, and I can't help but feel we arrived at the party too late.

"The housekeeper called 911 when her employer started having some problems. Looks like a heart attack."

His head nods toward the living room, where I see an elderly man propped up in a wingback chair. Across from him, on an antique settee, sits an equally elderly woman, lips quivering, cheeks streaked by tears. "As you can see, there's nothing for you here."

"On the contrary," Cain interjects. "Your stiff may have been involved in a much more serious crime, so if you don't mind, McCabe, we'll make ourselves at home."

Cain and the officer—McCabe, I take it—start in on the details of what happened, and when my mentor nods, I take the sign as an okay to enter the heart of the scene. Severo walks alongside me as we move into the living room, and I ask if he knows the officer on duty.

"I may have seen him around. But I get the idea Cain knows him much better than I do."

Nodding, I retain focus on the body. This man's prints were found at the church cremation site, but it doesn't add up. His body is old and frail, and I know I shouldn't be making judgments based on that alone, but he just doesn't seem to be murderer material.

While Severo inspects the body, I decide I can no longer ignore the sobs coming from the housekeeper. Besides, she may have information critical to this case.

"Hi," I say softly, letting a gentle tone alert her to my presence. "Sorry about Mr. La Roche. I was wondering—"

Her sobs break off for a moment as she stutters, *"Je ne c-comprends pas."*

"Severo, she speaks French."

"What, is that not one of your mastered tongues?"

My amused glare meets his, but I return my attention to the housekeeper. She continues, without knowing whether or not I can understand her. *"Il sort de l'ordinaire…."*

"She said it was something out of the ordinary." I translate to the detective as the lady's words mix with choked tears. She's dressed well enough, but as I crouch at her side, I pick up a mixed odor of mothballs and floor wax. "She got a call from Mr. La Roche and knew something was wrong."

"J'ai pris un taxi…."

"She took a taxi and when she got here, he was ill. When she realized he was having heart problems, she called 911."

"….Je n'ai pas entendu ce qu'il a dit…."

"He was trying to tell her something, but she couldn't hear what he was saying…."

"*…la brûlure…*"

I shove Severo to the side, twisting to see the victim, as the housekeeper keeps talking in spurts. "She said he was burned. Look."

"He certainly is. Look at that." Severo inches in and hunches beside me as I inspect the burn marks along the man's arms and hands. His face has been touched as well, but the remainder of his body seems relatively unharmed.

Leaning on the chair's arm, Severo looks at me. "However, it's no surprise, considering we found his prints at the crematorium."

"Yeah," I say slowly, "but it doesn't make him a killer."

A throaty guffaw escapes from Severo. "So, what, you're deciding this guy had nothing to do with Killarney's murder?"

"I'm just saying—"

"His prints were there, David. Prints that came up in the database. He's got a record for something. So don't go thinking this man's an innocent bystander just because he seems old and harmless to you."

I shush Severo, seeing that the housekeeper is watching us, looking to us for an explanation. "Hey, she may not understand what you're saying, but that smart-ass tone of yours could show a bit more compassion, don't you think? Besides, the AFIS report said this man's history was purely petty crime. Nothing like murder."

Severo's brow scrunches up and for a second he looks at me analytically. His eyes scan my face and then focus in around my lips. I shift restlessly and his attention diverts back to the housekeeper.

"Ask her what La Roche did for a living."

She says, *"Un boulanger."*

I translate, "He's a baker."

"Ten guesses these burns aren't from making Bundt cake."

The heavy throat-clearing alerts me to Cain's proximity. "Well, what do we have here? You two look so cozy together."

I get up from my squat next to Severo and disregard Cain's observation. "The housekeeper can't understand English, so go easy on her. If you want to ask her something—"

"Yeah, yeah, you can translate. What about Mr. Crispy. What's the deal with our suspect?"

Severo takes a stance against the floor-to-ceiling drapes and surveys the room. "Well, Agent David doesn't want to believe he's our suspect."

Cain settles in beside the housekeeper, keeping his eyes on me. "Talk it out, Angie. Tell me what you think."

I lean closer to the baker and point to his aged body. "How could he manage to get himself home, let alone carry Killarney's dead body back to the men's mission?"

"Maybe that's what prompted his heart failure," Cain says.

Severo is shaking his head, obviously not seeing my point. "His prints were at the scene. Either willingly or not, this man was somehow involved in what went down at that church."

"So? Maybe this guy's not the murderer. Maybe La Roche saw something he shouldn't have and that's what got him in trouble."

Cain's cough-filled laugh bursts out, and the housekeeper jumps in alarm. Her puffy eyes zero in on him, but she soon slips back into quiet sobbing.

"She's got a point, slick. Good thinking, Angie. You tell him." He pushes himself up from the settee and surprises me when he hands a tissue to the elderly woman.

She offers meek thanks by saying, *"Merci infiniment, monsieur."*

Cain simply says, "Yeah, right back at ya," before meeting up with the approaching officer on duty.

I stare down Severo while Cain and McCabe exchange a few words, but the detective does little but shrug at me. Stubborn. I know Cain warned me to play nice with fellow law enforcers, but I expect the same respect from them. That includes Severo.

Cain calls for our attention and leads us out to the foyer. "McCabe's team needs to get to work and prep this guy for the medical examiner, so we gotta move on out of here, folks. He's agreed to let us know when trace is through. Maybe there's something we can put to use we're just not seeing yet."

Setting the pad of his gloved thumb on the elevator button, Cain looks at me and says, "You made a point, kiddo, but try to keep an open mind. When we get back we can start up a profiling chart and put some ideas together, but in the end the evidence will lead us to the truth."

We may not have any concrete answers until trace comes in, but I can't believe La Roche is the murderer. There's gotta be more to it.

The bell chimes as the elevator door slides open at the ground floor, and Severo informs us he's off to tend to some personal business. I am about to follow Cain when my cell rings.

"David."

"Angie? This is your uncle Simon. I need to see you."

I wave a hand to both Cain and the detective, alerting them to hold off departure for a moment. "What is it? Are you okay?"

Simon's breathing is rapid and I can sense tension on his end of the connection. "It is your grandmamma, Angie. She is not so well. Please come. Angie, please."

Chapter 5

"I can take you," Severo says, stepping off the sidewalk. My feet remain firmly planted as he slides into the driver's seat of his Jeep. "Where you need to go?" he asks through the window.

"Gramercy Park. I thought you had something else to do?"

"Midtown West, but what the hell."

Cain honks his car horn and yells at me through the open passenger-door window. "You coming or going, Angie?"

I look to Cain, then back at Severo. Waving off my mentor, I slide into the seat next to the detective and buckle up. My curiosity is too much to ignore. "Isn't that out of the way?"

"We got a bit of time before McCabe shares his findings. Once we're out of the Village, Gramercy Park awaits. And Midtown? Hell, I'll get there eventually," he says, shrugging with little care, even though in my books that's a bit more crosstown driving than necessary. His hand extends to the middle console and I watch as his rough fingers fumble across the stereo controls. "You mind?"

"Not at all," I say, then make a face when Severo finds some obscure sounding station. "Nice ride."

"Thanks. I got it, uh, got it back when I was engaged," he mumbles, obviously uneasy with the notion of sharing this personal history. "I figured it was my last chance to buy something purely for me, ya know? Never had a brand-new car before. Then again, never had a fiancée leave me, either."

"Cain mentioned it," I say, treading with caution. "Sorry to hear about that."

"Hey, shit happens. At least the Jeep's still here."

His chuckle warms the mood and I keep my eyes on the road ahead, trying to ignore his offbeat lip-synching. The light behind us from the setting sun reflects in the mirrors and I close my eyes for a moment, taking in the activities of the day.

"Your grandmother lives with your uncle?"

The detective's voice jolts me from my lapse of reality and I clear my throat. "No. She used to live in the city, but moved with me to Michigan when I went off to school. Said she wanted to stay with someone who reminded her of her youth."

"So why are we going to Gramercy Park?"

My hands fiddle with the stereo and I let my fingers slide along the controls, looking for anything to keep my mind off my family. There's no point in ignoring his questions, but I'm not too keen on sharing my life with the detective. He is, after all, still a stranger to me.

"That's where my uncle's church is. Besides him, my grandmother is my only living relative."

"He's a priest?"

"That's right. When I went to Quantico, my grandmother stayed in Michigan, thinking she would eventually move back to the city. But after my father died, she felt kind of weird about it so my uncle saw that she had all she needed in Detroit, including a homecare nurse. We had plans to move her in with me once I got settled, but who knows? Maybe she'll be here sooner than we anticipated."

"What about your mother?"

I take in a deep breath before answering. If I don't get this out of the way, it only means he'll ask again, and I'd rather not dwell on the past any more than I already do.

"She died shortly after I was born. They didn't find out she was sick until she started prenatal care, so my father only had so much warning that he was going to be a single parent. But between my father, my uncle and my grandmother, I didn't lack anything growing up," I say, making sure there is no room for Severo to pity my upbringing. "I'm not saying it wasn't hard at times. Once I got the itch for analyzing crime, though,

I began to spend more and more time with my father. But Gran was great. We couldn't have been any closer," I declare, then let out a light chuckle before adding, "Especially when she was my roommate in college."

"That'd be interesting." Trying to use the rearview mirror to his advantage, Severo slants his eyes, intent on watching me. With the fading light of day, his features appear gentler, more humane than they tend to be on the job. "Is it serious?"

"Time will tell." I'm careful not to mistake his curiosity for compassion. I can't say I know him well enough yet to decode his facial expressions.

Turning right onto the side street, the detective pulls into an empty space near the church doorway. Without hesitation, he hops out and runs around to open my door, which is something I didn't expect. "I'll stay here. You go on ahead."

As I enter the nave of the church, the collection of prayer candles provides enough light to illuminate my path. Stained glass windows with artwork representing various saints reflect hues of blues and greens, oranges and reds. The kaleidoscope of colors leads me to my uncle.

"Angie! It is so good to see you now."

Urging my uncle to take a seat, I sit beside him in an aged pew and await the news.

"She is not so well, your grandmamma. The nurse tell me she is weak and she needs to be with her family. I know it is sooner than you expected, Angie, but we can move her now, yes?"

I slide a hand through my uncle's thinning hair and rest my palm against the back of his neck. "Yes, of course, Uncle Simon. Right away."

My uncle's hunched shoulders relax, but his expression still harbors concern. "I will get the papers."

I watch as his frail frame exits to a side room, and I think for a moment what it would mean to lose my grandmother so soon after my father's death. I don't think I could bear it.

It's been hard on the whole family to deal with this pain in separate cities. I hope that being in New York together will bring us all comfort.

"This, Angie," Simon says as he steps toward me. "We can sign this and your grandmamma will come here, yes?"

Reviewing the documents Simon has provided for me, I agree that signing them will bring some resolution to our issue. "Her personal caregiver will handle the rest, Uncle. She will be here soon, and then we can see she has all she needs. Okay?"

"Yes, yes, Angie," he says, wrapping feeble arms around my waist. His hair smells like scalp dander, and I brush a stray hair to the side of his forehead. "You are such a good girl. Angie, you make me so proud."

I lift my uncle's chin and say, *"Gratulor,"* thanking him in Latin. His small grin is enough response for me, and so I kiss both of his hands before leaving.

Outside, the detective holds the passenger door open for me and I hop in, relieved I will soon see my grandmother.

"Everything's okay?"

"For now. Any word on La Roche yet?"

"Nah, it's too soon." Severo pulls a pack of gum from the console, removes a stick for himself, then hands me the package. "You like working around the clock, don't you?"

The tangy zest of cinnamon bursts on my tongue and my stomach reminds me I haven't eaten in several hours. And that's only if you count vending machine products as food.

"I do what it takes."

Driving with one hand on the wheel, Severo straightens his hair with his free hand, repeatedly checking his reflection in the mirror. Who is he trying to look good for? Certainly not for me, and I don't know that Cain really cares what the detective looks like.

Once his shirt is straightened, he returns both hands to the wheel, but darts his eyes about, keeping attention on both the road and our conversation.

"Whatever it takes, eh? So, what are you in for? Life?"

"Excuse me?"

The scent of cinnamon drifts through the air and my stomach grumbles with every chew. I lay a hand across my belly, aware of the little bursts of sound it's giving off to let me know fuel will soon be necessary.

"Cain said you had bigger plans. Tell me about them."

Shifting in my seat, I turn to watch Severo as he

quizzes me on my career path. I don't know if he's just making small talk to pass the time or if he's actually interested in the answers, but Midtown West is still a ways. Better to make small talk than drive in silence.

"Eventually, I want to train with the National Center for Analysis of Violent Crime in Virginia, get into profiling full-time. But that's quite a long way down the line. In the meantime, all I can do is prepare in the field and try not to do anything stupid."

Severo laughs so hard I have to ask, "What?"

"You were just saying earlier how happy you were to leave Virginia to come back to New York City. And here you are, already talking about going back to Virginia? You don't think that's funny?"

My smile is hard to repress. "Well, if you put it that way."

"So for now, Cain's primping you for the big time?"

"That's the plan." I open my window a tad, to take in some of the evening breeze. The air is mixed with the scents of fresh bread from all-night bakeries, damp brown leaves dancing in the wind, and fresh coffee. "I'll probably spend at least four years with Cain, and then…who knows. I could be in the city for a long time before NCAVC takes me on. If they ever do, that is."

"You know they will. With Cain as your mentor— a man who has a killer reputation among his peers— and your upbringing by your dad… Hell, Angie, profiling is in your pedigree."

"I guess it is," I say, realizing how good I've had it. Training is one thing, but being surrounded by others who share the passion is a definite bonus. "You have a lot of respect for Cain, don't you?"

A sarcastic gust of air escapes from Severo's lips and he gives a playful jab to my arm. "I don't know that I'd go that far. Nah, I'm kiddin' ya. He's a good guy when you get used to him. He can be a bit hard to take, you know, when you're just starting out with him. But he's been around the block, knows his stuff. Wouldn't be where he is today if he didn't."

"How long have you known him?"

"Oh, man. Lemme think." Severo takes a right and slows his speed before turning off the engine. "A few years now."

"This is your stop?"

"Yeah," he says, sliding off his seat belt, but staying in the vehicle to finish his story. "I think I first met Cain when he was at the Newark field office, before he transferred over to New York. But I didn't really get to know him like I do now until after he became part of the task force. Hell, that was why he hoofed it over here to begin with. Didn't want to say no to that kind of opportunity."

"Sounds intense."

"It can be. It certainly was at times. But like I told you in my office today, I couldn't have asked for a better group of guys to work with. Including Cain. Anyways, we're late."

He exits the car, and for a moment, I just sit and watch him walking around to my side of the vehicle and then opening the door for me.

"Late for what?"

"Come on. You'll see."

My seat belt retracts from my body and I check where we are: east of Eighth Avenue, in the heart of Midtown West. I spy a small café on the opposite side of the street. The sign for La Costa is lit by multicolored patio lanterns, and the path leading to its front door is vibrantly illuminated in similar fashion.

"What are we doing here?"

"I told you I had to make a stop. This is my stop."

Before setting the Jeep's alarm, the detective reaches to the back seat and pulls out a gift-wrapped box, decorated with pictures of balloons and teddy bears. I shrug, not sure what to think of Carson Severo, the gift, the restaurant. Any of it.

He crosses the street and I hesitate, but my curiosity gets the better of me and eventually I follow his lead. When I reach his side, he hands me the gift and then opens the door, letting me walk in first.

A roomful of people, varied in age, look up, and at first they have the same expression on their faces that I am wearing. Uncertainty. Once they see the detective step from behind me, however, the room explodes in happiness and cheerful bouts of praise and pleasantries.

Severo's face lights up with a spirit I haven't seen before, and when an elderly woman approaches him, his arms open wide in a generous hug.

"Madre!"

Oh my Lord, it's his mother. I have no choice but to

smile when the woman looks at me with big, welcoming eyes, and when she squeezes me with a friendly hug, I let my arms fall lightly onto her shoulders, not sure what else to do with them, while juggling the gift.

Severo nudges me in the side and beams with happiness. "Angie, this is my mother. That there is my sister Maria," he says, pointing to a petite, extremely pretty thirtysomething. His hand continues to motion across the room, attaching names to faces I will surely never remember. "This is my other sister, Frances. That's my little brother, Marco. And this…"

With his dramatic pause, I watch as Severo scoops his arms around a young girl, whose face I recognize from the glitter-decorated photo on his desk. "This one is special. This is my niece, Christina, and today she is eight years old."

Guess that answers my question.

He smothers her with goofy kisses and the young girl giggles with delight, obviously happy to see her uncle. I am utterly in shock.

"Angie, this is my family."

The many smiling faces look to me with welcoming nods and greetings. Though being stunned at the situation, I let my lips curl into a grin, and say hello as I shake hands with a number of individuals.

One of the sisters—Maria, I think—pulls a chair out for me and sets a glass of wine on the table. "Welcome to La Costa. It's very nice to meet one of Carson's friends."

"Thanks," I say, not sure whether or not I should

clarify how I fit into the detective's life. "This is a lovely place."

Maria leans back in a modest pose, her hands in the pockets of her feminine apron. "Oh, you're kind. It's the family's. Been around for a long time, getting passed down from generation to generation." Her palms extend to her lips and a slight blush creeps across her already pink cheeks. "My manners! You must be hungry. Antonio!"

I follow her glance and see a neatly dressed young man with a cane nod back to her. Within moments, he arrives at the table with a younger family member, and they set out the dinnerware. "You and Carson should eat. You've probably had a long day."

They don't know the half of it.

Detective Severo takes a seat beside me, and a group of his kin fill in the remaining empty seats. A number of plates, topped with entrées, are spread across the table and Severo looks at me with a genuine smile. "Eat up, Angie. I'm tired of your stomach talking dirty to me."

I'm a little embarrassed, as his niece is showering me with a gleaming grin and I don't want to be rude, but have to say, "I don't know that we have time for this."

His fork, half raised to his lips, pauses and he shakes his head at me. "Angie, we've been working since this morning. I think you have time to eat at least once during your shift. Coffee doesn't cut it. Eat up."

Despite my concern for getting back to the office before Cain has a full-on freak-out, I oblige and sweep the guilt from my mind. Once I do, I am able to take in the aromas of Mediterranean and Italian cuisine. Bow tie pasta with blackened chicken, a fancy salad featuring sun-dried tomatoes, grilled shrimp skewers and a variety of breads are scattered about on this large banquet table, and my senses are overwhelmed.

"This is fantastic," I say, almost speechless at the welcoming spread and even more welcoming hosts. *"Grazie."*

Maria generously fills my glass and sets the bottle of wine between myself and Severo. "So, tell me, brother. Did you have a good day today?"

Dabbing at my mouth with a linen serviette, I watch closely as Severo replies to his sister. "I think it was fairly productive. Wouldn't you agree?"

Not sure whether to elaborate or keep the details to myself, I nod my head and agree with the detective. I don't know if he dishes the dirt to his family or keeps them protected by not unleashing the truth about the city streets. It's not my call, so I'm happy to leave it at that.

Carson's mother leans from behind his chair and pinches his cheeks. In Italian, she asks him who the pretty lady is, and I can only assume she's referring to me, on account I'm the only stranger in the room.

"Ma, she understands Italian. And speaks it very well."

Her eyes widen with disbelief and so I say, *"Capisco,"* to confirm that, yes, I do in fact understand.

She gleefully cries, *"Bene! Bene!"* which is naturally followed by her pinching *my* cheeks.

"Madre…" Severo trails off, but his mother is clearly pleased he has found someone in his life who not only understands her son, but quite possibly the entire family. So long as she doesn't get any strange ideas.

"Antonio!" Maria calls out to the man with the cane, and he carries a large birthday cake to the table. It is well lit with rainbow-colored candles, spreading joy across the little girl's face.

She is propped up atop a chair, and once everyone surrounds the table, the family leads into the birthday song as the little girl watches the cake with eager eyes.

Amid the pleasant commotion, I become aware of my cell phone's drilling ring, and move away from the table to answer the call. "David."

"Angie? Mother of God, you get caught in a parade or something? What is all that?"

There is a narrow hallway leading to the restrooms, so I duck behind the wall and cover my left ear while listening to Cain on the other end of my phone. "It's nothing. What's up?"

"Zip. Not yet, anyway. McCabe's team won't have any results until the morning, kiddo, so there's no point in chasing our tails tonight."

Peeping my head around the corner, I see that Christina is opening her presents now, and Severo is awaiting his turn for his niece to unveil the contents of his gift.

"Okay, so where do we go from here?"

Cain exhales from what I gather is a cigarette and says, "Home, Angie. You know that place you've heard of but see so little of? Go get some rest. We'll meet in the morning."

"Okay, I'll let Severo know the news."

"Hey, whoa, hold on there. You still with him?"

I lean into the wall, watching as the detective hands over the well-decorated box to his niece. "Yeah, um, he was just making a stop."

Along the wallpapered hallway, framed photos of the family, from both inside the restaurant and out, are hung on display. I raise a finger to a large photo, capturing the memories of a family gathering not unlike the one I am witnessing in person.

In it, Severo is smiling broadly, his cheeks covered in some sort of sugar or icing, and hanging off his arm is an attractive woman who appears equally amused by the situation. I wonder if this is the one that got away? I wonder if he thinks of her still, and considers whether he made the right decision to let her go.

"You two ganging up on me? You're not up to no funny business, are ya?" His question trails into laughter, and I'd give him a look of disdain if he were in my presence.

"Yeah, that's what we're doing. Having fun without you. Good night, Cain."

"Smarty pants. Well, g'night, kiddo. See ya tomorrow."

As I close my cell phone and slide it into my back pocket, I realize despite my sarcasm toward Cain, I actually meant what I said. I'm having fun with Detective Severo.

When I return to the table, he pulls a chair out for me and hands me a piece of cake, which I gratefully accept. For not eating well during this last shift, I'm certainly making up for it now. And I don't mind one bit that it's all been so delicious and surrounded by pleasant company.

"That was Cain," I say, setting a serviette across my lap. "I'm off the hook for tonight."

He hunches close beside me. "No lab results yet?"

Shaking my head as I swallow a sizable portion of cake, I explain my recent conversation. "So I'm free until morning. Who says I don't have time off?"

His laughter is light, like his company is right now. I'm admittedly all too surprised at this softer side of Severo. Of course, we all have intricacies to our personalities that take time to be revealed, but I never would have pegged the detective as such a family oriented man. It's obvious now, though, in this roomful of people, that he has a home to come to when he needs it, and warm bodies to surround him when he needs them.

Though in this situation I could easily reflect on my own family, I choose not to. My loved ones will be reunited soon, and for now I can surround myself with Severo's family and borrow some of their abundant happiness.

"Angie," Severo says, leaning close so only I can hear his words. "This has been nice, hasn't it?"

"Indeed," I say, feeling the wine color my cheeks.

"Good. Come on. Let's get you home."

My eyes meet his as he stands above me now, pushing his arms into his jacket. When he reaches a hand to me, I protest. "But we have the night off."

"And we both need our sleep, Ang. This case is just getting started, and you need to be in top form. I can't have Cain blaming me when his protégée falls asleep on the job."

Severo's lighthearted laughter is a slap back to reality. I shouldn't be here, anyways. I should be unpacking and making a home out of what's left of my father's apartment. The detective probably just felt sorry for my family situation and felt obligated to entertain me among his own. Well, to hell with that.

"You're right," I say, sliding into my jacket and reaching into my pocket for my cell phone. "I'll call a cab."

"No, don't do that. I can take you home."

Ignoring him, I seek out his mother to say thank you and take my leave. I look back at the detective as he follows me to the door. Raising a hand to let him know I've made up my mind, I say, "Stay. I'll get my own way home. I can take care of myself," before letting the door close between us.

Chapter 6

"Perk up, kiddo. It's gonna be a long Saturday."

Cain's voice jolts me from my relaxed position—my head lying on my crossed arms on top of my desk. Maybe Severo was right. I do need my rest. After the long hours yesterday, followed by an early morning walk with Muddy around the block in the crisp air, I'm still a bit groggy.

Cain places a mug of steamy brew on my desk and I stretch to welcome the start of our day. "Did the lab results come in?"

The black coffee sends a jolt of caffeine through my veins and I set the mug back down to let it cool. A few taste buds have already grown numb, thanks to its steamy temperature.

Clearing his throat, Cain seats his butt on the corner of his desk, then sips at his own coffee. "Yes, and it's time to put your mind to work, Angie. That old guy, Jean, he was gonna kick the bucket any day, or so the M.E. says. Guy was running on a short stick, if you know what I mean." As he says this, he taps his index finger to his chest, letting me know the baker's heart wasn't ticking as well as it should.

"Then I was right. It's doubtful he carried Matthias Killarney to the men's mission?"

"It appears as such." He slides photos taken at the examination room in my direction, and I glance at the unfortunate evidence. Mr. La Roche somehow got tangled up in this mess, and it's our job to figure out the details. "So, kiddo, if La Roche didn't carry Killarney, we need to figure out who did."

Scanning the contents of the folders, I peruse the crime scene photos as Cain's attention drifts from me. I follow his glance as he says, "Morning, Detective."

Through the glass door leading to the office Cain and I share on the twenty-third floor of Federal Plaza, I notice Severo is carrying a carton of half-and-half. "Sorry I'm late. Had to make a stop at the market." He sets the cream on the service counter by our coffeemaker and winks at me.

I take in the gesture, but return to my analysis of the photos. "La Roche is still a victim, though, Cain. Even if he had a bad heart, we know he was in the crematorium."

Severo yawns as he helps himself to the coffee. "What's the word from the examiner?"

As Cain explains the M.E.'s findings, the three of us get comfy in the office as our day begins to unfold. I'm glad we opted to meet here, rather than in Severo's cramped quarters.

The detective asks Cain, "Lab uncover any more prints?"

"Nope. Which means the only patterns found at the crematorium belonged to our victims, Killarney and La Roche."

There is a serious glare in Severo's eyes as he stares at nothing in particular, focusing his thoughts on the crime. "Then it also means our yet-to-be-discovered doer seriously knows his shit. To leave no trace anywhere?"

"Exactly," Cain says, and in his voice I notice a switch in tone, as though this is the moment he's been waiting for. The moment where a case provides enough information to formulate opinions and create the initial impression of a profile.

"From where we're at—and Angie, listen up— here's what I figure." As Cain begins to deconstruct the making of our man, he scribbles down his thoughts as quickly as he speaks. "This guy is middle age—maybe late forties, but I'm thinking early fifties? I say that on account of the victims and their age range. There's something about this guy to make me think he wouldn't go outside of his own peer group to make his point. Caucasian, that's for sure. We can assume he's intelligent and we know he's exacting in what he does. And as you've pointed out, Detective, he knows what he's doing. That's not good news for us."

I keep my ears open to the two of them as they begin to debate the clues, but I multitask by reviewing the material submitted by the medical examiner. Various substances were found on the body, and consequently at the scene, but not one stands out to unleash our killer's MO.

Gasoline, oil, lighter fluid…all the usual ingredients an amateur arsonist would utilize. I focus on these details, crossing fingers that a theory will soon come to fruition. There is only one idea I cling to at the moment.

"He wanted them to suffer."

Cain swallows some of his hot beverage and turns his attention from Severo to me. "Go on."

"Well, he wasn't burning them to death." Looking to my mentor, I explain. "He burned them, yes. They died, yes. But he wasn't killing them by fire alone."

I stand and circle my desk as I think aloud. Removing the crematorium's historical brochure from a desk drawer, I hand it to Cain. "Somewhere in there it describes the cremation process. For a body to burn as it should, under normal cremation circumstances, the fire must reach 2,800 degrees Fahrenheit, and burn for about thirty minutes."

I top up my mug, adding a pleasant dose of cream— thanks to the detective—and lean against the service station ledge. "Gasoline will only reach 1,500 degrees."

Cain looks at me, nodding to confirm my observation. "It wouldn't be hot enough to destroy the bodies."

"So if he wanted to kill them and destroy all evidence," Severo adds, "gasoline was not the way to do it."

I keep my eyes off the detective, not wanting to acknowledge his understanding, after our personal misunderstanding last night. "The fire would damage them, and the smoke could kill them, but the flames alone would not disguise the crime."

"And," Severo adds, "we know Matthias Killarney only suffered fourth-degree burns. It wasn't hot enough."

"Generally speaking," Cain says, and both the detective and I watch as he talks out the science. "Seventy percent of a body's skin needs to burn before death will occur. Severo, check the report on Killarney. What were the readings on his carbon monoxide levels?"

Severo flips through a few pages. "Enough to suffocate."

"Exactly," I say, beginning to grasp the evidence. "Killarney was alive during this whole thing. He suffered fourth-degree burns, but it was the carbon monoxide that killed him."

"Yeah, but you're missing one point," Severo argues. "How did he get from the cremation pit to the men's mission? And what about La Roche? He survived through it. Made his way home, too. Explain that."

"Killarney was carried. The killer moved his body."

"Proof?" Severo asks, eyeing me, then my mentor.

"His room at the mission was untouched. No trace evidence, not a drop. We know that much. Had he died at his residence, after walking up those stairs, he would have left a trail for us to follow. He had to have been carried in there by someone who knew how to cover his tracks, like Cain said. Someone who knew what we'd be looking for."

"And La Roche?" Severo asks, helping himself to a refill. "He was alive. You said it yourself."

I pace back and forth, staying clear of the detective's path. "Yes, he was. But the M.E. confirmed that La Roche would have been on his way out anytime soon. He was old and frail, with a weak heart. Being in the pit with Killarney, and the killer, he would have suffered similar effects from the smoke, creating oxygen starvation. Even if he didn't get burned, the lack of air in his lungs would affect the ability of his heart to perform. Essentially, he was poisoned."

Cain sizes up my argument and watches me intently, eager for me to take the lead in the criminal diagnosis. "Okay, kiddo. Why would the killer let La Roche go? If he was stable enough to make it home, there was no way to tell if he'd have a heart attack or not. For all the killer could tell, La Roche could've lived, identified him and closed the case."

Picking at the dried plant leaves that hang over the coffee service area, I pose a theory. "Not if the killer knew him. Not if he knew what state La Roche's health was in."

"You think the killer knew Killarney, too?" Severo takes a seat next to Cain, and the two of them sit side by side as I continue to pace the office.

"Yes, and that explains how a baker and a priest end up in the cremation pit."

Cain lets out a hearty guffaw. "Sounds like a bad bar joke to me, Detective."

"And," Severo adds, "it doesn't seem provable, Agent. It just seems mildly plausible."

I lean against the plain white concrete wall and press out a few kinks from my spine, but my eyes remain steady on the detective. "Maybe. But as far as I can see, our killer had to have known that La Roche could only go so far without dying of somewhat natural causes."

"Unless the doer wanted to get caught." Severo and I both look to Cain when he says this.

I begin to tape up the photos along the concrete office walls, so we can clearly see what we're dealing with. "Why would he want to do that?"

"Angie, this is where profiling comes in. Could be this guy is up to something, has something to say. We don't know that yet. But they all have their games they like to play. They want us to be amused by what their wicked little minds can do."

I think back to the victimology classes at Quantico, describing just that—little clues left by the killer to taunt the investigators. But it doesn't seem our guy has left us much to work with at either scene.

Cain's cell phone rings and he steps into the hall to take the call, away from me and the detective. I dump the remainder of my room temperature coffee into the small, rusted sink and wash out the mug. Severo's throat clears and when I turn my head to face him, he is looking at me with wide eyes.

"You want to tell me what's going on?"

I set the mug upside down on a stiff paper towel. "What?"

"Last night. What was that? I could have taken you home, you know. You didn't need to walk out like that."

"And you didn't need to follow me, Detective. You think I wouldn't notice your Jeep trailing my cab?" I stare into his eyes as I wait for whatever lame excuse he can provide for his behavior.

After I left his family at La Costa last night, during my cab ride home to Chelsea from the Midtown West café, I realized I wasn't alone in my travels. Severo was trying his best to shadow my cabbie from a distance.

From his expression, I see he had hoped I didn't notice him last night. "I wanted to make sure you got home okay."

"I've already told you," I say, pushing unruly chunks of hair from my face, "I don't need you to protect me."

"Hell, I know that. And listen, I live in Hell's Kitchen. It's not like I was completely off track getting myself home. So don't be getting all hissy on me. It was late and it was the gentlemanly thing to do. My apologies for being chivalrous."

I'm not sure I need to explain my stubbornness to the detective, but when Cain reenters the room, I don't have to.

"Looks like we got a live one. Oh! Bad choice of words," he says, chuckling in between rough breaths. "Maybe not alive, but I bet we ought to check it out." With his eyebrows arched into evil giddiness, my mentor looks at me, then at Severo.

"Is it him?" the detective asks, as I wonder the same.

"Could be. Who knows. But this one was found with the good book in hand, so it's worth checking out."

I look to Cain for answers. "The Bible?"

My mentor winks at me, then shrugs as he says, "Is there any better book to die with, kiddo?"

Chapter 7

"Thomas Devlin," Cain says, nudging at the victim. "Some kids were trekking through the shortcut this morning and found him here, stuck like a pig."

My eyes trail the narrow path, which leads from the building to the parking lot. It's obviously worn with traffic, but doesn't appear to be a main access point to anything other than dumping bins.

We've gathered outside the City College campus of CUNY, just west of St. Nicholas Park in northern Manhattan, and the winter chill that was only yesterday playing in the air is now on full-time duty.

A group of teachers and students, bundled in jackets and scarves, linger in the distance outside the North Academic Center, trying to capture a look at the scene.

I'm surprised to see so many here on a Saturday morning, but apparently bright yellow caution tape has a way of drawing people in rather than keeping them away.

"Devlin taught night classes to continuing ed students," Cain reads from his notebook. "Guess last night was his final exam."

I lean over the body, which seems carelessly propped against the brick building, and take in the sight.

The victim's body is pierced through with four swords. From each direction, they point inward, as though he were attacked simultaneously by four different assailants.

"Got to hand it to the students," Severo says, stepping up beside me. "At least the scene doesn't appear to be compromised. Damn good thing no one around here collects swords."

"Probably didn't want to lose their course credit," Cain retorts, stepping aside for a CSU photographer.

"What was he a professor of?" I ask, wanting to understand more of this man's life, as it could help us solve his death.

Flipping through his notes, Cain reads off in a monotone drill. "English. Philosophy. History. Myths and legends. You name it. The guy was a regular brain-a-holic."

"Then why the Bible?" Severo asks to no one in particular.

Cain lights up a cigarette, but backs away from me

when I glance at him with distaste. His overcoat is undone and flaps in the breeze, exposing an untucked shirt.

I squat down beside the body and evaluate the visuals. "Maybe he used it in class. To some, the idea of God is a myth. Or maybe he was just a follower. Anyone talk to his students?"

"The school's gathering a list. They'll have it to us shortly." Cain leans on the wire fence, which is apparently meant to block off shortcutters from the path. It doesn't seem to be working, for the crisscrossed wires bend downward, creating enough space to step through.

Severo is peering at me over the rim of his sunglasses. In his dark shades and bulky winter clothing he looks sporty and cosmopolitan, and I try not to get caught up in his stare. A crime scene is nowhere to dissect the mixed emotions I have developed for him.

"Why'd we get the call?" I get back to my feet, closing my jacket tighter around me, protecting myself from the tunneling wind.

"I told my captain about the crematorium," Severo explains while walking around Devlin's body. "With that scene being at a church, and this guy being found with a Bible, Captain Delaney must have figured we'd be interested in checking it out."

I pace around the victim in turn, trying to view the corpse from varying angles. "But swords? Seems a bit extreme, doesn't it?"

"Choice of weapon can tell us a lot about the killer,

kiddo," Cain says, walking up to Devlin's body. "Not every day you see swords on the street. It has to mean something."

"Hopefully there's prints to be found," Severo adds, before pointing a gloved finger to one sword's entry point. "Or blood. Chances are the killer would have sliced himself by accident while sticking it to Devlin."

"I'll be right back," Cain says. I follow his movements as he meets an approaching middle-aged woman halfway and takes a small stack of papers from her. They exchange words, and when he returns to my side, he seems to have found some optimism.

"What's that?"

"List of the professor's students. But get this," Cain says, handing me a sheet of printed paper. "Devlin was teaching them about the Lord, all right. In his myths class—Angie, good call—they were studying religious ceremony, Christianity, cults, you name it."

"Good to know," I say, admittedly a little smug.

"It's not the same MO…but there is a small chance it's the same guy," Severo says, a frown showing his frustration.

I watch the emotions he reveals, as I still can't figure him out. For the most part, it seems Severo keeps his guard up while on the job, as any good cop would, but when I least expect it he warms up. Hell if I can figure it. But I don't have the time nor the energy to think about the detective's mood swings. There's a more important—albeit less attractive—body in front of me, calling for attention.

"Which means," Cain says, bringing my focus to him, "we either have someone who has a lot of personal enemies or…?"

I finish his sentence. "We have a serial on our hands."

Severo steps back, pulling his shades off to reveal the sincerity of his emotions. "Now wait just a minute. First off, let's keep our voices down so as not to alarm any of these people," he says in a hushed voice, nodding toward the loitering public. "Secondly, we can't be jumping to any conclusions that this is a serial. I'll buy into the theory our killer knew Killarney and La Roche, but there's nothing here yet to tie him to Devlin. And even if there is, I wouldn't say that qualifies as a serial."

"Why not?" I ask, sounding more defensive than I intended. I simply want to understand Severo's disbelief.

"By definition," he says, "serials don't do people they know. They find victims to fit the mold of whatever plan they have in mind. It's usually more of a wrong place, wrong time type of thing."

"I know that much, Detective. But what about the Bible? You think it's purely coincidence our other two vics were burned up at a church burial site, and this one here dies with the good book in hand? I don't think so."

"I love it!" Cain chuckles, jabbing me in the side. "Play devil's advocate, kiddo. Let your mind take you somewhere."

Though he's prodding me along, I'm not yet sure

my theories are tangible enough to share. But something in my gut tells me there's a connection among these three bodies, and my father always said, "If in doubt, follow your instincts." He knew what he was talking about, so I go with it.

"Okay. Remember what we found in the crematorium? The carving in Latin? *In nomine Dei.*"

The two of them look back to me and so I translate yet again, "In the name of God. Which should tell us the killer has some religious score to settle."

With doubt in his eyes, the detective gazes at me. "Yeah, but Agent David, if the killer is all about God, or whatever, he seems to be targeting the wrong men, as far as Killarney and Devlin go. They're believers, not pagans."

I slide my tongue between my lip and inner mouth, tracing my teeth with its tip. I smack my lips, while thinking of what the possible answers could be. "Perhaps you should be thinking inside out, Detective."

"Pardon me?"

"The number one thing I was taught in training is to identify with the killer, not with the victim."

"So," Cain interjects, pleased with my statement, "how does it add up, kiddo?"

"If I'm the killer and I'm after what appear to be God-fearing men, perhaps it is I who is the disbeliever."

With a nearly burned-out cigarette dangling from his lips, Cain puts his hands together and begins to clap. I'm sure he means well, but the gesture is a bit annoying. Even if I am right, there's no need to carry on like that.

"That's my girl, eh? Eh, Angie. You got some smarts up there," Cain says, waving in the direction of my head. "Detective? You gotta love this woman. She knows her stuff."

Severo snorts with little enthusiasm, then says, "Then our list of potential victims just got bigger. Besides, seems like a lame reason to kick off a killing spree. Because these men believe in God? There has to be more to it than that."

"Detective, I have no doubt," Cain says, drawing us out of the way for the CSU to get closer to the body. "But hopefully we find this guy soon so we can ask him in person."

"How are we going to do that?" I step back from the scene, letting the icy air chill my senses. "So far he's left nothing to lead us in the right direction. We've got three bodies within three days. Without trace to guide us, how will we find him?"

"He wants to be found, Angie," Cain says, motioning toward the CSU vans. "He wants us to know how smart he is for making us look like idiots. There's going to be something that leads us to him. For now, we work with what we got."

As we drift away from the scene, I spot Severo's Jeep parked along the roadside and think of the previous night. Less than twenty-four hours ago, I was sitting in his passenger seat chomping on a stick of cinnamon gum.

It wasn't necessarily the highlight of my day, but I can't help but feel a discomfort has grown between us, with the way we parted at the restaurant. Maybe I shouldn't have reacted so childishly last night, but I'd thought we were having a good time. Who knows. Perhaps the detective was right in calling it an early night.

I watch as he disarms the Jeep. "You want a lift?"

Cain eyes me as he continues on to his car, and I see a slight grin crease his cheeks. Great. Now my mentor's going to think something's up between me and the detective.

"Actually, no," I say, realizing I have an opportunity to investigate our most recent scene a little bit more. "Hey, Cain? You mind if I check on something in the library?"

He looks at me quizzically. "What are ya thinking?"

"I just want to look something up, and since I'm right here, I may as well. If there's time."

"Yeah, sure, feel free. CSU is still digging through all that, so go ahead. You want me to stay?"

"No, I'm good on my own."

He nods back to me, then says, "Don't be too long, though. We're still on the clock, kiddo."

"I know," I reply, taking the foot trail toward the main library. "Just give me an hour."

I look back as Cain squeals out onto the road, and notice Severo is still sitting in his Jeep, watching me as I walk away. I give him a dismissing wave before entering the building.

The City College campus occupies about thirty-five acres of St. Nicholas Heights, stretching from 131st Street to 141st Street along Convent Avenue. Cohen Library is housed in the North Academic Center, close to where Thomas Devlin's body was found. If I wasn't here on business, I'd take a moment to explore the neo-Gothic architectural landmarks of the campus, but there is much work to be done.

When I find my way through the library to a vacant computer station, I roll the task chair snug up to the study desk and click on the Internet icon. Using a popular search engine, I type in the words *Devlin* and *sword.*

Taking the advice of my father to heart, I trust my gut will lead me in the right direction. My dad may not have been able to give me everything, but he gave me everything he had, especially the notion of instinct. There has to be a reason our killer used four swords.

As the results filter onto the screen, I scan through the site descriptions, looking for a possible lead. Irish genealogy, family heirlooms and a few book-review sites head the list, but I continue to scroll, not satisfied with the findings. On the third page of listings, however, I see the phrase "Devlin sword" and click to see what is revealed.

It's a Web site dedicated to coats of arms, and when I see the name Devlin cached, I click to open its accompanying image. The Devlin crest boasts a cross straight down the middle of the shield, at the top of which are two stars. There's another star directly below the cross, and all of these details are positioned underneath an iron battle mask. The only sword I can find is one set off to the side, and it's double-edged. The whole thing doesn't quite add up.

As I stare at the image, I let the visuals of Devlin's body sift through my mind. The head in the crest faces left, just as Devlin's did outside. The shield in the image covers what would be the torso of a real person…. And then it hits me.

I approach a staff member and ask, "Can I print from here?" anxious to show my theory to Cain and Severo. She accompanies me back to the computer station, enters a quick code and within seconds hands me a page I can take back to the office. It may not be much, but at least it's a possibility.

The idea that this may in fact be a serial killer makes my skin crawl. Not so much because it freaks me out, but that this could be huge for my career.

Maybe it's selfish, but nailing this killer, whoever he is, and proving my ability as a profiler will boost my chances of making it into NCAVC. And when it comes down to it, that's the most important thing in my life right now. It's something my father would have been proud of.

I exit the building, pocketing my findings, and begin to walk along the Convent Avenue sidewalk, but I'm caught off guard when I see Severo's Jeep still sitting there. He's not in the driver's seat, so he could be up to anything, but I hail a cab before I have a chance to find out his whereabouts.

There's something else I want to check on, just to see if we missed anything the first time, and I don't want to waste any time. "Riverside and 112th, please."

The cabbie nods his head and speeds off, heading

south out of St. Nicholas Heights. There has to be more than what we initially found. Maybe trace missed something. Maybe we didn't look hard enough. But our first and most critical clue as to what this killer is up to was found at the historical church crematorium. And if anything was left behind, I aim to find it.

The sounds of screeching brakes and a loud horn behind us divert my attention. Jerking my head around, I see two vehicles nearly meet bumper to bumper at the 125th Street intersection. The driver of the second vehicle is clearly pissed at the idiot in front of him for taking his sweet time passing through the intersection. At this moment, I'm a little pissed myself.

It's Severo's Jeep.

Evidently, he has a hard time hearing me when I say I do not need his presence every minute of the day. Thankfully, his mishap at the intersection stalls him, and before he has a chance to get back on course a taxi cuts in front of him, following my cabbie's path along Morningside Park.

Our car soon begins to coast along Cathedral Parkway, and I take a moment to relax, absorbing all this city has to offer. Just seeing the trees and even the buildings brings up memories of my youth. New York is incomparable to anywhere else, and it feels good to be back here, even under the circumstances.

I hand the cabbie some folded bills and exit onto the grassy slope of the cathedral property. As I slam the door with my butt, the taxi that was following our trail passes by and heads to the other side of the lot. Must be a tourist checking out the historic landmarks. At least Severo's nowhere in sight.

I get started along the walking path the team took recently. Passing by the water fountain and then the large statue of Christ, I head west toward the underground site. Crime scene tape is still draped along the entranceway, though I feel no shame in pulling it to the side as I descend the stairs to the dank and dirty underworld. The place still reeks of flesh and death, but my nose is slowly becoming accustomed to these occupational hazards.

My fingers trace along the carved words I found here, and the Latin meaning chimes through my thoughts, as if eager to reveal a greater meaning. In the name of God.

It's frustrating that there is no other evidence within these walls to set us on the right track. Three bodies in three days? There has to be something more to tie them together. At this tomb, however, it seems we got everything the first time. One clue to lead us, and nothing but broken links to confuse us.

As I lean against a wall of one of the labyrinthine arteries, desperate to discover any minute sign of misconduct, my nose is again alerted to a nasty smell. Beneath me, the ground is still damp and sour from the fuels used in torching the spiritual advisor, but my senses are telling me there's something more. Something fresh.

With careful footing, I step closer to the center of the crematorium and follow the scent of fuel. With the slight slope in flooring, a trickle of liquid passes between my feet and edges toward the back of the room. This isn't right. The fuel should have been absorbed enough not to run, so I follow the direction from which the tiny river is flowing.

For all I know it could be raining now, thereby pushing residual liquid down into the cave. As I find a slim trail dribbling across the middle of the room, however, I realize a shadow lurks at the entranceway.

Man, this guy cannot take a hint. "Severo, what the hell are you doing? Are you going to follow me everywhere I go?"

As I turn my head toward the shadowy light, I have a hard time distinguishing his silhouette.

"Severo? Come down here if you insist on tagging me like a lost dog. Help me give this place another look."

With slow-motion maneuvering, one foot steps down cautiously, then the next, and I shake my head at the dramatic entrance of the detective. But as his shadow falls slightly away from the backdrop of light, clarifying the silhouette, the person's shoulder width is very different from what I expect.

This is not Severo.

"I'm sorry, this is a crime scene. It's off-limits," I say, realizing some passerby has too much curiosity for his own good. You'd think the caution tape would have told him as much.

He stands firm in the staircase, with little light showing his outline, and his stubbornness is getting on my nerves.

"Sir? This is—"

"You will find nothing here you don't already know."

His voice catches me off guard, with its quiet, yet raspy sounding reverberation. "Excuse me?"

My heartbeat quickens and my hand instinctively reaches to my holster. This man may be a lost tourist, or he could be a cracked-out wanderer, but I can't afford to take any chances.

"Sir, you can't be here. This is a crime scene."

"You think this was a crime?"

As I move a few steps closer, now taking him a bit more seriously, I reach to my left side to retrieve my flashlight. When I light up the staircase to view the intruder, he raises his elbow to shield his face. He's wearing a rather long raincoat, vinyl or coated cotton maybe, but its black color makes it hard to see any distinguishing traits against the dark underworld.

"I'm going to ask you once more to leave this area."

My words do little to shake him, but as I move a step to the left, out of the stream of light, I begin to see the side of a chiseled jaw, with sunken cheeks leading to high cheekbones.

My fingers interlace with my Bauer .25 and I slowly pull it from its nest. For all I know he may be armed, and I don't want to make any sudden movements.

"Sir?" I beg, trying to get this man to understand my plea.

His voice, a firm whisper comes again. "I mean no harm to you."

My back stiffens as I grasp my weapon. "Okay, well, good. Let's take this back above ground, shall we?"

My feet scrape along the damp crematorium floor, shuffling along the residue of flammable fluids. "Come on, let's go." My weapon at the ready, I step closer, but he raises a hand, revealing a container of kerosene, to warn me off approaching.

"You will do best to stay where you are."

"Listen, mister," I say, trying to talk some sense into him. "I don't know you, but you just said you mean me no harm, and I want to believe you. I do. So, if we can go on back up there, and talk out whatever it is you need—"

He angles the container downward and fuel drizzles into the room. "Revenge. I'm sure you can understand that." Beneath my feet, kerosene swirls across the ground, sinking into crevices and spreading throughout the tomb.

"I'd like to understand. Let's talk about it outside."

I study the man's position, figuring how I can gain the upper hand in taking him down. He is too far away to get past safely, and still blocking the stairway. Plus I can't see what he's placed behind him, a few steps up.

I walk toward him with a firm pace, no longer taking this lightly. "If you don't turn around right now, I will have no choice in the matter," I say, releasing my handgun's safety.

He sets down the container of fluid. "Neither do I." He pulls a Zippo from his pocket and flicks it swiftly, bringing a flame to life.

My index finger slides to the trigger. I drop my flashlight and focus on my target as I shoot in the direction of the stranger. He dodges my attempt, knocking over the kerosene and dropping his lighter into a pool of fluid. Flames burst high and spread throughout the crematorium, and I leap away from the room's center, desperate to find safe ground.

Again I reel off a shot, trying to close the distance between us and end this charade. He's at least fifteen feet from me, but damn it, I'm not playing games. "Face the wall and put your hands in the air," I say, though with the increasing flames I can barely make out his whereabouts.

The fires are sucking in air from the open staircase, climbing into the depths of the cave, and I take careful breaths to preserve whatever oxygen may be contained in this room.

Coughing, I yell out to this man, "I'm thinking you didn't mean it when you said you didn't want to hurt me! Whoever you are, you better damn well get your ass over here and give me a proper introduction!"

Muffled words travel through the smoky space. Disoriented, I angle my weapon to take aim at any target I can, but a sweeping force knocks me from the side and I fall to my knees. "In time, Angie. In fact, I think we'll come to respect one another very much."

"What?" *He knows my name.* I scramble to grasp hold of my gun, which fell from my hand with the attack, but as I reach through the flames, another blow finds its way to my head and the shadows stop.

Chapter 8

The pulsing at the back of my neck muffles my clarity, but the shrill sound of ringing is enough to elicit some energy to lift my head. Through the dancing flames and toxic smell, I see my cell phone lying next to me, the small red light flashing as it rings. As I reach for it, my eyes take in the smeared blood on my hand.

With the phone cradled between my ear and shoulder, I push myself off the ground, but it's difficult to get any reception underground.

"Angie, where are you? Is everything okay?"

I slide along the wall of the main room, sweat mixed with blood dripping down my neck, as I try to find the staircase. "Severo? I'm at the crematorium. I need help."

Muted sounds travel through my phone and I cannot understand what the detective is saying. "Severo? I can't hear you. I'm at the cathedral."

But our connection soon fades and my phone is now useless. Shielding my eyes to protect them from the flames, I quickly dash through the fire, trying to find the entranceway staircase. I trip on something, and when I look to the ground, I see an extremely large wooden crucifix stained with blood. My guess is it's the weapon this guy used to knock me down. Bastard.

My lungs respond to the environment, and my coughing prompts my eyes to water as I stumble up to the doorway. It's stuck. Locked from the outside? My hand doesn't find the Bauer .25 at my side, and I desperately need something to force this door open. Air supply is running low in here and I don't know that Severo understood a word I said.

For once, I need his help. This much I know.

I pull my shirtsleeve up and over my nose and mouth to protect myself from ingesting the gases as I scramble to find something, anything I can use to apply force to the door. When my feet again knock the large crucifix, I kick it free from flames and return with it to the entranceway.

It's heavy, wooden and was strong enough to knock me out. Now I need it to save my life. With my neck pulsing shots of pain, I slam the cross into the door, screaming with every blow. The solid portal shifts a bit as I hammer at it, but doesn't yield. I must get out of here!

Small, deliberate breaths seep through my lips as I gain focus and find my center of gravity. Blocking out the external influences of my environment, I focus only on the door. When my head is as clear as it can be, I put all my strength into ramming the cross into it. The impact is enough to trip me up. The crackle of chain, though, lets me know I have succeeded. The lock has been busted.

Sunlight blinds my eyes as I crawl up the stairs to safety. Gasping for breath, I savor the New York air, and the cross falls from my grasp as I lie on the ground, my life no longer in jeopardy.

For a moment, fragments of words exchanged between me and the stranger drift in and out of my brain. Did he say he knew me? Did he know my name? If only my head didn't hurt so much.

Faint voices fill the air and I lift my head to see Severo running toward me, squad car sirens echoing in the near distance.

"Angie! What the hell happened?"

He extends a hand and envelops mine, steadying my stance as I find my footing. My eyes begin to take in the surroundings and I have to say New York has never looked so good.

"There was a guy, a man…"

"What man?" he asks, helping me walk to a church-yard bench a few steps away from the staircase. The squad cars slam to a stop by the outer lawn and soon the unit—accompanied by the fire chief—sweeps in to inspect what just happened.

My palms against my head, cradling the throbbing pain, I think of anything I can to make sense of this. "I don't know."

"You're a mess," Severo says, sweeping loose strands of hair from my face. Though his observation is less than pleasant, there is a calm, soothing tone to his voice. "I knew I should have stayed with you."

"Did you?" I turn my head to face him, and my neck spikes with cramping pain. But I have to look into his eyes for answers. "Why is it, Detective, that you are so hell-bent on following me? I can take care of myself, you know."

His playful chuckle irritates me as he says, "Yeah, I can see that." He breaks eye contact, though, as he stands to meet the squad and inform them of my physical state. I watch his actions as he gestures toward the crematorium, and as I look toward the place I just crawled free from, my thoughts begin to form.

"Severo?"

Wiping his brow, he returns to the bench and again squats in front of me, placing a hand over mine. "You doing okay?"

"Severo, I think he knew me. I think he said my name."

"You think, or you know?"

My eyes squint back at him, partially due to the smoke intake and partially because I wonder if he doubts my sanity. "I'm not making it up, if that's what you're asking."

"Okay, okay. We'll talk about it on the way. Come

on." He wraps a hand around mine, pulling me to my feet and steadying my wooziness. "That's a pretty bad blow you got. We need to get you checked out."

As he leads me past the crew, who are intent on stopping the flames below and seeking out any evidence left by my attacker, I have to wonder why this happened. I need to know who the man is. And why, it seems, he knows me.

After a much-needed check-in with the paramedics, Severo and I head back to the Plaza to meet up with Cain. Painkillers have toned down my discomfort and my wounds have been cleaned and labeled less than critical. Now the only pain on my mind is figuring out what just happened out there.

Severo hands me a mug of coffee, complete with cream, and sits down on the edge of my desk. He checks me over, stroking fingers across my forehead, and his eyes grow soft as he asks, "You okay?"

I slowly nod, but am careful not to move too much. The medic said I'd be fine, but I feel like I've been hit by a…well, a very large wooden cross.

Severo is again confusing me as to who he is. Hot and cold. Cold and hot. I wouldn't say he's turning into a softy, but he's certainly been extra nice today, ensuring I have everything I need to make this pain settle down. I guess I can't complain about that.

"Angie, kiddo, I know you're hurt, but I need you to think real hard for a moment," Cain says in his common rasp, though admittedly it's a little gentler right now. "The detective here informed me of what you told him, and I need to know for a fact. Did your attacker address you by name?"

I turn my attention from the detective and face my mentor. "I think so," I say, then quickly amend my statement. "Yes, he did. For sure."

"Then," Cain says, pacing to the office wall where our crime scene photos display the past three days' activities, "you may have just met our man."

Even the throbbing in my head can't stop me from reacting. "You think this guy is our killer?" My eyes shift from Cain to Severo. "Honestly?"

The detective reaches a hand out to dust my arm. "It's a possibility."

"Thing is, Angie," Cain says, arching a thumb to the wall of photos. "It'd be a little too coincidental for some wacko to follow you down there, even if he does know you, ya know? People don't usually wander into crematoriums for fun. It's not uncommon, though, for a criminal to return to a scene and admire his work."

A fever is breaking out on my skin, and I was warned I would likely encounter some nausea along the way, but I just can't believe this. "Then, if he's the killer…how does he know me?"

"Look. For all we know, kiddo, this guy followed you from somewhere you hadn't noticed. Somewhere he could have heard your name or seen your badge." My mentor slurps at his coffee, then wipes his chin dry before shrugging. "Happens all the time. Nothing to get too freaked out about. Not yet, anyways."

"What do you mean, not yet?"

Looking at Cain and Severo, I see the years of experience behind their outer appearances. They know what they're doing because they've seen it all. One day I'll be in their shoes, but for now I'm learning as I go along.

"Sometimes they like to make it personal," the detective says, and I watch him closely as he speaks. His voice is candid, but soft, and I suspect he's sharing information with caution, careful not to raise any alarm within my already shocked being.

"It's happened once or twice where a suspect takes it upon himself to add a little more to the game—you know, mind tricks and all. It's an easy way for them to feel like they have the upper hand. But you—you have nothing to worry about, okay?"

"How can you say that?" My anger takes me to the crime scene wall and I begin to rip down photos from the past few days. "If you're saying the killer wants to play mind games with me, who's to say I'm not going to end up like this?"

"Because you're smart, kiddo," Cain says, pulling the photo of Killarney from my grasp. "I didn't pick you out of a hundred mentoring candidates because you're an easy target. I picked you because you were the best damn intake the Bureau's had in years. I don't choose victims, Angie. I choose hunters. Your father had it, you have it. This," he says, waving Killarney's crime shot in my face, "is not your fate. You understand me?"

"Fine," I reply, feeling defeated by the reasoning. I don't know about Cain or Severo, but I don't take too well to the notion that some serial killer wants to play nice with me.

"Now settle down," Cain says, walking me back to my office chair. He makes me sit, then places his hands on the chair arms, leaning in as he speaks. "You cannot get riled up. You understand? I know it's tough, but you have to keep your focus. I need you to take it easy, let your wounds heal, and concentrate on this case. Remember why you're here."

His eyes look directly into mine, and I know underneath his crusty exterior, he means well. I came back to New York for two reasons: to be with my family, and to work with the best damn profiling mentor on the East Coast. Well, since my father.

He's right. I know he is. "Okay, so now what?"

"Let's figure out how this guy put a name to you," Severo says, tacking the photos back along the wall in an orderly fashion. "He had to have followed you from somewhere, to know you were going to the crematorium. So?"

The two of them look back to me, and I think of my decision to return to the cathedral. "I went into the library, like I said I was going to. I looked some information up and then when I was leaving…"

"What, kiddo?"

"I saw Severo sitting there. Or his Jeep, at least."

"Severo?" Cain asks, losing the focus on my eyes as he turns to face the detective.

"Yeah, so?"

"And what, mister hotshot, were you still doing there?"

He looks back to Cain, obviously gauging my mentor's tone. "I waited to see if Angie would want a ride after her trip into the library. When she wasn't coming out, I decided to leave. But not before taking a bathroom break, if you must know."

"Yeah, and then you followed me," I add, still wondering why he does that all the time. "You could have got yourself killed, you know? That car that nearly rear-ended you? And then that cabbie cutting in front—wait, that's it."

"What? What's it?"

"The cabbie. I was watching to see if you smashed up the Jeep, and then a cab cut in between us, and it followed me all the way to the cathedral. I didn't think anything of it at the time, as they drove off to the other side of the lot."

"But your attacker may have been the passenger in that cab."

My eyes meet the detective's. "Which would mean he actually followed me from the campus to see where I was going. You think he was watching me?"

I can't help but feel creeped out by the notion of this. Cain shrugs his shoulders, but I can see he's thinking about it.

"So, what made you go back to the cathedral, kiddo? He couldn't have known you were going there, unless of course you made contact with him. At the library, maybe?"

"No, I only talked to the lady at the help desk, so I could print this," I say, handing my findings to my mentor. "I didn't talk to anyone else. There was no way this guy knew where I was going. I didn't tell anyone, so…"

"So he was watching you," Severo says, his voice full of contempt. "If he knew you were working this case, he didn't care where you were going, only that he find you. Must have made his day when you led him right back to where it all started."

"Crap."

"Ah, now, come on, kiddo. There was no way you could have known. This guy, he's probably all messed up in the head. But we gotta keep an eye on you now. Now that he's made contact, he might try again. Could be this is just the start, ya know?"

"Great." Despite the aches within my body, I hoist myself out of the chair and stretch out the kinks. My muscles feel as if I've just endured another sixteen weeks of training, only with no break in between. "Something to look forward to."

"What's all this?" Cain asks, flipping through the printed pages I'd gathered from the coat of arms Web site. "I thought you were following something related to the scene?"

"I was." I sit back down in my chair, feeling a little woozier than I'd like to admit. "I tried to match up the name Devlin to swords, and sure enough, I came across the Devlin coat of arms. Have a look."

"I'm looking, but I'm not seeing your point, kiddo,"

Cain says, his brows scrunched up as he peers to the printed images. "What am I supposed to see?"

Cain makes room on the edge of his desk for Severo, who takes a look himself. "Well, there is a sword," he says, glancing at Cain, then back to the images. "But not much else of any significance that I can see."

"Then look harder." I get back out of my chair, my body fighting my determination, and pull the recent photos of Devlin off the wall. "Look. One sword enters in a direct line beneath the sternum. Another pierced from the left, through his heart. On the opposite side, one pierced his rib cage from the right. And the last one strikes directly downward, as though the killer stuck this into him from above, pushing it through his breastbone. So, if you examine the lines created by these swords...it almost forms a T. Or a cross."

"Ah," Severo says, pulling a photo of Devlin from my grasp to hold it up beside my library printout. "Now I see what you're getting at. Look, Cain. Devlin's rib cage is like the shield. These stars in each corner are kind of like where these swords enter here," he says, agreeing with my suppositions. "And then this sword is placed in relation to this star, right here, below the sternum."

"But there were four swords," Cain argues. "And only three stars. What do you make of that?"

I shrug. "The fourth sword enters his breastbone, but angles directly under his head. I'm thinking that's some sort of message to us. Or to Devlin, for that matter."

"Okay, kiddo, well done. But here's my next question. Why? What's the point? What else did you find at the library to tell us something about this Devlin guy?"

"Here, have a look at this." I shuffle the pages to some theories I came across this morning. "On the top of the shield, meeting up with the larger cross, is a smaller cross—kind of square in shape. It has a reference to Christianity, but more significantly, it occasionally refers to those families involved in the Crusades."

"Angie, my sweet little protégée, you are one smart cookie," he says, his grin spreading across his age-worn face. "We all know the gist of the Crusades being expeditions to recover the Holy Land from disbelievers. And you said so yourself, kiddo—we need to think like the killer, not like the victim."

"Yeah, but Angie was thinking this guy might be after believers, Cain, not disbelievers." Severo shuts off the office coffee carafe and dumps his stale brew. "I'm not sure it adds up just yet."

"But if we're going to think like this guy," I say, trying to find some rationale for what the killer is doing, "we need to really put ourselves in his shoes. Killarney, La Roche and Devlin all seem to be believers, at least when it comes to God. But…there's gotta be something we're not seeing. Something about them that would make the killer think they are not followers. Of God, of the church…"

"Of him," Severo says, his lips pursed as he thinks out loud. "We don't know, right? All we have at this point is the little bits of trail he's left for us to piece together. And if he does know the victims personally, through some association or another, anything is possible."

"He's a wacko if that's what you mean," Cain grumbles. "He may have some score to settle with these churchgoers, but I couldn't give a flying rat's tail about it, ya know. I just want to nail his ass and get this thing done with. Who knows what's on his agenda? But it's our job to make sure it ends now."

"When's trace coming back?" I ask, anxious to get back out on the trail. My enthusiasm causes me to lose my balance and stumble, but Severo steadies me. "Anything from Devlin's scene to solidify a connection?"

Cain cracks his neck as he gets up from his desk and looks at his watch. "Should be soon. The lab's picking at it now."

As the detective piles some of the paperwork together I get the feeling he's leaving. "Where are you going?"

"We," he says, handing me my jacket, "are taking you home."

"What?"

"Cain's going to talk to Devlin's students and see if anyone saw anything that can point us in the right direction. I'm taking you home so you can rest."

"But—"

Cain hushes me, waving his hands. "Kiddo, that was a nasty blow you got and I don't want you dropping dead on me. You've been going strong since you got here, but I want you to take some time, refresh, and get back out there with a clear head."

He ushers me to the door, Severo ahead of me with my files, and I feel like a child being told what to do. "Tomorrow being Sunday, what better day to rest? Besides, we got enough lifeless bodies to deal with today. I need you in top form, Angie. Especially seeing how this guy's taken a personal interest in you."

Chapter 9

Little beams of evening sunlight shine through the balcony doors in my living room, hitting the hardwood floors and, sadly, making me notice the dust bunnies that have taken up residence. With a few tissues in hand, I scoop up the telltale signs of bad housekeeping on my part and quickly dispose of them before Severo gets back.

He was kind enough to take Muddy for a walk around the block while I changed into some comfy clothing and heeded my mentor's command to rest up this evening. As much as I know I need a full night's sleep, I wish I didn't have to sacrifice valuable time on this case.

According to Cain, he and the detective will wrap

up any interviews with Devlin's students, pick away at the trace findings and prep me when I return. But I won't get any field experience sitting at home.

At the sound of my phone ringing, I rush to answer, wondering if Cain has already found something. But when I answer, I am much more pleased with the delicate voice that responds, and a smile spreads across my lips.

"How are you, Grandma?"

"Oh, how I miss your face! My sweet, sweet dear, I cannot wait to see you tomorrow."

"Tomorrow? Wow, that was fast," I say, taking a seat to rest my body. "When can I expect you?" Looking at the mess known as my apartment, I wonder how I'll ever get this place in order before she comes back to the city. I haven't even unpacked my stuff from Virginia yet, let alone made my father's old bedroom suitable for my grandmother.

"I couldn't wait, Angie. My bags have been packed a long time, waiting for this day to come. All I needed was for those papers to come through and now they have, thank goodness. This place is no good for me. There's nothing but old people here, and they're all such bores," Gran says, and I laugh at her candor. "It's like they're all getting ready to die with the way they carry on, moping about. Miserable old croaks."

When I left Michigan to train in Quantico, my grandmother took up temporary accommodation in a "mature residence" while deciding what to do with herself. She has her own apartment that her caregiver frequently visits, but the entire building is inhabited by elderly folks, and apparently my grandmother doesn't consider herself one of them.

"But how are you feeling? Uncle Simon says you are not as good as you should be."

"Oh for goodness sakes, your uncle makes it sound like I've got one foot in the grave, which I don't, of course," she says matter-of-factly. "It's just my hip, Angie. Old age is defeating me, is all. Otherwise I'm feeling mighty fine. Coming home will do wonders for me, I'm sure."

"Yes, I'm sure it will, Grandma, and I can't wait to see you," I say, absorbing her softness, underneath that stubborn exterior. Guess I know where that personality trait comes from.

"I should be at the church by noon, sweetie, so I expect to see you for lunch. I'm going to visit with that uncle of yours and set a few things straight with that boy. He's always been such a sentimental softy, but he needs to know I'm not checking out anytime soon."

"Well, I'm glad to hear you're in good shape, and in good spirits," I say, meaning every word of it. I wasn't sure what to expect, the way Simon described her, though I won't disagree my uncle can be a bit overreactive at times. "It'll be nice being roommates again, won't it?"

"You bet your silver dollar it will," Gran says, sounding as though she's geared up for spring break. "We're going to go out on the town, shake what the Lord gave us, and make some boys drool, all right? To hell with my hip."

"Sounds good to me," I say, restraining my laughter. Gran's always had a fiery spirit, and I love spending time with her when she gets feisty. It's like having a much, much older sister to hang with. I'm sure having her here will do me good, too.

With the sound of my door creaking open and the familiar footsteps of Muddy trotting along the wooden floors, I know Severo has returned, so I close my conversation with Gran.

"I'll see you tomorrow, sweetie," she says. Then, before hanging up, she adds, "It's Saturday night, love. You better have some fun plans made. Just be sure to save some energy for when I get there."

"I will, I promise," I say, then hang up to embrace Muddy. "How's it going, baby? You have fun with the detective?"

Muddy rubs by me, more interested in visiting his water dish, and I quickly check my appearance to make sure I'm not entirely indecent. I threw on an old college sweatshirt and some drawstring bottoms, but am now second-guessing my casual attire. Ah, hell, it's my home. I can dress however I want. I'm not trying to impress anyone, after all.

"It's freezing out there!" Severo says, rubbing his hands together as he rounds the hallway to meet me in the living room, which is really just an extension of the dining room, which is kind of an extension of the kitchen. This apartment isn't the biggest on the block, but it's got all the comforts I need, and memories of growing up with my father, so I couldn't ask for more. "That Cain?"

"Here, warm up," I say, handing him a mug of freshly brewed French roast. "No, it was my grandmother. She'll be here tomorrow, so I need to get this place cleaned up. Hey, you want something to eat?"

"Who's taking care of who here?"

"I'm not bedridden, Severo. The way you make it sound, I should be counting my lucky stars I can even stand up."

"I'm just saying there's no need to treat me like a guest." His voice is childlike in defense. "You don't have to entertain me or anything."

"Good." I nod toward the fridge as I begin to pick up stray newspapers and toss them into the few packing boxes I have managed to empty. "Then you can make me something to eat."

"Yes, ma'am." When Severo opens my fridge, though, he grunts something inaudible, then turns to face me. "Hey, Angie? You may want to call 911. It seems there's been a robbery. Someone apparently ran off with all your food."

"Very funny." I reach his side and look at the sparse contents of my fridge. "Look, there's…well, there's some pickles. And yogurt. And there, what's that?"

"Some strange lump of flesh?" he says, holding out a tinfoil wrapped plate. "What is this, a science project?"

"That," I say, pulling the plate from his grasp, "is my leftovers from Thanksgiving. It's turkey."

His laughter erupts and he watches as I peel back the foil. "No it isn't. Turkey isn't gray, Ange. That boneless, burned lump can't possibly be a proper bird."

I feel my cheeks flush a bit as I pick it off the plate and toss it into the trash. "If you must know, it was one of those precooked meats they do now. It's all about convenience, Detective. You think I have time to fool around in the kitchen?"

"I'm not making any judgments," he says, backing away from me slowly and playfully, as though I may attack him for making accusations against my culinary skills. "Perhaps, though, we should order in and see to it that you get some real food in you. You need your strength."

"Fine, you choose," I say, then return to tidying the main living space. My grandmother will undoubtedly scold me for keeping such a messy apartment, as she was always so nutty about order when we shared a place during my college education. I'd hate for her to show up and start cleaning this place herself, even if she swears she feels fine. If her hip is bothering her, the last thing she needs is a messy apartment to tempt her stubborn nature.

As Severo makes the call for takeout, my thoughts turn to curiosity. It's only been a few days since I met the detective, and I really know very little of him. Where he's from, why he chose to work in homicide, and what he does when he's not working.

I don't need his whole life story, but knowing a bit more about him will maybe make it easier to understand those mood swings he gets. Mind you, he's been very accommodating today, and I have to appreciate that.

As I push a sweeper across my floors, attempting to nab the little bits of hair and dust, I ask, "Why homicide?"

"What?"

"Why did you choose homicide? I'm assuming you could have worked in any number of fields, so why this one?"

The detective shrugs a bit as he speaks, and I watch as he loads my sink with the empty coffee mugs my counter has accumulated over the past few mornings. "Why not? It's got everything a man could hope for. Lies, deceit, betrayal. And let's not forget murder."

"That's a given."

"Yeah," he says, his voice dry. "But it's an interesting lesson in the human spirit. Why people kill one another, how they do it. It's all so dramatic. Then again, you come across some clean-cut cases, too."

"Clean-cut?"

"You know, your basic shot-in-the-heart case, with the killer still at the scene. The confessionals. The wives who turn themselves in even before we find their poor excuse of a husband. Good old homicide. Those are the ones that are open-and-shut cases. You know?"

I take a seat at the kitchen table, resting for a moment to ease my muscles after the day I've had. With the painkillers settled in, I'm not hurting too much right now, but my bones are arguing the artificial sense of strength. "Yeah, I guess so."

"Plus, it's not just homicide I deal with. There's the links surrounding murder. Drug rings, counterfeit ops.

That's what I tend to work with. It usually ends in murder, though."

He piles the now clean mugs to the side, looks under the counter, then back up at me. "You got some all-purpose cleaner or something? This could use a good wipe," he says, running a finger along the countertop.

"You don't have to do that, you know," I say, getting up from my seat.

"Yes, but I want to. So sit down and tell me where your cleaning stuff is. Or are you as adverse to cleaning as you are to cooking?"

"Aren't you just full of compliments," I joke, pointing to a side cupboard where I've stashed the few supplies I own. "I think tomorrow I'll head out and pick up some things so this place is presentable when my grandmother gets here."

"How's her health?"

"Oh, she's fine." My fingers wrap through the mug of my hot beverage and I think of how lucky we are that she is okay. "I guess Simon is just worried about her hip problems, but otherwise she's the same as always. Stubborn and direct."

"Sounds like I know someone just like her," he laughs, and I toss one of Muddy's chew toys in his direction. Of course, Muddy trots along after it, settling down at Severo's feet to gnaw on the rubbery plastic.

"What about you, Severo? You're pretty tight with your family, aren't you?" He hasn't actually mentioned them in conversation, but with the introduction I got last night at La Costa, I could see he has a lot of love for them.

"They're the best. Truly. My sisters, my niece. My little brother. All of them. Great."

My memory drifts to the night before and I recall the numerous excited faces, so proud when the detective walked into the room. "What about that one guy? Antonio, I think. He had a cane. What happened to him?"

"Yeah, that's Antonio. Maria's husband. Good guy. Four years ago he was working late with Maria." Severo turns his head toward me as he scrubs down my countertop, and I simply nod in agreement. "It was late, nearly midnight, and in comes this guy, walking through the restaurant doors, and he's got a gun."

My brows arch as Severo explains, and I try to imagine the scene within the walls of the quaint establishment.

"So, he comes barreling through, aims this shotgun, of all things, and wants the cash. But they ain't got none. Nothing substantial, anyways. The restaurant's not exactly a hopping joint, but it does well enough to keep afloat."

"What happened?"

"Antonio tells Maria to go to the back safe, which they don't have. Nothing more than some shoe boxes in the upper apartment," he adds, leaving no detail behind. "And while she's gone, he's trying to talk the thief out of the situation, calm him down. Naturally, the shooter ain't so complacent."

"And?"

"The guy starts panicking, but Antonio keeps talking to him, wanting to get him out of there as fast as he can. When Maria comes back in, she says she can't find the key to the safety box—which doesn't even exist. You know, trying to stall the guy, but it doesn't work."

Severo ties a knot on a kitchen garbage bag, then searches for a fresh replacement as he continues to explain the situation, which I already know won't end well.

"He gets in a fuss and aims the gun at my sister, threatening her if she doesn't take him to the money. But Antonio, he hops over the counter and tackles the guy. Maria calls 911, but my brother-in-law gets shot in the leg as he wrestles with the thief."

"No one else got hurt?"

"Nope. My niece was upstairs, fast asleep, and she was too young to remember it well, thank God. Antonio got hurt pretty bad, but he did what he did to protect my sister."

"Sounds like a great guy," I say, feeling the respect Severo has for his sister's husband.

"Yeah, he's a good man." Severo twists around as a buzzing noise interrupts our conversation. "What's that?"

"The door. Must be our food."

He motions for me to stay put as he buzzes in the delivery guy and then waits at the door for our takeout. Although I wasn't expecting the detective to stay this long, his company has been pleasant and I'm glad I have a chance to get to know him a bit better, seeing how we're evidently going to be working together for a while longer. At least until we get this case wrapped up.

On his return, he balances multiple cardboard cartons and a plastic bag of treats. My nose takes in the aromas of curry and spice and my stomach wakes up from its slumber.

"Indian?"

"You bet," he says, laying out the cartons along the kitchen countertop. "You need some fire in you if you're going to get back out there and get all that experience you need."

Reaching his side, I open a container of butter chicken, eyeing its gooey goodness. "So what do you think of it all?"

He pours butter sauce over a scoop of rice, then leans back against the counter to address me. "The case? Hard to tell. I don't like the looks of it, though. Especially with you being followed today. How ya feeling?"

I dip a finger into the butter sauce and lick it before saying, "Considering? Not that bad, really. I mean, I was freaked out about it at the time, that's for sure. And even now, I suppose. But hopefully Cain'll get something from Devlin's students, and if the lab comes back with anything from the scene, we'll be on our way."

The detective places a peeled-off piece of naan bread on my plate and we settle onto the living room floor to spread out files and relax a little as we review our data to date.

"I've brought as much as I could from the office," Severo says before spooning a large portion of saucy chicken into his mouth. Sliding a few official documents toward me, he lifts a finger to wipe his chin free of curry. "Pass me a water?"

I hand him a bottle from behind me, and grab one for myself to wash down the spicy tastes. Other than last night at La Costa, this is probably the best meal I've had since returning to New York.

Severo leans back to rest on his arms, his legs crossed in front of him, knees slightly touching mine as I sit opposite him, cross-legged.

"What do you make of the Devlin coat of arms?" he asks, and my attention diverts from his presence to his question. "I get the whole crusade theory, mind you, but this guy has to be after something tangible. He's gotta be making a point."

"Wait." My memory is foggy and the painkillers aren't helping, but I think I may have something to work with. "You know when I was down there, in the crematorium, I could swear he said something about revenge. I think."

Severo rubs a piece of naan bread along his buttery plate. "Revenge? Well, that's common enough, I guess. If it's not money or power they're after, it's usually revenge. What did he say?"

"That's the problem. He didn't really have much to say at all. Just something about revenge and me understanding it or… I don't know that I really remember all that well."

"Maybe it'll come back to you," he says encouragingly, his eyes soft and relaxed. The more I get to know Severo, the more I see his less edgy side. It may take some time for him to turn off that cocky detective attitude, but when he does, it's worth it. "I don't think we should discount his trying to get close to you, though. He seems to have taken a liking to you, ya know?"

Severo gets up from the floor, taking our plates to the kitchen, and I, too, get up to stretch out my legs. Standing motionless in my kitchen doorway, as though contemplating the wonders of the world, he traces his eyes over me as I walk to the living room balcony doors. Clearing his throat, he speaks softly. "About last night, Angie. At the restaurant? Why'd you take off like that?"

"Oh, I was just tired. And cranky." I realize now I may have overreacted a tad. It's just that I was having such a good time with Severo and his family. I didn't really want to call it a night as quickly as he suggested.

"Okay. If you want to drop it," he says, approaching me now. As he rubs his hands along the sides of his pants, I'm not sure if he's wiping them free of curry or busying them in a state of boyish nervousness. "I just want you to know I wasn't blowing you off."

"I don't know what you're talking about."

In the hush of the night, I can hear my pulse beating beneath my layered clothing. I doubt Severo can hear it above the whistling wind outside the glass doors of the balcony, but to me, it sounds like a million drums rapping against my skin.

"I think you do." His words are soft as he closes the distance between us. I'm not sure if I want to step back a foot or step forward and close the space between us.

The sound of his breathing has overpowered my own and I grow conscious of his smell. Severo has this spicy scent about him, though I'm not sure if it's from a cologne or his genes. Either way, it's welcoming, like warm cinnamon toast.

With a hand raised in front of him, he slides his fingers down the side of my face, slowing against the curve of my cheekbone, then again under my jawline. With the other hand, he threads fingers through my hair, and the lingering scent of my citrus shampoo wafts through the air.

"Detective," I say softly, knowing the answer before I ask. "Are you trying to kiss me?"

His lips curl upward, a devious smirk spreading over his face, and his gaze skims across my shoulder, up my neck, then focuses in on my eyes.

"Could be."

He centers the pad of his thumb on my bottom lip, and with a slight pressure, leans into me so I can feel his warmth. I twist a few inches, resting my back against the shockingly cold balcony doors, and the contrasting sensations send shivers across my skin.

With his opposite hand, Severo smooths my skin like he's buttering toast, letting the slight roughness of his fingers contrast with my own softer flesh. Then he reaches downward, along the side of my rib cage, and even through my old college sweatshirt, the tickle causes my skin to react.

Leaning into the detective, I guide my lips and nose along his neck, taking in his woodsy scent. It's overwhelming, as I have not been this close to a man for a number of years. I guess I wasn't one to engage in social entertaining during college, especially with my grandmother as a roommate. Since then, my social circle hasn't expanded much, what with my constant training.

Oh, I've had a few flings, but nothing worth remembering. But here, now, with my body close to Severo's, there's a gentle reminder of my less professional needs. Needs that haven't been met in some time.

I raise my chin, again facing him. Our heartbeats have combined, or overlapped, and I cannot distinguish which is mine and which is his. Severo's eyes, half closed, peer at me as he leans closer.

My lips part and I instinctively lick them, but he soon pushes his own against mine, pressing warmly, then gently sucking them closer. He pushes my mouth open, flicking my upper lip with delicate dabs, and I close my eyes to savor the moment. He begins to explore the inside of my mouth with care and precision, and I find myself drawing in his breath.

Leaning my body into him, I wrap my hands around his neck and offer him my whole mouth as I tilt my head upward.

There's an aroma of body heat between us and I slow my pace to inhale the intoxicating scent. When my eyes open, I run my gaze along Severo's neck, up his jawline, then meet his eyes. The dark centers are serious now, the pools of chocolate still for this moment.

Looking directly at the detective, I sense the worry he has recently developed for me, and though it bothers me that a part of him thinks I may be in danger, I can at least appreciate his concern.

With a slightly devious smile, I lean in to place my lips on his again. But he pulls back, just enough to strike me as odd. "Severo?"

Straight-faced, he glances into my eyes and then at the files of paperwork scattered about on my living room floor. "Angie, I don't think—"

I step back, sliding from between the glass doors and the detective. "Yeah, you're right," I say, as our professional connection kicks some reality into my stuttered senses.

"Angie?" Severo says, a bit of a plea in his voice. But I can't figure out his motives in the context of this situation. "Would you just hear me out? We should think about this. With everything that's happened today, I just don't know the timing is right, is all."

"I get it, Severo." My voice rises to cut him off, but I try to gather some composure by straightening my clothing. I turn toward the hall leading to the door, and look at Severo once more before opening it. "I think you better go," I say, gesturing to the passageway. "The drugs are starting to wear off and I need my sleep. Good night, Detective."

He brushes my arm as he passes me, avoiding eye contact as he collects his belongings, leaving me to an empty apartment.

Chapter 10

"Come on, Muddy!" His aging body trails beside me as we head out onto the street to enjoy a bit of early morning shopping in Chelsea. I'm eager to discover the new developments of the neighborhood and revisit old favorites from my youth. If Cain wants me to relax, Chelsea is the place to do it.

Artsy folk have always taken up residence in this area, but recently it seems more and more professionals, like doctors and lawyers, are finding a home here as well. Can't blame them. From Fifth Avenue to the Hudson River, this area has some of the best independent shops on this side of the city. I learned early that I could go without the department stores of Lower Manhattan, finding everything I need right here within walking distance.

The farther south you go in Chelsea, the pricier real estate seems to get. In my corner, though, along Tenth Avenue north of West Twenty-ninth Street, prices remain reasonable, probably on account of the proximity of the Lincoln Tunnel Expressway. But with Chelsea Park and a plethora of shops within a few blocks, my street is just as good as the next.

Muddy and I head south along Tenth Avenue, but I look behind me when I hear my name being called.

"Angie, wait up," Severo says, jogging toward me from the east side of the street. Great. Just when I was about to enjoy my day off.

Though I'm being pulled forward by Muddy's leash, I stall a bit for the detective to catch up. "What are you doing here?"

"Just had breakfast with Cain downtown, but figured I'd come by and see how your head's doing. Where ya going?"

"Shopping. And I'm fine," I say, then turn back the way I was headed.

"This early? Mind if I join you?"

"Why?" I say, not facing Severo as I keep a steady pace. "You want to play some more games? If you recall, Detective, we don't have time for that sort of thing. We're on a case."

"Oh, would you just cut the sarcasm and wait a minute!"

As he says this, I stop in my tracks, pivot with force and look at him. But the early morning sun glares against his shades and I have a hard time making eye contact as he speaks. "Listen, about last night…you know I didn't mean it like that. It's just…with what happened to you yesterday we both need to be at the top of our game, ya know?"

"Yeah, you said so last night."

"If you must know…" His voice cracks and he peers around as one of my neighbors walks by. He nods to the stranger, then continues in almost a whisper. "If you must know, I like you. I do. And I'm thinking you might even like me a little, when you're not pissed at me for one thing or another. But…"

"You didn't want to take advantage of a wounded woman?"

"Exactly," he says, standing next to me now and I hear the sincerity in his voice. It's not like I had a concussion for crying out loud. Though I suppose I can forgive him under the circumstances. I won't deny there's an attraction between us that's developed rather quickly.

Maybe this is something we should explore later, after we finish this case and I get settled into the city a bit more. I consider how hard that would be while looking at him, as he asks, "So, mind if I join you?"

"I guess not," I say, in my best indifferent tone. I don't want him to think I can be won over so easily. "But you better have comfortable shoes, Severo. I have a lot to accomplish this morning."

"That I do," he states, as he picks up the pace and trails alongside Muddy. "So what's on the agenda?"

"The market opens at ten o'clock, so I figure a few

stops along the way, and then I can gather up some food so I have something to offer my grandmother."

"You're going to see her for lunch, right?"

I rewrap my scarf around my neck, since the wind keeps pulling it loose from its knot, and I take in the scent of fresh ground coffee as we round the corner, nearing a small café.

"Yeah, at the church. I don't know if she's planning on staying with Simon for the night or heading straight over, so I need to be prepared."

We enter the café, busy with neighbors enjoying a beverage this fine, sunny Sunday morning, and I order a café latte to go.

"Same for me," Severo says, and when he pulls his wallet from his pocket, I protest.

"This one's on me," I insist, letting my attitude settle, remembering how gracious the detective was yesterday despite our personal incident. "You got dinner last night, so this is the least I can do."

Lattes in hand, we head south toward some independent shops and I take in the familiar scenery. I spent many Sunday mornings wandering this neighborhood after sharing breakfast with my father, and seeing the old buildings and fruit stands brings back sweet memories.

"You had breakfast with Cain?" I ask, stepping up to a vendor selling flowers. The gerbera daisies are looking nice for this time of year, so I select a few bright orange and a few cheery red, then one yellow for spunk, and pay the man for the bouquet. "Any news to share?"

"He met with some students, but none of them really knew of anyone strange hanging around the campus. Not like anyone really pays attention to strangers in this city, ya know." He takes Muddy's leash from me so I can balance my latte and the wrapped flowers. "After breakfast he was heading back to the Plaza to check on forensics to see what the lab came up with, if anything. Said he'd give us a call if something surfaced."

"I would hope so," I say, then motion for Severo to enter the next shop. "I want to go in here."

He slows for a moment to attach Muddy's leash to a sidewalk bicycle rack, then looks up to the store's marquis with bewilderment. "Records? Your grandmother need some music to make her feel more at home?"

"No, but I do," I say as I step through the narrow aisles, working my way to the jazz section. "My father and I used to come here all the time. Look, they still have those old-fashioned listening booths. He'd bring me here when I was a kid and introduce me to all the classics, one Sunday at a time."

"Very cool." Severo nods, pulling an old vinyl album of Nina Simone off the rack. "You really like this stuff, huh?"

"Yup. Know it better than whatever it is you listen to, anyways," I say, recalling the obscure CD collection I spied on his desk a few days ago.

His laughter catches a wandering shopper off guard, and I smile at the sound of his voice. When in good spirits, the detective can be rather charming and pleasant. Getting past our kiss and the aftermath is easier than I expected, with the way his warm side creeps back in, making me forget there was ever an uncomfortable moment between us.

"I like to fight for the underdog," he says, but my dumbfounded look prompts him to explain. "You didn't recognize any of the names, right? There's no reason you should. It's not like they're busting off the charts. Not yet, anyway."

"How do you find these bands?" I'm curious to know more about Severo and what brings life to him outside of working hours. He seems to be comfortable with who he is and what he's made of, and I'd like to know the intricacies of what makes him tick. "Or is there a process?"

"Oh, there is indeed." His voice is enthusiastic now, as though I've hit a joyous nerve that was waiting for someone to tickle with curiosity. "It's a very technical process, actually. I go into a record store, not unlike this one, and I do one of two things."

My fingers slide along the E section, skimming for a Duke Ellington oldie. "I'm listening."

"Either I ask the nerdiest kid in the joint who the latest and coolest unknown band is and take his word for it, or—" he closes his eyes and runs his fingers through a stack of records, blindly pulling out a group I don't recognize "—I do this."

"You're kidding me?"

"Nope. Random choices sometimes lead to a real

nice surprise," he says, defending his system. "Sometimes you don't know what you're looking for until you find it."

"Fair enough." I grab the latest mystery album from his grasp. "How about I test out your theory, then? If I like it, I owe you a beer. If I hate it, you owe me a beer."

As we walk to the cashier Severo looks at me with a grin. "Then I win either way."

"How do you figure?" I pay for my albums and hold the door for the detective as we head back to the sidewalk to meet Muddy, faithfully awaiting our return.

"Because either way, I get to enjoy the pleasure of your company, regardless of who's buying."

Now it's my turn to grin. "Point taken."

Balancing the collection of daisies and the leash on Muddy, Severo walks elbow to elbow with me as I study the back of the unknown album. He's trying to read over my shoulder, and when we come to the intersection he pauses, unsure which way to go.

"We should head to the market," I say, so we cross over to the east side of the street, heading toward Ninth Avenue. "Once I get some edible items for Gran and me, I'll have to get back to the apartment and see if Mrs. Schaeffer will keep an eye on Muddy while I go to my uncle's."

"I could always hang out with him, ya know. We're bonding, can't you tell?"

I watch as Muddy rubs up against Severo's leg, the old dog bumping into him periodically as we strut down the sidewalk. "I can see that, but I'm afraid you already have plans."

"I do?"

"Of course," I say, matter-of-factly. "I'm returning a favor. You're having lunch with my family."

"Thanks, Mrs. Schaeffer!" We head down the stairwell from the second floor and I say to Severo, "She's so sweet."

"I noticed. For the record, I don't know that I've ever seen a dog smile, but Muddy sure seemed happy to see her."

He pushes through the door, holding it open for me as I pass through with hands full of flowers and the wine I decided last minute to pick up for my uncle. It's nice that Simon's having us all over for lunch, and I want to show my appreciation.

As Severo disarms his Jeep and I fumble to make sure the door closes behind me, a delivery guy from a reputable courier company catches the handle. "Georgia Schaeffer?" he asks, peering above his delivery log, and I nod my head toward the stairs.

"Second floor, to the right."

"Thanks," he says, and I watch the bald guy heave it up the stairs, his hands spread out, carrying a rather large package.

"Wonder what that is?" I murmur to Severo, my curiosity aroused. "I never get presents delivered to me."

"Is that so?" he asks, one eyebrow raised and lips devilishly curled into a grin. "Well, never say never."

Despite our mended attitudes this morning, there is little conversation as we drive from Chelsea to Gramercy Park. This is the first time I'll be in the same room with my uncle and grandmother since my father's funeral, and it's bittersweet. I'm so happy to be reunited with the both of them, but my father's absence is still hard to take.

I don't know that you can put a time limit on healing, and I don't want to lose the memories of my father, but for the sake of my family I need to put on a brave face. It's the only way we'll get past this pain and find the place where memories turn to sweetness, instead of hurt.

When my cell phone sounds, I answer quickly, eager to keep my mind from falling into the past. "David."

"Hey ya, kiddo. How's your head today?"

I smile at the personal interest Cain has taken in my well-being. "I'm fine, but thanks for asking. Hey, Cain," I begin, as the thought occurs to me. "If you don't have plans for lunch, you're welcome to come by my uncle's church. My grandmother's arriving and we're having a little get-together. It'd be nice if you could join us."

"Nah, I'm heading out to see my kids for the afternoon. Maybe hit the zoo or some weirdo museum that'll impress them. I appreciate the offer, though. But listen, you have yourself a good time and be sure to rest up."

"I will," I say, and then add a goodbye. Looking toward Severo now, I ask, "You know Cain has two kids?"

"That I do. Met them last year, in fact, at some Fourth of July barbecue he hosted in Brooklyn Heights."

"Really?"

"Yeah, at some community park near his bachelor pad. It's too bad he doesn't get to see them all that often, as I know he loves those kids more than anything. But what can you do?"

I think of Cain and what he told me of his defunct marriage. Far be it from me to deny he can be a bit work oriented, but I just can't see why his wife would hold that against him. I loved that my father was so focused on the job. Then again, I had ambitions to grow up and be just like him, so our situation was definitely unique.

It must be hard for Cain. With his kids off at a private school and his ex-wife living with another man, that is. He doesn't wear it on his sleeve, but it must get under his skin on some level. Poor guy.

As we arrive at my uncle's church, Severo can't stop fussing with his tie. "Does this look right?"

"It's fine, trust me." Despite my argument that it wasn't necessary to be so formal with my family, he insisted he present himself as a fine, upstanding man of the law. I laughed pretty hard at that one. I have to wonder why he keeps a stash of spare clothing in the hatch of the Jeep, but then again, he's a complicated guy. "Just relax," I say, as we enter the rectory.

When we pass through the hallway leading to my

uncle's private residence, I become aware of an argument in motion.

"Mama," my uncle is pleading to my grandmother. "Please, please sit down and relax. I am taking care of this."

Severo looks at me, confused, as I watch my two family members playing tug-of-war with a serving platter. "How old do you think I am, Son? Two or two hundred? Damn it all, I can set a table, Simon, so give me that damn plate!"

"Mama, please! Not in the house of the Lord," my uncle says, letting go of the plate to hold his hands to his head. "I don't care what you do, just no speaking like that, please."

"Am I interrupting something?" I ask, and as soon as my mouth opens my grandmother quickly shuffles to me, leaving the debated platter behind.

"Angie!"

As I hug her snugly, taking in that familiar grandmother scent, I look over her shoulder to see Simon still upset by her choice of words. "Gran, you got to go easy on him, or it'll be you taking care of him," I joke.

"That boy is so stubborn. Thinks I'm too old to do anything. Why the hell does he think I moved back here, anyways. To sit on my tush and waste away? I don't think so."

Simon is waving his hands about, obviously feeling beaten by my grandmother's vocabulary, but I'm sure he'll get used to it very quickly. Gran always had a way of being direct. Leave it to her to abandon decorum in the house of God.

"Now, who might this be?" Gran asks, stepping up to Severo. Her petite stature—maybe five feet—seems so small in comparison to the detective's height, but with her head erect and her posture full of pride, I'd say the scales are fairly even.

"Grandmother, this is Detective Carson Severo," I say as they shake hands. Simon joins us to do the same. "He's a good friend of my mentor's, so we've been able to do some work together."

"And how's my girl holding up out there?" Gran asks, without missing a beat. "She as good as I suspect she is?"

Severo chuckles, looking at me for a quick second to gauge the reality of Gran's direct nature, then very seriously replying to her inquisition. "Yes, she's doing quite well."

"Mama, come sit, please," Simon urges, placing a bottle of wine on the table. "You make me so nervous. Angie, tell your grandmamma to sit down and rest her hip."

"Oh, for heaven's sake," Gran says, taking my hand as she pulls out a chair. "Didn't I tell you that one's a mama's boy?"

"He's got a point, though, Gran. Don't be doing too much too soon, okay? Remember, we need to save some energy for hitting the dance floor."

I begin to pour wine for the group, but my attention diverts for a moment when I hear the door down the

hallway creak. "You expecting someone else, Uncle?"
I ask, about to check it out for myself.

"That's probably just Denise," Gran says, and her
statement catches me off guard. I didn't see that coming.

"I thought it was just going to be us." I don't want
my defenses to get the better of me, but I can't understand why Denise would have been invited.

"You brought along the detective." Gran says, wearing a triumphant expression.

"Hola," Denise says, rounding the corner and laying her eyes upon us. "Hello, Simon, and Mrs. David,
and…hello, Angie. Nice to see you again, so soon."

My grandmother peers at me, obviously curious as to
what Denise is referring to, but I just shrug off her glance.

"Likewise," I say, swallowing my childishness.
Whatever feelings I have toward Denise, I need to suck
it up and fast.

My father loved this woman and, apparently, my
family is not going to forget that too easily. "Here, let
me help you with that," I say, taking a tray of dessert
from her hands. "Denise, this is Detective Severo. He's
a…well, he's a friend of mine."

Caught off guard by what exactly to say about
Severo, I don't think anyone would care how I introduce him. He's not much more than that at this point,
unless of course I want to get into the details of our situation. But what would I say? That we're hunting down
a murderer and making out a little on the side? Yeah,
that'd go over well, I'm sure.

We spread out around the simple wooden table in Simon's compact dining room, topped with a healthy selection of market finds and homemade treats. Baguettes and dips, cold cuts, salads and fruits make up our easy lunch.

While my grandmother holds my hand, sitting next to me, she recounts stories with Denise. I suppose they haven't talked to one another since my father's funeral, so they likely have much to catch up on. I'm a little jealous of my grandmother's time, but I know I'll have her to myself very soon.

Across from me sits Severo, and when I look at him he meets my glance, offering a subtle wink as my uncle tells him some story about the church's history.

Despite the pleasantry of this scenario, thoughts of my father fight for my attention. This is exactly the way we used to spend family time, sitting around the table, enjoying wine and an assortment of foods, sharing stories of our days at work, play and rest. I miss him so much. These past four months have been a constant heartache for me and I wish I could spend just one more moment with him.

Having my grandmother back in the city will be great, as I really need to feel close to my family right now. With both her and my uncle aging, I want to spend as much time with them as possible and gather memories to last beyond their years.

"It was bad timing," my uncle explains to Severo, and I realize now he is telling the story of how my father died. "Joshua was undercover, working on something completely unrelated, when that robbery was taking place."

The detective cautiously looks at me as he says, "I read about it in the papers." His eyes are soft, and I know he's being delicate with the situation, understanding how this is such a sore spot for me. Uncle Simon was the one who brought it up, though, so I have no reason to be bent out of shape.

"Yes, yes. It was everywhere," Simon says, shaking his head in permanent disbelief. "Those young kids, with futures ahead of them. Terrible to get caught up in such horrible acts."

"They never found the weapon, did they?" Severo asks.

"No, but once you kill one cop," I say, keeping my emotions contained, "the system doesn't take it lightly when you do it again. Concrete evidence or not."

Whatever situation brought my father in proximity to that ill-timed robbery, operated by two minors out to score some cash, is irrelevant. When he got in their way, apparently, and figured out what they were up to, his life was cut short.

Shot by a minor, who'd been only recently let out from a juvenile facility after shooting an officer, my father died indirectly while in the line of duty. That kid, no matter the gun wasn't found at the scene, didn't stand a chance. He was there, and with enough evidence of their crossed paths to convict him, he'll be behind bars for a long time to come. It's too bad he didn't learn from his earlier mistakes that crime, indeed, does not pay.

As Denise sets out dessert plates, thankfully interrupting my uncle's storytelling, I decide to check on Mrs. Schaeffer and see how Muddy is doing. I would have brought him along for the company, but Simon has a slight allergy to dogs.

As her phone continues to ring, unanswered, I wait for the beep and then leave a message. "Hey, it's Angie. It's almost two, so I bet you're out taking Muddy for a walk. I'll be home soon, but you know where to reach me if need be," I say, then close my cell phone and return to the company.

"Everything good?" Severo asks, as I take a seat beside him. His tie is a little crooked, so I reach a hand to straighten the silk against his tailored shirt. Man, when this guy dresses up, he looks pretty good. Mind you, I have nothing against a uniform, either.

"Yeah, they must be out for a walk," I reply, then lean into his shoulder, pleased we are no longer on the topic of my father's death. "We can go anytime you want, you know? Gran said she's staying with Simon for a few days so they can catch up and so I'll have a few more days to get the apartment ready for her."

"Good," he says, pushing a finger through my hair. "Because if you ask me, you still got a lot to do to make that apartment presentable." He laughs as I pinch his side, and moves out of harm's way. "Hey, it's not like I didn't try to help you clean up, Agent. Plus, you seem all recovered now. Maybe we should head back and see what else we can do to make it feel more comfortable."

My eyes move slowly from his to my family's,

checking to see if anyone overheard that invitation. When it appears my conscience is clear, I move in closer to Severo, whispering so only he can hear, "How fast can you drive?"

The ride back to Chelsea is definitely more pleasant than our earlier drive to meet up with my family, as Severo and I share stories on everything from training and work to childhood and the holidays. Even when I mention my father, in this casual conversation my memories focus on the good times I had with him and not so much on the pain I've been dealt since his death.

Severo parks his Jeep off to the side of my apartment, and we make our way to the three-story walkup. His hand is wrapped snugly around mine, and with the afternoon sun shining down on us, I feel pretty good right now. We may be weary of what we're doing, with our connection as coworkers, but there's just something between us that's hard to restrain.

As Severo holds the door open for me and I begin to trek up the stairs ahead of him, I'm surprised to see Muddy sitting on the second floor landing. It's not like Mrs. Schaeffer to let him roam freely in the hall. There are only three small apartments in this narrow building, one on each floor, but we've never let Muddy take over the common walkways, out of neighborly respect.

His tail wagging, he approaches me, and as he does I shriek with panic. "Shit! He's bleeding." Muddy's nose is streaked with blood, and I quickly check for any sign of injury. The blood is slightly sticky, yet I cannot seem to find its point of origin.

"He doesn't seem to be hurt, though," Severo says, lifting his paws one at a time, then looking behind his ears.

"Oh my God," I say, running to the door. "Mrs. Schaeffer!"

Muddy and Severo follow after me, as we enter the unlocked door and scramble to find my neighbor. "Mrs. Schaeffer!" I keep yelling out, and with no answer to lead me I search through her kitchen, bathroom and bedroom. "What the hell?" I look to Severo, bewildered by her absence. "Where could she be?"

A muffled sound comes from inside her hallway closet, and as I approach to check it out, Severo releases his handgun and cautions me to take it slowly. With his weapon leading the way, he slides the closet door open and then relaxes briefly as we see Mrs. Schaeffer sitting on the floor, her mouth secured by duct tape.

The fear in her eyes is crying out to me, and I drop to my knees, careful to pull the tape slowly from her delicate skin. Her eyes dart to the side, and as Severo follows the direction she's looking, he whispers, "Angie, stay quiet, okay?"

I nod to him as he slowly walks through her apartment, and I try to hush Mrs. Schaeffer as I peel the last of the tape from her face. "Shh, it's okay. You're okay now," I say, then wrap my arms around her in a hug. As I do so, I notice my neighbor has no blood on her whatsoever, and I am confused as to how Muddy picked it up. "Mrs. Schaeffer, what happened?"

She first gasps for air, stretching out her mouth, and then she informs me of her bound feet. As I untangle her from the mess, she speaks softly, obvious fear keeping her on guard. "There was a man, Angie. I don't know who, he just came to my door, and I opened it, thinking it must be you or Mr. De Salvo downstairs. Because how could someone get in without buzzing?"

"But Mr. De Salvo's in Florida visiting his nephew."

Her sad, fearful eyes stare back at me for answers and tears begin to run down her cheeks. As I raise a hand to wipe her face clean, my attention is caught by Severo yelling from a distance.

"Angie! You're gonna want to see this!"

Chapter 11

Hopping up every other step to the third floor, I follow Severo's voice and race to my apartment door, where I see Mrs. Schaeffer's spare key in the lock. When I walk in and see what Severo sees, I gasp.

"No. Oh, no, no, no!" Careful of my footing, so as not to disturb any evidence, I step closer to the courier box sitting in the middle of my living room floor.

It's torn open a bit, and I can see where Muddy must have chewed on the corners, thereby getting blood on his face. I don't know that I want to look inside the stained cardboard box, but I don't have a choice.

"Okay, see you soon," Severo says, hanging up his cell phone. "Cain's on his way right now. Angie? Hey, come on. Maybe you should sit down."

"No." Whatever this guy is up to, he obviously wants to make a point by leaving me something to come home to. I just can't believe I let him in the building. What had he looked like? Bald, I remembered. Thinking on it now, I should have paid more attention to a Sunday delivery.

Taking a latex glove from the work pack I keep at home, I peel back the top of the large box, and when I lean in to get a closer look, I cover my face with my free hand. Inside this courier box, which is big enough to hold a computer monitor, a man's head sits on a platter.

"You should gather some personal things together," Severo says, his voice calm but firm as he reaches out to me. "You can't stay here tonight. I'll call my captain and make arrangements for Mrs. Schaeffer to stay in a hotel. What about the guy on the first floor?"

My head shakes back and forth as I take in the sight. "He's in Florida, but we should see when he's scheduled to come home."

"Okay. I'm going to take Muddy to be with Mrs. Schaeffer right now, just to keep him out of here. And I'll let her know to pack some things." His hand strokes my arm, and I look to his eyes to read his concern. "I'll be right back. You yell if you need me."

As he leaves my apartment, I stare at the bodiless man. I know from his mouth we'll be able to pull DNA and hopefully find out who he is quickly, and see how he plays a role in this charade, but I really can't stand it anymore.

Our killer is obviously not settling down anytime soon, and who knows how many more possible victims are out there? With each attack, though, one thing is for sure. He seems to be getting closer and closer to me, and this makes no sense whatsoever, mind games or not.

Sirens begin to wail, and I know Cain and the others will soon be here to dissect the crime scene at my apartment. I prepare to abandon my home once again.

The one thing I can't figure out is why this guy has taken a liking to me. Why leave this head here? What do I have to do with any of this?

I wait in the living room, where CSU members are making themselves at home. For someone who wasn't planning on having guests over so soon, my apartment sure seems like a hot spot right now.

"Hey, kiddo," Cain says, appearing at my side as I watch the team begin to poke around for clues as to what and how and who. "You doing okay?"

"Fine. Weren't you supposed to be with your kids?"

"I was. We met in Central Park, so it wasn't nothing to get over here. This is much more important, you understand? I'm here for you now."

"I just want this over with, Cain. We have to get this guy before he does this again."

"And he will, ya know," Cain says, handing me a file folder of crime scene photos. "Check it out."

I review the same images I've been staring at in the office the past couple days. Killarney, burned to death. La Roche, suffocated by the burning of Killarney. Devlin, pierced by four swords. "What?"

"Angie, remember we saw something odd with the Killarney photos?" Cain taps a finger against the image showing that bizarre cut on his right foot. "Well, look, kiddo."

I watch as he pulls a photo of La Roche into view, and can't believe it. "He's got a cut, too?"

"Two, actually," Cain says, pointing at the detail. "Same foot. Same type of wound. But two small slices."

I review the photos carefully, and don't know how I didn't see these before. "Devlin has the same thing, Cain. Only there's three cuts. I bet wherever this guy's body is, it'll be the same story," I say, taking in the unsettling news.

"Which leaves us no doubt," my mentor states, sliding the photos back into their folder. "He's counting them off, one by one. Angie, congratulations. You've got your first serial case."

"Gee, thanks," I say, nervous about the possibilities to come. "Cain, I have to tell you something. This guy, I let him in my building. I thought he was a courier and I didn't even think twice when I held the door open for him."

"Do couriers even deliver on Sundays?" he asks, shrugging his shoulder. "But, Angie, kiddo, don't let it get to you. This guy was coming here no matter what. It's not your fault. You may be luckier than you think, not being here when he came and made himself at home in your apartment. Is your neighbor okay?"

"Yeah, Severo's precinct is putting her in a hotel for

the night, but thank God she wasn't hurt," I say, and as I do shivers run up my skin. The idea that Mrs. Schaeffer could have been seriously hurt—or worse—is enough to make me feel nauseated.

Cain and I watch as a CSU investigator lifts the head from the cardboard box and places it in protective plastic. The same process is done for the accompanying platter, but as it's bagged I take note of its design. "Hey, hang on a sec."

The investigator holds off packing the platter and lets me and Cain have a look at the ornate images decorating the gilded dish. "Cain, you seeing this?" I ask, and as Severo returns to my apartment I call him over to take a look, as well.

"What is that? Some biblical symbolism?" Cain asks, and I gaze at him, not believing his question.

"Are you serious? It's the Last Supper, Cain. How can you not know this?" The platter displays a scene from the Bible, where Jesus is surrounded by his apostles for the last time prior to his death.

"I know what it is," he says, defending himself quickly. "I just couldn't see it so well smeared with all that blood. But we better call the archdiocese. If this guy's got serious angst toward the church or God or whoever, we gotta put the word out. There's no telling who's next."

As Cain makes the call, Severo raises a hand to brush my hair from my face. "Mrs. Schaeffer is fine and I've got someone calling Mr. De Salvo's nephew. But how are you, Angie?"

"Um, well, considering we just found a head on my living room floor, not bad under the circumstances," I say, then nudge the detective in the side to compensate for my terse remark. "I'm okay, really. But we have to find out what this guy wants. This is day four, and the fourth victim. I don't like it."

"Me either," Severo says, then turns his attention to a CSU member. "Don't forget that," he says, and I follow his glance to my dining room table, where I see my newly acquired rosary.

"No, that's mine," I say, approaching, then taking a step back when I see it's been moved and something else is there. "But what do you think this is supposed to mean?"

The rosary is laid across the table, and beside it, written in blood, is a question mark. That's it. Just a question mark.

"I'm not sure, but what do you mean that's yours? It wasn't here when we left, Angie."

I think back to when Severo and I came up to my apartment in between shopping and heading out to my uncle's, and can't recall where the rosary was. I realize it had probably been in plain sight on my dresser. "It's mine. Some guy gave it to me the other day."

"What guy?" Cain asks, meeting up with us as we inspect the blood drawing. "When was this?"

"On my way to the cathedral. I hopped a cab and some homeless man was coming out of Denise's shelter. We shared the ride and when I was getting out, he handed it to me."

"Jesus, Angie, what did he look like? Was it the same guy?"

My eyes turn to meet Cain's and I think hard, but shake my head before I respond. "No, no, it wasn't. This guy was real scruffy and obviously homeless. He had ratty long hair and, okay, so I couldn't see him too well under his baggy clothing, but—"

Cain's hand wraps around my arm as he pries for more information. "Could he have been the same guy who was here today? Or for that matter, the same guy who followed you to the crematorium? Angie, think, damn it. Exactly how long has this guy been following you?"

Severo pulls my mentor away, seeing my discomfort. "Cain, take it easy, would ya? If you recall, that was just yesterday, so her head's probably still a little sore."

"Kiddo, I'm sorry," Cain says, leading me to sit down. His voice now softer, he looks into my eyes, and I see he means well. "It's just…what do you remember? Angie?"

I think back to my contact with all three men. The one in the crematorium had been dangerous, but the other two appeared harmless, and none of them seemed familiar. "The guy in the cab was quiet and real rough looking. I figured he was shy or ashamed or something. He looked nothing like the courier. Although…. I guess they could've been about the same size."

"A shower and a shave can change a lot, kiddo."

"Then Cain," Severo says, pulling out a chair to sit

beside me. As he runs a hand across the back of my neck, he speaks with a monotone, but firm voice. "If it is the same guy, he would have been following Angie long before yesterday. He could have been following her from day one."

"Even before the shelter?" I ask, angling in my chair to debate this idea. "That was the day after our first body was found at St. Augustine's. If he's been following me since then, what does that say? That he was at the men's mission watching us? He was there the whole time?"

Cain taps his knuckles against the table, next to the blood-smeared question mark. "That's exactly what we gotta figure out, kiddo. Because if this guy's got some personal business to settle with you, it doesn't matter how many bodies we find. It'll be yours that means the most to him."

"Bag it," Severo says to the CSU, who then picks up the wooden rosary and adds it to the collection for trace. Little specks of blood are on the beads, and I wonder if Muddy accidentally played with the evidence. Time will tell.

"So now what?" I ask, unsure of where we go from here. With no clear theory of how this guy chooses his victims, it's hard to figure out how to save his next one. Now that the archdiocese is aware of the situation, thankfully, word will get out that someone may be trying to send an ungodly message.

"Well, you can't stay here," Cain says, and I nod toward the detective.

"Yeah, Severo said the same thing. I'm going to pack some stuff, but I can't go to my uncle's. He's allergic to Muddy."

"And I have a crappy bachelor pad, kiddo. So, what'll it be. Hotel or the office?"

"She can stay with me," Severo suggests, and both my mentor and I look to him. Though Severo and I were perhaps planning on spending some social time together today, I don't know that my mentor needs to hear about it. "Besides, if this guy likes to follow her around, it's probably best I stick close, ya know?"

My eyebrows arch as I glance at the detective, hear his words. That has got to be one of the lamest excuses I have ever heard from someone trying to get me up to his place.

"Sounds good to me," Cain says, surprising me. "He's got a point, kiddo. Who knows what this wacko is up to. Best you're not left on your own."

"Do I have to remind you of my skills, gentlemen? I ranked at the top of my class at the academy," I say, defending my ability to take care of myself. "I know how to—"

"Take care of yourself," they say in unison, and then Cain grabs my hand, holding it tightly as he kneels down in front of my chair to speak to me. "Kiddo, I have no doubts you can kick some serious ass. Hell, you could knock me out in a second. But you can't take this lightly, you hear me? There's no sense in risking it, just to prove yourself. You don't have to prove anything, not to me. You are your father's daughter. You got in you some of the best breeding the Bureau's seen in a long time. I know that, the detective knows that and we sure as hell know you know that. But right now, I'm asking you a favor. Stay with Severo, just for the night, and then we'll figure something else out tomorrow, if that's more to your liking. Okay?"

With their eyes on me, awaiting my reaction, I absorb all that Cain has said. I know this is the best thing for me, and he's right. I have no problem staying with Severo. I do, however, have a problem with not having control of this case.

"What are you going to do?" I ask my mentor, getting up to retrieve my overnight bag.

"I'm going to follow CSU and wait on the lab results. This guy may think he has the upper hand, but that's far from true. If—no, when—I get the ID on this guy and we know what's what, you'll be the first to know. We'll get this one, Angie. Mark my words. NCAVC is going to eat you up when you apply."

In the heart of Hell's Kitchen, south of Port Authority, Severo's comfort lies within a second floor loft overlooking the cheap eateries and quaint little shops on the street below. Though I hadn't really given much thought to what would be revealed inside his residential walls, I'm a little taken aback by his decorating skills.

"You do all this yourself?" I ask, curious to know if perhaps his ex-fiancée planned it out. His apartment is bigger than mine, and definitely more tidy. Guess that's why he felt so at home doing my dishes yesterday.

"Yeah, I just figured I may as well make it livable. I don't spend as much time at home as I'd like—you know, with the job being the way it is—but I figure I may as well have something decent to come home to," he says, handing me a beer.

Two plush leather sofas and a reclining chair are the focal point in the main living space, but along the exposed brick walls are a number of bookcases, with neat stacks of magazines, hardcovers, a few ornaments and framed photos. A fireplace is nestled into the wall, opposite a big bay window, and Muddy seems content to have found a place to curl up.

Severo flops down into the nearest sofa as I continue to inspect his space. I'm not at all surprised to see a large and eclectic music collection, ranging from groups I recognize as household names to the telltale blind choices, as he explained earlier today. I slide a disc from an odd-looking case and set it in the player, waiting for an unknown band to make itself known over his surround sound system.

"You have a lot of toys," I comment, taking in the high-tech audio and visual equipment.

"I'm a sucker, what can I say?" he jokes, as he watches me peruse the display of his personal lifestyle. His space is more mature than I would have suspected. Rather than skimping on style by simply framing poster prints, he's decorated his walls with actual framed paintings.

"Well, I'm impressed, to say the least," I say, as he pulls on my hand, guiding me to sit next to him. I fall into the plush sofa and feel the buttery leather wrap around my form. Very nice, indeed.

He places a thumb under my chin, drawing my attention to him as he speaks. "So am I."

My eyes meet his, and my expression must show my confusion.

"You've been in the New York office for less than a week," he says, straightening up from his slouch to place his beer bottle on the wooden trunk coffee table. "Not only have you managed to get accustomed to working with Cain and the rest of the team, but you've gained the respect of half the NYPD without a wink. I'd say you're doing pretty good."

"I don't know about that." I sip at my imported cream ale. "You might need a reminder that I've also managed to make friends with a serial murderer, nearly get myself killed in a crematorium, of all places, and put a neighbor's life in danger. I've had a busy week, all right. I just don't know that it's been all that productive."

"Oh, come on," he argues, leaning in with a look of disbelief. "I can top that one. Remember Zeus? Just a few days ago you went undercover and spoke, what was it? German?"

"Yeah, German."

"Okay, you spoke German to a serial rapist and murderer, and not only that, you nabbed the guy right then and there. And you had just arrived in the city. So don't expect a pity party from me if we haven't figured out this guy's deal within four days," he says, proud to have made his point.

"But shouldn't we have?" I ask, and in all sincerity I don't know. Yeah, four days isn't much time to work with, but tell that to the four dead guys our killer has left behind. "Shouldn't we be further than we are, or at least know who we're dealing with on this, Severo?"

"We will. He's going to slip up, Angie. It's like Cain said. Guys like this want to get caught. It's the only way we'll know exactly what he wants to tell us, so he'll slip up. One way or another." He reaches for my hand, tugging at it playfully. "And I'm pretty sure you can call me Carson now. I think we made it past the official business part."

"Okay, *Carson,*" I say mockingly. "But you mind telling me what the hell that is?" I ask, angling a thumb toward the stereo. "Is that a banjo I hear?"

"Hey, it's good stuff," he laughs, and then as I push myself out of the sofa to change the music, he pulls me right back down, closer to him. "I bet you have a little hillbilly in you, just waiting to be discovered," he jokes, then reaches a hand to skim my shoulder, rubbing it with warmth, and I meet his glance with laughter.

"Detective," I ask, playing the same game that got us in trouble the other night, "are you trying to seduce me?"

"Could be," he whispers, inching closer to me as he raises a hand to my face, smudging his thumb along my skin, letting the contrast of his ruggedness mix with my softer flesh. His scent draws me back to that night at my apartment, when his lips were on mine, and I ache from within for their fast return.

My voice is soft but demanding when I say, "Then kiss me."

Rubbing his thumb along my bottom lip, he tilts his head toward me, and with his other hand reaches to stroke my hair. My right hand grabs hold of his, and I cradle it as I lean in to close the distance between us.

Our breaths are shared for a moment before I place my mouth on his, letting its warmth brush against my cool lips as he responds. His flavor is sweet, and salty, as his lips press against mine in a cautious yet controlled caress.

I twist on the couch, turning my whole body to offer more of what I want him to explore. I place both hands on his face, letting my fingers dance along his cheekbones. His eyes soften as they skim over me, down my neck and along my shoulders.

Leaning into him, I move my legs across his so that I'm facing him, straddling his body. My head tilts and I place my open mouth on his, letting his warmth heat me again. His tongue begins to explore and, beneath me, I can feel his erection expand.

Raising my arms, he slides my shirt overhead, tossing it to the side and then getting rid of my bra before returning his lips to mine. Slowly, he moves them down my neck, and I arch my back at his touch. My hands unravel the necktie he donned for lunch, and then I pull his tailored shirt from the formfitting jeans he's wearing, and slide the cotton off him, exposing a bare chest, warm and welcoming.

His skin is slightly tanned, and on his lower rib cage

I see a streak of scar tissue, giving evidence to an event I know nothing of.

I trace a finger along his ragged scar, then press my breasts against his muscular breadth. My nipples react at the contact and I inhale his scent, sucking it in with a deep breath.

His kisses continue, pushing harder against my flesh as he slides his face from my neck to my shoulders, until finally he reaches my breastbone, tickling my skin as he strokes his tongue against my bosom. My breathing intensifies as I let his mouth tease my skin, and I long for more of him.

With my mouth on his neck, I nudge him down onto his back, still straddling his length. His musk intensifies as I rub myself into him, and the friction between our jeans causes my skin to ache.

With one hand on the sofa, supporting my weight, I slide the other to my waistband, loosening my belt first, then unzipping my jeans. Severo shoves a hand down my side, his fingers momentarily stopping at my midsection to linger on my skin. Then he assists me with removing the jeans, and I kick them off, letting my legs wriggle into his.

He returns his attention to my lips, sucking the heat from my mouth and pushing his tongue deep within me. I absorb this briefly, before wriggling down his chest, licking as I go, until I reach the closure to his denim. There, I let my fingers tease the doorway to his flesh, and his hairs stand on end, excited by my touch.

Pulling hard on his waistband, I rip those jeans off

fast, and he lifts his head to watch me get what I want. His flesh is now protected only by cotton boxers, and his size is pushing against the fabric, crying out for release.

Sliding them off, one leg at a time, I then remove my last remaining garment and return my attentions to the hard flesh beneath me, rolling on the condom that appeared as if by magic in Carson's hand. Carson's breathing is now harsh, and his skin is dotted with little beads of sweat. My tongue traces along his abdomen, licking up his salty taste before I arch onto him, letting my moisture slowly envelope his ready-and-waiting penis. Pressing into him, onto him, I find the fullness of him brings an ache, while my body adjusts to take him in.

My hips guide my movements, as I begin to circle around, letting my arousal climb through my veins. The detective's hands are hugging my hips and he lifts his head to dart his tongue at my exposed nipples. The combined sensations cause my body to shiver, and I know my insides are screaming for more.

I grab hold of one of his hands and stick his fingers in my mouth, moistening them well, and then lead him to my pubic region. Pushing his fingers between his flesh and my clit, I direct him to stimulate me in a pattern I know will guarantee satisfying success.

With one hand pressed against my throbbing clitoris, the detective grasps my shoulder with the other, pushing himself in farther. He pulses into me, tighter, stronger, as I writhe beneath his touch. The heat within me rises, scratching at my veins, and the fluttering shivers begin to stretch from my center to my limbs.

I press into him hard, letting the motion penetrate me deeper, as I absorb the reaction of my climax. Beads of sweat drip along my neck, some landing on Severo's slick chest, and I press my mouth to his, tasting his saltwater skin.

The pulsing slows and I release my weight onto him, our chests again pressing together. His eyes meet mine and I let my gaze drift over his features before I lift my head, taking notice of the accompanying music. "Now what is that?"

"A washboard." He chuckles softly. "It's bluegrass."

"Well, all right then," I say, lifting myself off him and reaching for my empty bottle. "You got another beer?"

It's half past six but I can't sleep. A theory has come to mind, and with Severo's laptop on hand, my research has proved somewhat useful.

When I awoke from my slumber, I listened to a message on my cell phone from Cain, letting me know the name of our fourth victim. Paul Aaron White. It took me some time to wrap my head around it, but I soon realized our killer's angst toward godly men is even more freaky than we could have ever imagined.

In fact, had it not been for the symbolic platter accompanying Paul's head, I might not have even come this far. With the image of the Last Supper in mind, I scroll through the Web sites I have found thus far. Matthias, Jean, Thomas and Paul. Four men who have something very unique in common. More interesting than their lives—according to these Web sites—is their deaths, at least in application to this case.

"Come on, wake up," I say, straddling Severo's back, as his body is squished facedown into his comfortable bed. His head rises slowly from the down pillows. Much as I'd like to hop back into the sheets with him, time is not on our side.

"What time is it?" he asks with a yawn, as he slowly stretches his arms out. I climb off of him, satisfied I've finally woken him up, and seek out my clothing.

"Almost seven," I say, removing his tie, which somehow wound up on me last night. A few rounds of good cop–bad cop was fun while it lasted, but we have some serious work ahead of us. "I'm going to hop in the shower, so maybe you can make some coffee?" His grumble barely acknowledges my request. "And then we need to meet up with Cain."

"Can't we just stay in bed a little while longer?" he begs, reaching for my hand as I walk by to retrieve my overnight bag. "Cain's not going to be in for a while, ya know."

"Oh yeah? Well, I called him and told him to meet us right away, so hurry up."

"Why would you do that?" he asks, rising up on his elbows, as Muddy hops onto the bed for company.

"Because I figured it out, Severo. I know how this guy chooses his victims."

Chapter 12

"I can't believe none of us thought of that sooner,"
Severo says, following me through the glass door to the
Plaza office. Cain is slumped over in his chair, both
hands wrapped around his coffee mug. "Morning,
Cain," Severo says, then looks at me. "Coffee?"

"You have to ask?" I say with a smile, then pull together the crime scene photos to spread them out in
front of my mentor.

"This better be good, kiddo. I hate Monday mornings, and for you to haul my ass in here early... I'm
just saying, this better be damn good."

"It is," Severo declares, handing me a fresh mug
of office brew, topped up with cream. "Go on, tell
him."

He takes a seat on my desk and I sip at my coffee before clearing my throat. "Apostles."

"What? Kiddo, I don't do well on Monday mornings, so talk to me like I'm an idiot. Spell it out for me." Cain sits up in his chair, looking worn-out, and I wonder how long he stayed with trace last night. Regardless of what the forensics lab uncovered, I just hope he got *some* sleep, at least. It's going to be a very long day.

"After I got the message you left on my cell phone," I explain. "About the identity of the head? Paul Aaron White? Well, I got to thinking about all of our victims, trying to see what ties them together, what they have in common."

Severo perks up, enthusiastic about my theory. "Get this, Cain. Matthias, Jean, Thomas and Paul."

I proceed, in case there is any confusion. "This is what unifies them and made them a target in this guy's hunt."

Cain stands up to walk around his desk, then looks at the photos upside down, though I'm not sure why. When he twists them to view them properly from his angle, though, I see there is no reason to his maneuver. "Now I'm not saying that's a bad theory, kiddo, I just need you to clarify for me. Are you saying what I think you're saying?"

"Yes. Those are all names of apostles. And you want to know the punch line?"

"There's more?"

I pull some printed pages I obtained online this morning, via Severo's home computer, and hand them to Cain. "Oh, there's more all right. After I thought about their names being those of the apostles, I did a few searches to see what I could find."

Severo traces a finger along the first page Cain is looking at. "She found this. A Web site detailing how they died."

"The apostles?" Cain says, looking to me for answers.

"Yes! And just look at it, Cain. According to that site, and several others I cross-referenced, the apostle Thomas died at the hands of four soldiers. Pierced through with swords."

"I don't believe it," my mentor says, clearly astounded at these findings. "Would ya look at that?" He shows the detective, who has already heard my entire theory.

Severo says, "Yeah, so not only does that coat of arms thing hold up with the idea of this guy ridding the earth of believers—or disbelievers, depending on how he views it—but this only intensifies the issue."

"And John the Apostle escapes after being burned, but then apparently dies of natural causes," I say, then clarify when Cain looks at me quizzically. "Jean La Roche? The name John in French is Jean."

"You don't think it's all a little strange?" he asks, his head nodding as if it's too much to take in. "Them sharing the names of the apostles?"

"No," Severo declares, urging my mentor to grasp this information. "It may not help us understand why he chooses who he does, but it certainly helps us understand how. Look, he followed Angie for days without anyone noticing him. Maybe he sets his eyes on his prey, gets to know them a bit on a personal level, like he did with Angie, and then makes his move."

"Okay, I'll go with that thought for a moment. What about the other two? Matthias and Paul?"

"Well, not that I need to point those out, but Paul was beheaded, and Matthias was burned to death. Cain, do you not think this is right? That this has anything to do with our guy?"

He sets the photos down on his desk, looking toward the floor for a moment as he thinks about it. "I don't know what to say, kiddo. Thing is, if your theory holds up, we're in big trouble."

"Why's that?" I ask, curious to know his thoughts.

"Because, Angie," he says, his voice very firm with unease. "There were twelve apostles, were there not?"

I see his point. We may have four victims on our hands currently, but unless we find this guy soon he may cause a lot more damage. "Yes, and we know from those cuts on all the victims' feet, that he's counting them off, one by one. If we can figure out what else they have in common, if there's any other reason these men are being chosen—" I pace past the dying plant in the corner "—then we can try to get a step ahead of him. Stop him before he does it again."

"Well, we know they all have some sort of connection to either the church or to religion in general, right?" Cain says, flipping through files to check his facts. "Like Devlin, who was teaching his students about myths and Christianity and such."

Severo nods his head, agreeing with Cain. "And Matthias Killarney was a spiritual advisor, so that's a given."

"Which leaves us with Paul and Jean," I say. "Jean was a baker. I don't know what role he plays in this, but maybe we can talk to his housekeeper again, now that we know to question from this angle. And what about Paul Aaron White?"

"I'll check into it," Cain says, then pats me on the shoulder. "Good work, kiddo. It's bad news for us, knowing there's another eight possible victims on the list, but good work figuring that out. I like the way you think."

As much as I want to enjoy this moment of commendation from my mentor, one thing is still bothering me. Why did the killer decide to make contact with me? As my thoughts wrap around possible links, however, Cain's cell phone rings at the same time as Severo's, and I listen for the inevitable.

"Let's go. Number five is still alive."

I ride with Cain, as per his request, and we follow the detective's Jeep to the scene at a sewer drain along the West side. "What do you think he's doing?" I ask Cain, shocked to learn our fifth body is still breathing. "You think he's setting us up?"

"No way to know for sure," Cain says, keeping his eyes on the road ahead as he speeds along the streets.

"If he's up to something fishy, we'll use it to our advantage, kiddo. If this guy's as good as he thinks he is, nothing comes by way of accident. If he left this victim alive, it's for a reason."

There's a bit of nervousness in Cain's voice and I share his obvious concern. I don't know which scares me more—another dead body or a possible trap to snag us. But I listen to my mentor as he preps me for what's to come.

"Just do what you do best, Angie. Use those instincts. We're going out there with all eyes open, and if you keep in mind everything you were taught—at the academy and by your father—you'll do just fine. Okay?"

His car reels into place alongside the sewer passageway, and we exit to meet up with Severo, not knowing for certain what to expect. As we step forward, armed and ready, I am drawn by an unidentified voice. There is no one visible. The man's speech is coming from behind some concrete slabs.

"And he found in the temple those selling cattle and sheep and doves," the voice says, and thanks to my uncle Simon's private sermons, I recognize the words as a Bible passage.

Growing up, I gained a solid education in the ways of religion, even though I've never claimed to be a churchgoer. Even when I skipped out on official Sunday preaching to spend time with my father, Simon made sure each of my visits with him was spent discussing the old ways of the world. At the time I didn't care one way or the other what I was being taught, but now that I've grown up and work in the real world, it's amazing how much of those life lessons come in handy.

The detective walks at my side, with Cain just a few feet behind. Not sure what to think of the situation just yet, we pace ourselves, not knowing if our killer may still be on site.

"…and the money brokers in their seats."

As the voice preaches its message, my fingers wrap tightly around my handgun as a precaution. Severo nods his chin to the left and I mimic his movements, staying close against the concrete, creeping nearer to the source. The sewer drains are rippling with water, and the faint smell of refuse and rotten perishables fills my nose.

Cain has remained at the sewage entrance, and I see he has met up with paramedics who are waiting for word to go in and see what help this victim requires.

It was a jogger on this out-of-the-way path who came across a stranded vehicle, and when he noticed the body inside, not knowing if it was dead or alive, he called 911.

It's not a good idea to assume the killer has left the scene, not when we can't even see it yet, so I prepare for the worst. This could be the day his identity is blown and this case moves from open to closed.

We're edging closer to the end of our concrete protection and I ignore the words "he poured out the coins of the money changers," until I hear a new noise filter through the air. I sidle closer to Severo and realize it's the chime a car door makes when it's ajar.

Rounding the edge of the barrier between us and the car, the detective and I make eye contact, giving one another the go-ahead to step into the scene and crack down.

Gradually, I peek out into the open and see the teal-green sedan with the driver's-side door open. My foot loosens some gravel and the minuscule disturbance triggers a reaction from something, somewhere.

"This is Detective Severo with the NYPD," Carson announces, his voice echoing through the sewer drains. "Come out with your hands where I can see them."

My breath sounds louder than the preaching voice, but no one is making his presence known, other than a few sewer rats. We step forward, cautious of any nooks that could act as a hiding place, but no one appears.

In the distance, the wailing of additional sirens grows closer, but Severo loses his patience and begins to walk toward the car. Other than the voice, there is no indication we aren't alone, and when he approaches the sedan, his hands move through the air as he shrugs.

"Cassette tape."

Not too quick to shrug off the possibilities, I take my time approaching, but he's already affirmed where the voice is coming from. I reach his side and he points into the car, where the keys are turned in the ignition to keep the battery going, but the car is stalled.

My guard down, I lean into the car and offer a smile

to our victim, but he appears lifeless except for the faint movement of his chest. "Cain, bring the medics!" I yell, letting him know our killer is out of sight. In the driver's seat, the man is propped tight against the headrest. The nylon seat belt has been cut, then wrapped snugly around his neck.

"Nice." The detective looks up and down the sewers and shouts out, "I hope you're enjoying your little game!" which surprises me, since I don't know who he's yelling at. "Just in case," he says, looking back at me. "You recognize the voice from the tape?"

"I'm not sure," I answer, trying to remember what my attacker sounded like that day in the crematorium. His voice was raspy, but my mental clarity isn't top-notch right now.

Cain is approaching with backup and the paramedics, but I keep my eyes on the details of the crime, determined to find any evidence to lead us to our killer.

"Must have got him from behind," Severo says, aiming a finger at the back seat. "The belt's wrapped around several times, but it's tied at the back. See?"

"Yeah." My attention diverts to the car's exterior. While there's no way our killer could have covered his tracks out here, our chances of finding his trail look grim, with the muddy earth and flow of drainage fighting against us.

Cain approaches me, notepad in hand, and I await the news. "According to the plates, this is Mario James Anderson. I don't know what that does for the apostle theory, kiddo."

Cold drops of rain begin to fall upon us on this second-last day of November, and combined with the crispness of the gray weather, my skin begins to get goose bumps even under the layers of clothing.

"Mario's not one of the Twelve, but James is," I say, shrugging my shoulders, wondering if my attempts at figuring out this guy's pattern will hold up.

As the paramedics take away our victim, alive but not in the best of shape, and CSU begins to inspect the scene, eager to pull trace yet again, I look to Cain for answers. "Anything else about Anderson? Anything that might possibly indicate his religious involvement?"

The pellets of rain are increasing and the three of us, Severo beside me now, slide under the sewage tunnel to stay dry. "I dunno, kiddo. This guy was no saint. His plates came up with a flag on him. He's served time before."

"What for?" Severo asks, clicking off his car alarm and leading us in that direction. The collar on my jacket is filling with rain, so I shake a bit, trying to get the wetness off me.

"Perjury, of all things. Gotta love a man who lies and gets caught. Especially in front of a grand jury."

I slide into Severo's Jeep and he quickly turns up the heat to warm us from the sudden cold shower outside. Cain, however, remains in the rain, determined to have a cigarette even without an umbrella. As a compromise, I keep my window down halfway, so we can hear him read off his notes, and I simply sit back to avoid the drops of rain.

"Our perjurer here didn't do much for the friend he was trying to protect. Guy's locked up. Doing time, big-time."

"But he's alive?" I ask, somewhat relieved there may be a lead we can follow. If the convict knows today's victim, he may also know the killer.

"Interesting choice of words, kiddo."

"Why's that?"

"He's up the river."

"At Sing Sing?" Severo asks, leaning into me to listen closer to Cain's words.

"Yup. Death row, too. Philip Martin. Seems he and Mario James Anderson here were involved awhile back on some level," Cain explains, looking to me for confirmation that this name is also that of an apostle. "Counterfeit ops, drug rings, you name it."

"We have to talk to him," Severo says, and I agree. "If he knows anything, it's not like he's got something to lose by sharing it with us."

"You're probably right on that one." Cain wipes the rain from his brow, then backs away from the Jeep as an approaching CSU member calls to him. "Hang on a sec, you two."

"This is good, Ang," Severo says, and I twist toward him as he leans over the middle console. "This might be it, you know? The day we figure out what the hell is going on with this case."

"Hey, look," I say, watching Cain and the CSU member.

With my window still down a notch, Severo and I

lean over to hear Cain ask, "Whatcha got?" as he accepts a clear plastic sleeve the investigator is carrying. I can't believe we may finally have some evidence to work with. That, and a possible connection with this Philip Martin guy.

"Maybe a family photo," the investigator says. "Found it tucked into the visor. Best look into his next of kin."

"Oh my," Cain breathes, his voice crackling through the cool rain. "Angie."

"What is it?" I can't see well enough from my seat, so I hop out of the Jeep and reach for the bag. But Cain pulls away and takes a step back. "Cain, what the hell is it?"

Severo has also left the comfort of the vehicle and walks around to meet me as I stare at Cain, hungry for answers. Rain is pounding down on us and I scrunch my neck into my collar, trying to keep the body heat inside.

"I'm not sure, Angie. I'm not sure you should see this."

Severo leans toward my mentor, also wanting answers. "Cain?" he asks, but doesn't wait to be acknowledged before he grabs the bag and looks at it closely. His eyes move up to meet mine, but I can't read his expression.

"Jesus, you guys, you look like you've seen a ghost." I move my hand quickly and snap the bag from Severo's hold, shaking my head at their absurdity. But when I see the image stained with age and damp with today's rain, my breath catches and I feel my throat tighten.

"Angie?" Severo pleads, his voice muffled by my thoughts.

My eyes do not leave the image I am holding when the words escape from my lips. "It's my father."

"I'm sorry, Agent David," the CSU investigator says coldly, as he reaches for the photo. "But I'm going to need that back. It's evidence."

"I know that! Just give me a minute, will ya?"

Heat rises to my face even in this chilled weather, and I feel somewhat faint despite the surge of adrenaline pushing through my veins.

Severo's hand reaches to my shoulder and I feel his fingers wrap securely around my wet clothing. "Angie?"

"And that's me. God, I must have been six years old when this was taken. He looks so young."

"Okay, let's give it back to these guys, kiddo," Cain says, wrapping one of his hands around the sleeved evidence and grasping my arm tightly with the other as he looks into my eyes. "They'll need to trace it for any prints, fibers…and, Angie, kiddo, we're going to figure this out."

I let my eyes meet my mentor's, unsure of what this means. Cain's right. This is evidence, and for some reason, it's been left here for me to see. I aim to find out why.

"Okay. He knew we'd find it. He knew it would affect me. So let's get on with it," I say, trying to keep focus despite my unease. "Let's talk to the guy at Ossining."

"Hold on just a minute, kiddo," Cain says, speaking softly against the rain. "I don't know that you should be going up the river. This might be a good time for you to take a step back. Step away from the case for a bit. You know?"

"I couldn't disagree more! Cain, he's making it personal. This guy obviously has something to say to me and I want to hear it. Philip Martin may know who's behind this. I'm not going to give up on this because of a photo. Hell, he could have taken that from my apartment yesterday."

"That's true," Severo states, and I look to him, relieved he sees my point. "But, Angie, this is a lot to take in right now. Are you sure you're up for it?"

So much for siding with me.

"Yes, I'm up for it. I don't know what this means any more than you do," I say, looking at the detective, then at my mentor. "But I'm sure as hell not going to sit around and wait to be knocked over the head. Again."

"All right, all right," Cain says, leading me to Severo's Jeep and urging me into the passenger seat. "Then you go with the detective. Technically, this is his case, so he'll need to get clearance to talk to this guy on death row."

"What about you?" Severo asks, nodding to Cain.

"I'll go to the hospital and see if Mario James Anderson feels like talking. His life was spared for a reason, so he must have something to say."

Chapter 13

With Sing Sing nearly an hour away, I get comfortable in the passenger seat as Severo and I head out to meet Philip Martin. With Monday morning traffic to compete with, this may be a long ride. Hell, it might take an hour just to get through the core and out to the expressway.

Despite my unease with seeing that photograph at the scene, I have to focus on what to ask the convict. Whatever he has to say may lead us to our killer, and nabbing him off the streets is the most important thing to me right now.

"You think he'll cooperate?" I ask Severo, angling in my seat to watch his reaction.

His hair is damp from the early morning rain, and

his eyes are intent on the road ahead, but I'm glad he has accepted my determination in finding this killer. There is no way I'm going to sit back and watch as everyone but me takes action with what could be our best possible lead yet.

"You never know," he says softly, and I can tell he's a bit worried about my apparent involvement in this case. I don't know what the killer wants with me, but he'll find out soon enough that I don't play nice with strangers. "Have you ever met someone on death row?"

"Can't say I have. Though I've heard stories."

"Yeah," Severo breathes, almost with a laugh, but his voice is undercoated with a reality I can't yet relate to. "We can pretty much expect one of two scenarios."

His face turns a bit to his right, and meets my glance for a moment before focusing again on the drive. "This guy will either be newly repentant and want to amend his ways by helping us out, like it's some sort of debt he needs to repay to society before he goes. Or…"

"Or we'll be the last people on earth he'll want to talk to," I admit, realizing the odds are probably not in our favor.

"What we have on our side, though, is that we're not after him, exactly. That may make it easier for him to talk to us, seeing how we're not trying to dig into his past, per se."

"Philip was one, too, ya know," I say, my eyes skimming the printed-out pages from this morning's research. "An apostle, that is. Damn it, Severo, how did he do this? How did this guy figure out who to kill? And for what?"

His subtle shrug shouldn't be confused with uncertainty. I can see Severo is wrapping his thoughts around this case like it's the only thing that matters to anyone right now. And, well, it is. If there are another potential eight targets out there, we have to stop this man before he goes too far.

"I think it's safe to go with the name connection," the detective says, making the transition onto the expressway. "I also think there's another reason he chooses them. Could be the connection they each have to some religious organization or whatever, but there has to be something with that. Despite the textbook definition on serial killing, this guy has already tossed any tested theories out the door. He seems to know his victims personally, and they are anything but random."

"Does that scare you?" I ask, hoping to get an honest reaction to such a simple question. As part of our jobs, we're supposed to know what's going on and have the confidence to set it straight, but we can't be robotic about things. Human nature isn't always just, but it does leave room for fear, even among the good guys.

"A little. It just means we have to work that much harder, that much faster at putting the pieces together. Now that we know the superficial elements," he says, leaning toward the dash to wipe a condensation smudge off the inside window. "It's time to go deep."

As I reach to the stereo to turn on some music, anx-

ious to pump some adrenaline into my blood, Severo's
hand meets mine and stops me at the volume control.
"Hey, Angie, about that photo—"

"I'm fine. I'm just pissed off," I say, showing my
anger. "I'll have to have a better look around the apartment and see if anything else is missing. Creeps me
out, is all."

He holds my hand and gives it a quick squeeze before returning his to the wheel. "Whatever this guy's
up to, he's trying to make it personal. But don't let him
do that. Don't let him get the better of you. It's what
he wants, ya know?"

Though I nod my head in agreement to keep this di-
alogue short, I don't know. What could this killer possibly want with me? I can't help feeling he saw me as
the weakest of the three and decided to angle his taunts
in my direction, hoping to get a reaction from me.
Well, that's not going to happen.

My determination to go into profiling, once I get the
required field experience, is to dissect the minds of
criminals and see what it is that makes them do what
they do. If this guy thinks he's getting what he wants
by reeling me in closer to his game plan, he has it upside down. In the end, we'll get him behind bars, but I
will have gained the understanding of what and who
he is, readying me for NCAVC one day.

As we near the end of our drive, I think of the history of Sing Sing. I've never been here, but it is perhaps one of the state's, if not the country's, most
famous prison grounds.

My knowledge of it stems mostly from the press, relating to the infamous escape attempts made in the early years. Now, though, it still houses a good collection of felons, ranging in age and severity of crime, and pretty much anything is possible within its historic nest.

We head along Hunter Street, and I'm beginning to see the great structure against the backdrop of the lengthy Hudson River. The original wall surrounding the prison was made of handmade bricks. Those now have a place in history, and the newer, more modern blockage is designed for maximum security with a combined fence and state-of-the-art cement wall. Tough to get in, tough to get out.

We pass our first security clearance and wind through the gateway to the entrance. Once parked, Severo and I trail back on the footpath to find a way inside, and neither of us can resist looking around, as though we're tourists. The enormity of the place is worth at least a moment of awe. This will be my first time stepping inside the famous walls, but hopefully the last.

"Philip Martin," Severo says at the front desk, showing his identification as he signs a collection of forms.

"Says here, he'll be out in a week," the guard says, and when she says "out," I know she doesn't mean free.

Another guard ushers us through a maze of hallways, and my adrenaline is increasing at the thought of conversing with a man on death row. As we walk through multiple security lockdowns, it occurs to me

I failed to ask what Philip was in for. He may have a history of counterfeit, but they don't hand out death sentences like candy. There must be something more to his deal. Then again, I may not want to know the details.

The door buzzes open as Severo and I are guided into a stale visitation chamber, a plain room with a few glass windows along the side to allow guards visual advantage. The place is maxed out with security, both human and technological, so I know we're safe in here.

"Who the hell are you?" The man drops hard into his seat.

"Philip Martin? I'm Detective Carson Severo of the NYPD and this is Special Agent David with the FBI." As we sit down across from the convict, I push a button on my tape recorder so we don't miss anything, and then I quickly make eye contact to establish decorum. "We're looking into a case you may have some connection with."

My eyes meet Martin's, and his glassy pupils stare back at me, intrigued. "I don't need to talk to you."

We were expecting a little friction, so I take my time warming him up with a feminine voice. "I know you probably don't care what's going on out there. I also know you're on a short leash, so I won't waste your time. But believe me when I say you could prove to be a big help for this case."

Philip stares in silence, eyes peering at me as though they're looking through me, somehow.

"I'm willing to sit here all day, if that's what it takes."

Still nothing.

Severo leans his elbows onto the institutional desk, his attitude adjusting to accommodate the situation. "Maybe there's something you want? Something, perhaps, to make your last days a little more pleasant?"

Bribery is not my strong point, so I'm glad Severo has taken this step. I realize whatever this guy has done wrong is well in the past, and if offering up any material possession will bring him joy, it'll only be a temporary satisfaction.

"You got gum?"

My brow arches toward Severo as Martin says this. "Gum? Yes, I think I do." I reach into my bag and then halt, looking back at him. "Or were you kidding?"

"I like gum."

"Okay," I say, locating the spearmint sticks in my bag's side pocket. A guard approaches me, inspects the chewing gum, then approves it for the inmate. I don't see how such a simple pleasure could coerce his opinion any, but who am I to judge.

Severo gets right back to business. "So, Philip. Anything you can say to help us out would be greatly appreciated. We know of your history with Mario James Anderson, but that's not what we came to talk about."

The blank stare returns as Severo begins to draw out some files. It occurs to me this man may be more responsive to my voice, so I take the chance. "We're looking for someone you may know. He's been after a group of men who appear to be connected in some way, though we can't really share the full details with you. I hope you'll understand."

His shrug does little to state his interest or lack thereof. Severo nods to me, though, and I'm glad he thinks I'm making progress, and doesn't mind me cutting in.

"It seems he's been killing men by replicating the deaths of the apostles. These men also share the names of the apostles, and the method of murder."

Philip straightens in his chair, and I don't know whether to take it as a sign or if he's just feeling restless. I look to Severo, then back at Philip Martin, and cut the tail-chasing short.

"Do you have any idea what I'm talking about? Because if you do, and I know you probably couldn't care less whether or not we put someone away for murder, but if you do—"

"Yeah, I get it."

Both Severo and I sit up at his words.

"Excuse me? What do you get?" I ask.

Philip leans into the space between us, his body angled slightly over the table, and I hear his breathing pulse in a calm rhythm. "You mean Jude. Right? You're talking about Jude."

I slide my documents outlining the names of the apostles to Severo. Though the name is a variation of Judas, this can't be a coincidence. There's no way.

"Yes. Yes, I think so. You know this man, Mr. Martin?"

Philip leans back in his seat, glazed eyes looking directly at me. His voice is calm, as though he's been sedated into complacency, like a lap cat. "I do. Jude Barnaby, or Judas, as he likes to call himself. Stupid ass."

The detective tries again to get in on the conversation with our convict. "Do you know about the murders?"

"Nope. Got nothing to do with it," he says, without taking his eyes off of me.

I glance across the notes we've brought along, and some accompanying photos. Normally, I probably wouldn't feel so inclined to share inside knowledge with a convicted felon, but I'm getting the feeling Philip doesn't mind talking to me, and that maybe he can help in more ways than he has already.

I slide a photo across the table, letting him touch the image. "Do you recognize this man, Mr. Martin?"

"Thomas Devlin."

I glance at Severo, then exchange the photo for another.

"Matthias Killarney."

I shift to another photo, then another. He names off the four victims we have, as though they were standing in front of us in a lineup. We already know of his counterfeit history with Mario James Anderson, so that makes it five for five.

"How are they all connected, Mr. Martin? My guess is they all know each other. After all, you seem to know them by name."

Philip nods to the pack of gum set on the table between the detective and me, and I hand the guard the entire pack, knowing we're getting our end of the bargain.

Severo shifts in his seat, resigning himself to take notes as I continue to converse with the convict. I'm grateful the detective feels so confident with me leading this exchange, rather than wanting to dominate what is, in fact, really his case, after all. I guess he's putting the job before his ego, which is admirable.

"Years ago, maybe ten or so," Martin begins, and I pay close attention to his words, "we all got started on a project. Didn't amount to much. I guess you can figure that, with those success stories in front of you."

"What kind of project?"

Philip takes another piece of gum, begins to chew, then looks down at his hands, worn and dirty. "Guess you could say we were a bunch of do-gooders." Though I find this hard to believe, I listen intently as he explains. "Back then, we were all a bunch of good guys. You know, respectable men with jobs and futures ahead of us. Not like now."

He pauses, but I don't speak. His voice is slowly warming up, and I don't want to risk not retrieving valuable information by interrupting.

"Jude was a minister at the time. So was Matthias. The rest of us were just churchgoing folk who wanted to make a difference. When Jude came up with this idea, it sounded good."

He stops and I wait for him to continue, but the pause grows longer. "What idea was that?"

"Like what you guys call a community watch,

nowadays. It was just the group of us, looking out for our neighborhoods, trying to keep the streets clean. We wanted a safe place to call home, but it was tough with all the drugs and sex happening in our own backyards."

Severo speaks up, asking, "What did you do to control it?" But he returns to taking notes when Philip Martin keeps his eyes on me as he replies.

"Nothing really. Except," he says, now using his cuffed hands to gesture. His wrists are worn like leather where the metal meets his skin. "When something was going down on one of our blocks, the other boys would come in to help. Police didn't do much for that sort of petty crime, but it was important to us."

I let my eyes measure his face, cautious to appear sympathetic. "Where did things go wrong?"

"Jude starting getting a little more out there with his ideas. Wanted to make our group into something it wasn't. He called us the Apostles of Peace and we all changed our names accordingly. You know, so we'd have names like James and John, and the like."

His eyes drift briefly to Severo, who is feverishly taking notes, but then his stare returns to me. "Some of us didn't have to do that, like me and Thomas, as that's just what our folks called us, being godly people and all. Hell, it made sense at the time, but instead of focusing on the good we could do, he started getting fancy ideas on how to cleanse the earth. Rid the world of scum and the like."

Even though I see the tape recorder is running, I feel

the need to repeatedly check it. Severo's notes will be useful, too, but the more concrete testimony we have regarding this case, the better. I don't want Cain to miss out on any of the information, as this is proving to be the best lead yet.

I look into Mr. Martin's eyes. "What kind of fancy ideas?"

"He wanted our group to be a larger organization than it was. He had big dreams, but we were just a bunch of guys. We had jobs, and we couldn't do all he wanted us to." He pauses as I settle better into my chair. They certainly don't make the furniture around here very comfortable. Guess it's their way to discourage long visits.

"So, he gets it in his head he wants to make this a bigger stink than it is, and some of the guys had doubts. But he doesn't care. Jude's on this power trip, ya know, and no one could say shit to him about it. He's got a mind to do it and wants to get money together to create an empire, spread out our resources and tackle the world's troubles from more than one city. Clean off the streets, so to speak. Idiot."

"Where'd he get the money from?"

"That's where the trouble starts. Jude's asking us and asking us to give every cent we've got, but no one wants to turn their hard-earned cash over to this guy, no matter it started out with good intentions. So at first he skims from the donations at the church."

Philip asks for some water and a guard brings a paper cup to him, half-full. "Then he moves on to bigger opportunities. trying to get other churches to give up their coin, and when the doors start slamming in his face, he loses it. Gets in with the wrong group of people."

With what Philip is providing, I know we're not going to have any problems tracking down Jude Barnaby. To top it off, we'll have his life history to shove in his face as we nail him for four murders, and intentions for a fifth.

"Then the laundering starts. He's got money coming in from God knows where, and I can bet my life some of it's counterfeit. I know it when I see it," he says, a hint of regret in his voice. "He's setting up deals he can't possibly commit to, and before you know it, he's peddling crack with brokers to make a buck for this thing none of us even want to be associated with anymore. It just got out of hand."

"Did you leave the group?" I ask, wondering if Philip's life behind bars stems from his involvement with the Apostles of Peace.

"Not at first. But then Jude got busted and ends up jailed. He's trying to get out, and trying to get out, but you feds keep him in here as long as you can, and ya did right by it, too. But I knew it wouldn't be long till he got out on some sissy ass excuse or another and hit the streets again. I suspect he's seeking vengeance on those who betrayed him. It's messed up, though, since I think he even had a suit or two in on the profit."

Severo looks up into Philip Martin's eyes as he hears these words. Martin just goes on, matter-of-factly.

"You know, cops making a buck and keeping their mouths shut. If only I had his luck. Instead, here I am, waiting to bite the dust."

"Do you remember who they were? Whoever it was Judas had an arrangement with?"

"Nah, he always kept that side of the business to himself. He didn't want any of us knowing too much, you know, in case we got found out one day. Can't spill what ya don't know."

"Okay, when was this? When did Jude get out?"

There had to be an event to trigger these crimes. After his release, there had to be some moment in Jude's life to make him act on his anger and seek to kill members of the former fellowship.

"Just recently, I think, but I can't keep up with the news. I have limited resources here, as you can imagine."

"What happened to everyone? How did they disassociate with him, knowing he had a bad streak?"

"Hell if I know. I got thrown in here so I'm off his list. Just the others who have to deal with that son of a bitch."

I flip the cassette tape in my recorder and return my eyes to Philip. There's no reason he'd be lying to us. It's a freaky tale, to think a minister started this whole thing, but it has to be true. The bodies prove it.

"And you?" I begin, knowing I'm asking more than I need to know now. "How did you end up in here?"

A buzzer sounds and I realize it must be prison lunchtime. My stay with Philip Martin is coming to a close, so I need to get as much as I can from him before he heads back to his cell.

"Well, I dropped my relationship with God when I made a friend of heroin. When the counterfeit turned out bad, I busted into a bank and had to shoot my way out, taking down a few cops on the way. Hey, shit happens."

Severo flinches briefly at these words, but I reach a hand under the table to brush his knee, quieting his reflex.

"Philip Martin, you've been a great deal of help. If there's one more thing I can ask of you," I say, clicking the cap off my pen to take a copy of these notes for myself. "Can you tell us the names of the others? If Judas, or Jude, is aiming to take revenge on those who betrayed him, there's a few lives we'd like to save."

Both the detective and I jot down the full names of the yet to be found apostles, and I am so relieved to know we'll be able to stop any more deaths at the hands of this former minister.

"And I don't know that he's sitting around, waiting for company to show up," Philip says, shrugging his upper body. "But last I heard, Jude was hanging around some new stomping grounds. I think somewhere in the East Village?"

Severo clears his throat and I meet his glance. That's the same neighborhood where Jean La Roche lived. With so many places as possible hideouts in that area, it'll take some hefty legwork to find him. Then again, I've always been a fan of hide-and-go-seek.

"Philip," I say, reaching across the table and shaking the prisoner's cuffed hand. "You have been extremely helpful. I know you didn't have to tell us everything like that, but I'm glad you did. I only wish I had more gum to thank you with."

For the first time throughout our conversation, a smile slowly makes its way across his lips. "Hey, I can arrange for a conjugal if you want to express your gratitude that badly," Philip jokes. I look back at him and let a simple grin destroy his attempts. "Hey, ya can't blame a guy for trying."

"No, I can't. Thanks, Philip. Take care of yourself," I say, then regret the words as I realize how idiotic it must sound to someone who will be put to death in a few days. He gave us more than we could have imagined, and I'm glad at least one person will be able to remember that man for something positive.

As Severo and I are about to pass through the secured entranceway, I pivot and hold off the detective from departing just yet.

"Hey, Philip," I ask, while I still have the chance. "Do you remember the name of the federal agent who brought in Jude?" If we can locate who was on this case before, we may be able to gather background information to nail this guy even more.

"You're joking, right?" the convict asks, as a guard leads him to the exit on the opposite side of the room. My look of confusion clearly surprises him, and he says, "I thought that's why you came here, Agent David."

"I don't get your meaning," I say, then I look at

Severo, who also seems caught trying to make the interpretation.

"Maybe I'm the one who's confused," Philip states, looking into my eyes with sincerity. "Sorry. I just assumed you were related or something. The guy who brought in Judas was also a David. Agent Joshua David."

Chapter 14

"Right. That's the last of them. We'll be right over."
Severo closes up his cell phone after his conversation
with Cain. His hand wraps around mine as they meet
on the console of the Jeep, and he lets out a throaty sigh
before facing me.

"Cain's going to talk with Captain Delaney, get
some squad cars out there and find these other apostles before Jude has a chance. Angie," he says,
squishing my tense, balled fist. "Right now our priority is saving those men's lives. But as soon as we
know they're safe, we're going to find Jude Barnaby.
Got it?"

"I can't believe it," I say, my voice evidence of the
shock I'm in. "He's after me because my father locked

him up? What the hell is that going to prove? What kind of kicks is he getting from this? It makes no sense."

"Don't, Angie. Don't try to make sense of this man's actions. There is none," Severo argues, turning the ignition of the Jeep so we can get off this prison ground and back to work.

"It's like what Philip Martin said in there, Ang. Jude's after vengeance for those who shook up his plans, that's all. Your father being the one who put him away years ago? I'd say Jude's just as bitter and pissed as the day he was locked up. He wants to make your life hell, because that's what your father did to him. And rightly so."

"So why not just come straight after me? Why bother with all the rest of it?"

"If he feels betrayed by his fellow apostle players for ditching him when things turned sour, he has more than one score to settle. You're probably just the icing on his cake."

Severo is right. If everything Philip Martin said holds true, and there's no reason he would need to lie, my father was the one who put an end to the Apostles of Peace the day he got Barnaby locked up. Some peacekeepers they were.

"How do good people get involved in such bad shit?" I ask, twisting in my seat to relieve the tension. "That man we just spoke to, that man on death row…he did wrong, I'm not saying he didn't. But you saw it, Severo. He really did have good intentions at one point. How does that happen to people?"

"That's just how it works, Angie." His tone is soft

against the ever-increasing rain, which is apparently not letting up today. It's now just after noon. The rain's been falling for hours, and this Monday is evidently living up to the gloomy reputation.

"I see it all the time, and you will, too. It only takes one wrong move, doing something stupid without thinking. People get in trouble, and then while trying to get out of their mess, they end up causing more damage along the way. It's like they get caught in a ripple effect."

Philip Martin may have robbed banks and shot cops while trying to escape, but behind those imprisoned eyes I saw the man he once was. He got involved with these men because he wanted his neighborhood to be a better, safer place. There's irony in that. It's a shame, for what people feel they have to do to feel safe in their own backyards.

"I know it may not seem like it, but there is good news," the detective says, now picking up speed along the north end of the expressway. "At least we know this Judas guy isn't necessarily trying to kill you. He just wants to make your life hell, for what your father did to him."

"Yeah, great news," I say, swallowing the reality. "What I don't get, though, is how he knew I'd be on this case. How could he have known I'd end up working it?"

"Nothing is random, Angie. We know that with this guy. Hell, for all we know he was waiting on this, just letting it boil within him, until you came back to the city. If he knew you were Joshua David's daughter, he must have known you'd come back someday. For all we know, he just sat tight until that day came, like a bomb waiting to go off," he says, theorizing the possibilities.

"Whatever it took for him to remain patient," Severo explains, "you know this guy's been planning the whole thing for a long time. There was a lot of detailing to do, and this plan of his didn't happen overnight."

"And then what?" I ask, realizing we may never know the full story. "He followed me from day one? Was he there when I unlocked my apartment door for the first time last week? Was he there the first day I signed in at the Plaza?"

"Angie, listen to me. There was nothing you could have done to stop this guy from doing what he aimed to do." Severo's eyes peer at me briefly, trying to make eye contact while still focusing on the road ahead. "Yes, he followed you. From the shelter. From the campus library. Wherever. Just don't underestimate what he would have done to make sure this fell out exactly how he wanted. He's likely been planning this since the day they put him away."

"But this started out as your case, Severo," I argue, trying to pinpoint which of my actions led Judas right to me.

"Yeah, and he probably knows the system well enough to know exactly where to leave a dead body. Killarney lived in my precinct. If the killer saw us together, even once, he may have started with a murder that would catch the attention of both of us. I don't know. But I'll tell you one thing," he says, as we speed back into the main artery of the city streets. "You're going to have the opportunity to ask him that yourself."

Back at the Plaza, Cain is talking with some other agents in the common area, but instructs the detective and me to wait in the office. Severo decides to call his captain, and I take a moment to check in with Denise, who was kind enough to keep an eye on Muddy for me today.

Severo said he didn't want to leave keys to his loft with any of his neighbors, which I can appreciate, and I knew Denise would welcome the invitation to have a place in my life, even if only to watch the dog.

I feel bad for Muddy, being shuffled around these past few days, but being the good friend he is, he seems to adapt well enough. I suppose, too, he remembers Denise, as she wasn't necessarily a stranger when my father was alive.

"He's doing just fine," she says, reassuring me I'd made a good decision. "I'm just glad I had the day off to help out, Angie."

"I want you to know I appreciate it. Denise, I realize I haven't been the friendliest with you, now or in the past, and I apologize for that," I say, my words filled with sincerity. "I wish I would have been more accepting of you being with my father. I just…well, I hope you forgive me for being such an ass."

"Angie," she says, her tone soft and warm. "You

were always the gem in your father's life. I didn't mind taking second place to you, and I know you always meant well for him. Though I acknowledge your apology, and am so happy to open my arms to you, there is no need for that now, okay? It's been too hard on all of us these past few months. Let's put that behind us now."

"Fair enough. Give Muddy a big hug for me," I say, relieved to get that discomfort over with. "And save one for me."

As I close up my cell phone, I notice Severo smiling at me. "Good for you," he says, and I realize he must have heard some of that conversation.

"Yeah, well, I guess there's enough for me to deal with without keeping that wall between me and Denise. She's a good person. Always has been. I should have just accepted that from the start."

Cain pushes through the glass door, closes it behind him and looks to me and then the detective. "Have a seat."

Severo and I pull up a pair of office chairs and I unpack my tape recorder from our meeting with Philip Martin so Cain can hear all of what was discussed.

As Severo retrieves his files with the notes from our session, he nods to Cain, getting right to the point. "What about the others? You get to them all on time?"

Cain sits on the edge of the coffee service counter, shaking his head as though he doesn't seem all that enthused we've made this progress.

"Yeah, between your captain and me we ran all the

names, found their whereabouts and put out the cars to get them out of harm's way. All of them are in a safe house as we speak, while we figure out what to do with them."

"What do you mean?" I ask, feeling like I'm missing out on a point. "They're all safe, right?"

"They are. A few have records worth looking into. A couple have been active lately and we'll need to follow that up, as well, but that'll be for NYPD to work on."

"We'll need to question a number of them," Severo adds, and I keep my ears alert to the process that will bring down Jude Barnaby. "Though Philip Martin provided a solid testimony for us, we'll need to hear it from the others just to cover all the bases for when this guy goes in for sentencing."

Cain reaches over to the coffee carafe to fill up his mug, and I sense there is more unease within him today regarding this case than there was before we even knew our target.

"What is it, Cain?"

He slurps at his mug, tapping a foot against the gray carpet, and when he looks at me, his eyes are serious and his irises wide. "I'm more than a bit concerned with what the detective here told me. About Jude Barnaby seeking revenge for being put away by your father."

"So what? We go after him, we nab him, case closed."

Wheeling up an office chair to take a seat, my mentor shuffles closer to me, his emotions calm but strangely freaking me out. I've never seen him so tense.

"We will do just that, kiddo. However, he may not be so easy to find. Right now we have undercovers out in the East Village, going up and down every single street, seeing what options we may have to his whereabouts. Chances are, if he is watching you as he has been, he'll know we're after him and he may have already fled. Or worse."

I shift in my seat, look to Severo, then back to Cain. "What do you mean, worse?"

"He's made it very clear he's more than a little upset at those who destroyed his hopes and dreams, regardless of how idiotic they may seem to us," Cain explains, moving his chair closer to mine so he is sitting directly in front of me. "If he thinks he can act out his revenge against your father—God rest his soul—by causing harm to you, we may need to keep a watchful eye to make sure nothing goes wrong."

Severo gets up to pour coffee for the two of us, and as he does, I absorb my mentor's words and those Severo shared on the way back from Ossining. "But if all he wanted to do was kill me, he would have found a way days ago. Severo says this guy probably wants to play a game, make me fall into his panic trap or whatever, and if that's the case, I say bring it on."

"Angie, you cannot play on the same level as this guy," my mentor says, placing his hands on the arms of my chair, urging me to hear his words. "Don't let yourself get sucked into it. He may or may not have bigger plans with you, but we cannot afford to take that chance."

"You're not suggesting she move off this case," Severo asks, handing me a warm mug. "If he wants her, Cain, our best bet is to keep her on this, where we can watch his moves."

"And use me as bait," I say, offering myself up if that's what it would take to get this asshole off the streets.

"That's not what I'm saying," Cain says, raising his hands in the air. "Not at all. However…" His eyes look directly into mine. "You just need to beware, kiddo. There's more to this than we could have ever imagined."

I look at Severo, who clearly has the same reaction I do. "What? What is it?"

Cain gets up to pull some paperwork from a file. "I don't know how to tell you this." He speaks slowly, cautiously, as he takes a seat on the edge of the wooden desk. "But the lab found something. Something we weren't expecting."

"Cain, what the hell?"

"That rosary of yours? The one he gave you, the same one that was lying on your kitchen table? It had blood on it."

"From Paul Aaron White." I state the obvious.

"But the cross on that rosary had a twist-off compartment, Angie. Kind of like a little vial, or something."

Severo pulls the lab report from Cain's hand and his

face goes blank as he reads the findings. My patience is running low. "Well?"

"It turns out, kiddo… The blood found in the rosary matches up to a sample our office kept on file, in the personnel department." Cain scrunches down in front of me, looking at me on eye level.

"Angie, I'm sorry, kiddo. But that blood matches up with a sample belonging to your father."

Chapter 15

I can take no more news today. Not when every fresh piece of information that comes to light makes this case more and more about my father.

"How?" I demand. "How did he get my father's blood?"

Severo crouches down beside me, resting a palm on my shoulder, and I instinctively reach a hand to his, desperate to feel something good in the face of all this bad news.

"There's a possibility, kiddo," Cain says, getting back up to lean again on the coffee service counter. "That Jude Barnaby may have been involved in your father's death."

"How is that possible? My father was shot in the line

of duty, after getting in between some kids during a robbery. It makes no sense, Cain. If it was Judas who shot him, why the hell is he seeking revenge with me now? And what about that kid who's doing time for murder? Is he suddenly innocent?"

Severo's tone is serious but calm as he remains beside me. "Did you look into Agent David's case files? See what it was he was up to the night he died?"

"Yeah, that I did," Cain says, handing copies of the file work to the detective. Severo spreads them out on my desk and we lean in to review them together. "It seems just before Agent David was killed, he was working on something related to Jude Barnaby. And yes, he was working undercover that night, kiddo."

"Then we have to look further into that," Severo says.

Cain nods, and adds, "But Judas, if that's what we're supposed to call him, seems to have been up to no good from the day he got back out on the streets. My take on it is your father probably found out something new to work with, something that would put old Barnaby back behind bars."

"Philip Martin did say that Judas was in on a deal with a badge," Severo mentions, straightening up to walk around the desk. "Some sort of hush arrangement. Maybe Agent David had a lead on this. But what about that day? And those kids?" he asks, and I sort through the files to find the report.

It's an odd feeling, reading the official statements on my father's death. Of course, the details were provided to me over the phone, when I was informed of what happened, immediately after the fact. At one point I was shown the brief reports outlining the highlights of that night. I also heard the story retold to me by coworkers filling the void of silence at my father's funeral in July. And more than once, I've thought about that fateful night. But seeing the reports for myself, without any of the details missing, is another thing altogether.

"There's nothing to suggest Barnaby was there, let alone the shooter," Severo says, and I have to agree. My father was working an undercover operation that night, the reports confirm, and got caught off guard when some young thieves happened to be conducting a petty robbery in the same neighborhood.

The official statement is that a stray bullet, not necessarily intended for my father, made its final stop pushing through his throat, where too much blood loss led to his death. From the files, I know my father was wearing a bulletproof vest that night on account of his operation, but there's not much anyone can do when the windpipe is busted and lungs fill with blood instead of oxygen.

My eyelids close, as I fear the tears welling up will soon release down my cheeks. This graphic information must not interfere with my ability to see this case for what it is.

I've been working at grasping the knowledge that a minor, with a history of shooting cops, accidentally took down my father. And now with this possibility? No matter where that shot came from, it was an accident.

The only way someone could have purposely made

a precise hit through the throat like that would be if they were standing right in front of my father. With his instincts and abilities, added to the situation described in the reports, there is no way that was a possibility. It would have taken more than one person to hold down my father, and the CSU investigators who followed up that scene would have realized it, if it had gone down like that. But it didn't.

"Which still doesn't answer our question," I say, clearing my throat to restore my focus. "Where Judas could have got ahold of my father's blood."

"Kiddo, there's no telling what this guy has done either in the past or in the present." Cain's eyes are soft in consideration of my pain. "The only thing we know right now, for sure, is that he has a mind to settle the score with you, as your father's daughter. He likely wants to set things straight with the David name, once and for all."

"If that's the case," Severo says, his tone harsh and somewhat agitated, "Angie's not the only one in danger."

I huddle in my seat, staring at the detective to measure his innuendo. "What do you mean?"

"I agree," Cain says, gathering his personal belongings. "Angie? Don't get alarmed now, but I think the detective here is trying to say we should also keep an eye on your family."

"What? Why? It's me he wants. It was my father who put Jude away. Why doesn't he just come after me, damn it!"

"Shh," Severo says, hushing my anger as I feel my

face tense up and color flush my skin. "Just as a precaution. We should make sure your uncle and your
grandmother are not at risk. There's no way to know,
or control, what this guy has on his agenda. And Simon
shares a name with an apostle."

"My sentiments exactly," Cain says, nodding to the
door. "Come on, kiddo. Let's put your mind to rest.
We'll get this bastard one way or another. Hopefully
before he has a chance to do any more damage."

"You've had quite the week," Cain says, as I look
to him from the passenger seat, thinking how that is
such an incredible understatement.

I decided to ride with Cain so Severo could grab another officer to accompany us to my uncle's church.
Plus, I need to hear the wisdom of my mentor. With his
experience, he's undoubtedly encountered a number of
cases such as this. If he can help me understand this
one, I'll be grateful for more reasons than one.

"You holding up okay?" he asks me.

"It's messed up, is what it is," I reply, acknowledging the bizarre events that have unfolded these past few
days. "Never in my life would I have imagined this to
be my reality, Cain. When I made that transfer request
to come back to New York, I figured it would do some
good to reunite with the past. Just not to this extent, by
any means."

"I'm real sorry this has turned out the way it has,"
he says, nudging a hand against my shoulder. "But I
suppose if something funky did happen between your

father and this Judas Barnaby, or whatever his name is, it's best to know about it. It'll put your mind at ease and then you can get back to doing what you gotta do, to work your way toward NCAVC."

I nod my head as I realize how strange this has become. From my father's untimely death to learning of his putting away the man who is now a serial killer, not to mention the remote possibility that a kid is doing time for a crime he may not have committed… It all intertwines in my mind, and I'm not sure what to think of any of this.

All I know is I'll be glad when this case is over and done with. My family has been through enough these past few months. They do not need to feel unsafe now, with this guy out there seeking revenge.

"Just know this, kiddo," Cain says, and I watch as his face turns very serious. "Your father wouldn't let something like this get under his skin, ya hear? He would have done all he could to make sure justice, in his mind, was carried out. I suspect you and he are alike in that way. So you need to prepare yourself, kiddo. The worst may be yet to come."

It's not long after we pull up to my uncle's church that I see Severo's Jeep following behind. Cain waits for the detective, but I immediately go in to gently share the news with my family. The sound of Alex Trebek's voice informs me they are watching *Jeopardy!*, but they have no idea of the new game they are about to learn.

"Angie!" My uncle's thinning body pushes free

from the old recliner and he approaches me with arms wide. My grandmother follows his lead, and she looks at me with a mixture of happiness and confusion.

"Were we expecting you, love? I didn't think I'd see you until tomorrow," she says, placing her arms around my neck. "Not that I'm complaining, of course."

Cain, Severo and another officer make their entrance, and I look back at them cautiously, then return focus to my family. "Go ahead, sit down," I say, leading them back to their comfortable seating. "There's something you need to know."

"What is it, Angie? Is everything okay?" My uncle's words are pitched high, and I don't like that I have put them in an alarmed state. I know my mentor and the detective are right, that there may be a chance this guy wants to execute harm upon my family, but I wish it weren't so.

"It's okay, Simon. Grandma, it's okay. You remember Detective Severo? And this here is my mentor, Special Agent Marcus Cain." A few pleasant hellos are exchanged quickly as my family watches us, not yet understanding the purpose of our unexpected visit.

"It seems there is someone out there," I say, slowly explaining the situation, "who may have vengeance on his mind."

"I do not know for what you mean, my Angela," Simon says, his face puckered with bewilderment, his reading glasses resting low on his nose. "What is this about?"

Cain pulls a chair from the dining set and places it in

front of my family members, his face full of sincerity and compassion as he explains the situation. "There's a man we're working on, a murderer in fact, who seems to have taken an interest in Angie," he says, and as he does so my grandmother's breath catches in worry. "Now, there's no need for you to be concerned, really, as we're on it and we plan on taking this guy down tonight."

My grandmother, ever the wise matriarch, leans in to look at Cain, her eyes narrow as she judges his words. "And yet, Mr. Cain, you feel the need to come here to tell us of this? Why do I think there's more than you are letting on?"

Despite the severity of the situation, Cain chuckles as he looks at me. "Sheesh, runs in the family I see."

But then, with a serious tone once again, he looks directly into my grandmother's eyes as he says, "You are right on that one, Mrs. David. Our man may have a score to settle with your family in general. In fact, we think he is seeking revenge for being put behind bars by your son, Agent David."

"Joshua?" Grandmother questions, looking to me for answers.

"Yes, Grandma. Dad put this man away years ago, and since his release a while back, he's apparently been planning this elaborate scheme to ease his pride."

"We don't want to alarm you," Severo says, his voice warm and familiar with my family, whom he just met yesterday. "But for the sake of caution, we're going to make sure you are both completely safe."

"What of my Angela?" Simon asks, obviously feeling I have been left out of the safety equation.

Severo looks at me as he answers, "She can take care of herself. Agent David's fully aware of what she's getting involved with, and neither Cain nor I have any doubts as to her ability out there."

My grandmother looks to me with pride, then shifts her gaze over the detective. "You're a smart boy, I see."

She then reaches her frail hand to mine, squeezing it as she checks me over. "You are your father's daughter," she breathes, then looks away for a moment as the detective answers a call on his cell phone. "I have no doubt you can and will take care of yourself. After all, my darling Angela, you have a family who needs you to take care of them," she says, her voice saying more than her words.

"I know, Grandma." I place a kiss on her forehead.

"We may have found him," Severo says, closing his phone. "Got a street tip. Someone who meets his description was seen heading into a church."

"Let's go," Cain grunts, getting up from his seat to follow the detective. "Come on, Angie."

"Wait. Someone needs to stay with them." I look to my uncle and my grandmother, see the slight worry in their eyes, more for me than for themselves, I know.

"The officer here can do that, Angie," Severo says, nodding toward the man who accompanied him. "We need to get going."

"Severo, this is my family we're talking about. No offense to your squad, of course, but someone else has to stay here. Someone who knows what Jude is up to and what he's capable of."

"This is my case." He shrugs. "I have to go. And you? If you stay, you're just putting yourself and your family at risk. So now what?"

We both look at Cain, who stares back at us. "Well, hell, I guess I could stay with them. I don't think there's a need, but if it's what you want."

"There's no time to argue about it," Severo says, leading me to the doorway. "Cain, you stay. You might also want to get in touch with Denise, just so she knows what's going on. I'm sure Simon has her number. We'll call you when we know Judas is there for sure, so you'll know it's safe to leave this family to enjoy their evening."

As Severo and I turn away, my mentor offers some last words of wisdom. "Hey, kiddo. Keep your guard up, and whatever you do, don't let it get personal."

"Cain," I say with more sincerity than I have ever felt. "I think it's a little late for that. Getting personal doesn't even begin to explain what I'm about to do with Judas."

Chapter 16

At East Tenth Street, between Second and Third Avenue, we take in the sight before us. Judas could be here or at least in the area. Either way, he was spotted heading into this church, so we're off to a good start.

Squad members from Severo's precinct fan out in the immediate radius, stepping quietly but with forceful intent across the wet earth, as the detective follows me toward the entrance.

This is one of the oldest churches in Manhattan, and lately it's developed a reputation for being used by the city for community events and historic presentations. My interest in sightseeing, however, is set aside this evening as we stride up the shiny sidewalk, slick from today's rain, and prepare ourselves for the worst.

Passing the entranceway and into the nave, we make our presence known throughout the dimly lit place of worship. Candles are burning along the sides and at the front, and the hint of light is enough to lead us.

Stepping cautiously, I am aware of the fact that Judas could be looking at us, spying on us from a safe location as he likes to do. He won't be safe for long this night.

Severo nods to the right of the altar, and I step behind him as he follows his senses toward one of the side chapels. There's something I'm hearing, and though I can't make out anything distinct, I'm willing to have a look inside.

As we round the doorway, candescent flickering casts dancing shadows against the wall, and we prepare for any confrontation that may await us. The sound of distant voices reaches my ears, and when we clear the entrance, I see there is a camcorder sitting at the foot of a statue of Mary.

I hear my own voice coming from it, and recognize my words from the scene at the City College campus in St. Nicholas Heights, when we were trying to figure out why Thomas Devlin had a Bible on hand.

"Maybe he used it in class. To some, the idea of God is a myth. Or maybe he was just a follower."

"Angie?"

I tilt my head to meet Severo's glance, his silhouette barely distinguishable in the dim light. "That's us," I whisper, looking hard at the footage. "Look, there's you. And Cain. Judas was right there."

I think back to Saturday, when Jude followed me from the campus to the crematorium. He was watching me the whole time. Hell, he was watching us. I suppose if we knew what to look for then, his presence would have stood out. As it was, he would have blended in with the grouping of teachers and students, looking on as we dissected the crime scene, right before his eyes.

Severo nudges me, and I follow him as we step cautiously out of the prayer room and into the nave again. Judas has to be here, watching us. It's his style. I know that now. There's no way he would lead us to this church only to run off. This, I'm afraid, feels much more like an invitation to get nice and personal with his devious mind.

As we pass through a hallway leading to a study room, I take in the bookcases along the wall. On them, I see there are stacks upon stacks of Bibles, some old and worn, some leather bound, and since Judas was previously a minister, I'm guessing he knows his way around the verses. Open notebooks with pages of handwriting also catch my attention, and you just gotta know he's written some strange diary entries in those.

The creepiest feature leading down the hallway, on the opposite side from the study room, is the collection of crucifixes hanging from the walls, ceiling, doorways, and propped up on the floor. There's a balanced mix between those upright—and those turned upside down. They vary in color and shape. Some have a figure of Christ. Others are ornately decorated with rosary beads, and I think of the rosary containing my father's blood.

Apparently Judas has made himself at home here these past few days. With this church being as popular as it is, even throughout the week, he had to have done something intense to take its interior over and claim it as his own. I wonder if he's been administering to the public. They'd have no reason to suspect the horrors contained beyond the untouched nave. As for the resident priest, I'm not too naive to realize innocent lives could have been taken in trade.

Severo pokes me in the side and directs me down the hall, toward a room we cannot yet see. Even stepping lightly along the old wooden floors, I can't stop the creaking beneath my feet. If Judas is here, he'll know he has company. Yet there is no sign of him anywhere.

In this room, which I assume is the office, we find pinned to the sadly painted drywall a few Polaroids of each victim, taken long before their deaths. For the first time, I become acquainted with Matthias Killarney's original appearance, before he was burned in the crematorium. His eyes are warm and kind, and the smile in the photo gives no indication he knew what was to come. My eyes scan the snapshots, reviewing those whose lives have already been taken from them, but I am grateful we were able to save the others from the wrath of Judas.

As we head down the last hallway, leading to the rectory, I become aware of a shuffling sound from within a hallway closet. Thinking of where we found Mrs. Schaeffer yesterday, I flash my light at Severo, signaling him to back me up while I turn the doorknob.

Another officer approaches, handgun drawn, as we prepare for who or what is inside. As the door creaks open, an elderly man stumbles toward me, bound at the feet and hands, with his mouth closed off with duct tape, just like my neighbor was. As he falls toward me, his eyes are fiercely teary, and I grasp his weight, steadying him.

"Shh," I request, not knowing where our sought-after man is hiding. "You'll be okay." The attending officer takes the burden from me and begins to unravel this man's bindings.

Severo leans in, speaking quietly. "Where is he?" and the man, who by his clothing I gather is the priest of this church, nods down the hall.

Looking at the officer, Severo instructs, "Get him out of here and see that he's taken care of." The priest, untied and breathing freely, is escorted in the opposite direction as the detective and I continue on down the hall.

I begin to hear a few voices and I look to Severo, who nods before we round the corner. Weapons drawn and blood pumping, we enter the priest's chambers and spot one of Severo's squad members taking photos for evidence of this new crime.

A man is bound against a floor-to-ceiling crucifix, his body stained with blood. His eyelids flicker, so we know he's alive, but obviously in pain, as his chest heaves anxiously.

I watch as a CSU member passes a small flashlight over the man's eyes, checking his level of awareness. Another officer begins to peel away the ropes, careful not to cause the man any more bodily harm than he has already endured. His limbs are bound fairly tightly, enough to suspend him against the cross.

The detective looks at me and says, "This can't be an apostle. Cain said we got them all. They're supposed to be in a safe house."

"Could be another church member?" I wonder, though my conviction isn't strong as I take in the sight. I think for a moment, and trace my memory for any indication of what the symbolism of this man could mean.

From the testimony given by Philip Martin, we have all of the living apostles, though there is one other thing to consider. "Technically, Severo, there were thirteen apostles. But why would Philip Martin hold anything back? He seemed to be so honest with us."

We move in and Severo's gloved hand pulls duct tape slowly from the man's mouth. He gasps for air, sending saliva flying as he breathes freely. As I walk toward him, my foot catches on a small step stool and I move it out of the way so no one else makes the same mistake.

Doing so, however, makes me wonder why there is a step stool at all. Unless whoever tied this man up was extremely short, there was no need for one, as this man's body was hanging fairly close to ground.

The man's chest is heaving as he is relieved of the

last bindings and held up securely by two officers. His eyes narrowly watching me, he blows air against his upper lip, sweat dripping onto his mouth.

As he does so, I look at him intently, staring into the black centers of his eyes, where I see a small, distorted reflection of myself.

As I aim my Bauer .25 toward the man, he licks his lips, a smirk crossing over them.

"Judas," I say, my words barely audible above the commotion of the room.

"Hello, Agent David. It's so nice to see you again."

Severo and every squad member present unleash the safeties from their guns, and all aim directly at this man.

I step in closer, wanting to have a good look at the man who has killed four men and nearly a fifth. The man who followed me and trapped me in the crematorium. The man who took control of others' lives and led them down a path of destruction. The man who somehow came into contact with my father's blood.

"Nice is not exactly how I would describe it," I say, my face a mere inch from his. Severo pulls on my arm, urging me away from Judas as the officers quickly cuff him.

"How the hell did he manage to tie himself up like that?"

I face the detective, the blood pumping in my veins. "You said it yourself, Detective. Never underestimate the mind of a monster."

Chapter 17

"Angie, this is Captain Delaney. Captain, this is Special Agent Angela David," Severo says, introducing me to the commanding officer of the Fifth Precinct.

The captain's eyes are direct as he sizes me up from his towering height. "I've heard several positive things about you, Agent. Glad to have you in the city."

"Thanks very much." Though I maintain a polite exterior, my insides are surging with adrenaline as we sit in a conference room, complete with a window that also acts as a mirror for the interrogation room beyond the glass.

Judas is in custody right now and we're simply awaiting protocol to clear the belongings off his person. An officer will soon escort him in for questioning, and my body is itching, waiting for us to get started.

Though I doubt we'll have much to debate regarding his plea. With all evidence and testimony pointing to him, he needn't say much. Besides, he practically confessed to the apostle murders by binding his body against that crucifix.

Hell, he knew we'd find him there. As Cain has told me time and time again, people like this want to get caught. Whatever Judas wants to get off his chest, I'll listen. But I don't expect to find reason in this man or his actions.

"Who you calling?" I ask Severo, when I see him enter digits into the conference room phone.

"Cain. He needs to know we have Jude. Your family will be glad to hear that."

I think of my grandmother and my uncle, who have already been through so much these past few months with the death of my father. Despite Jude's intention to rattle my family's sense of security, I'm glad they were not victim to his taunting.

Me, I can handle it. But I will not tolerate seeing my family suffer. And when I get in that room, face-to-face with this indescribable criminal, I'll put to rest, once and for all, whether or not this man was in fact present the day my father was shot.

"Great," Severo says, and I listen to the final bit of his conversation with Cain. "Give them my best. See you soon."

The captain hands me a cup of water and I nod in thanks, appreciative of the small comfort as we wait in these closed quarters. Not unlike the room Cain,

Severo and I shared just a few days ago, when I first became familiar with the Fifth Precinct, this room is anything but cozy. It serves a purpose, though, and that's all that matters.

"They're fine," Severo informs me. "They're all fine. Denise is with them now, and Muddy, too."

"But Simon's allergic."

"Muddy's in the office, curled up and staying out of sneezes' way," the detective jokes, and I think of how great he's been with my family over the past two days.

He's only just met them, but for some reason he has taken to them rather quickly. Kind of how I feel about him, I guess. "And Cain's on his way over soon. Says he got caught up in a game of cards with your uncle."

"Oh, that can be dangerous." More than a few times my uncle has walked away a richer man due to his hush-hush poker pastime. "Thanks for doing that. Checking on them, I mean."

"It's my job," Severo says nonchalantly, then leans closer to me so his captain doesn't overhear. "But for you, I would've done it anyway."

My grin is fast to fade, however, as the sound of metal chairs scratching against tile floors draws my attention to the window. An officer escorts Jude Barnaby into the interrogation room, and as he sits down they cuff one of his hands to the chair. The only place this guy is going anytime soon is back behind bars.

His eyes stare through the window, and I imagine he knows the mirror facing him leads to us, staring back at him. Looking at him now, I find he doesn't seem like much of anything. I recognize the sunken cheeks and chiseled jawline I first laid eyes on in the crematorium, and his hair is shaved.

He may think his ability to disguise himself has trumped us, but no matter what he looks like on the outside, I know there is nothing to this man's soulless interior.

"Shall we?" Severo asks, opening the door to lead us around the other side. I take a deep breath, prepared to meet the man who has caused such chaos in my first week of being an agent in New York City. I came here to work the field, but I was not expecting this as a welcoming party.

"Agent David," he says, his voice as raspy as I remember it. "You're looking good."

"Wish I could say the same."

Severo slides a chair toward me, taking a seat himself across from the first criminal to know me by name. I can't say I like the feeling.

"Why don't we start off with the basics," the detective says, slouching a bit in his chair as he reads the expression on Jude's face. The prisoner seems intent on staring at me, but then again, I'm returning the glare.

"I'm not interested in talking to you, Detective," Judas says, sitting up in his chair as his eyes follow my every move. A clock on the wall provides a steady beat as the second hand clicks by, drumming along with my pulse.

"Fine." I slide my chair tight against the table so I am as close to him as I can get without taking a seat

on his lap. "You got something to say to me? This is
your lucky day, Judas. Spit it out."

He slides the end of his tongue along his top teeth,
and the sound of wet flesh squishing against the
crooked edges causes my back to tense up. I watch as
this man attempts to control my emotions, cracking his
knuckles and curling his cuffed hands into fists.

"You have nothing to say?" My voice rises above
normal volume, but I maintain a steady, concentrated
tone. "After following me day after day, tracking my
every move, it comes down to this. Silence? Well done,
Jude. Well done."

Severo and Jude watch as I lift myself off the chair
and walk to the door. "Sit down," the criminal com-
mands, his voice explosive in the silence.

"Why? You're not holding my interest, Judas. Did
you think you'd impress me by killing those four men?
Or maybe by pulling off those disguises? Because I'll
tell you one thing," I say, now leaning over the table
and staring him down. "You haven't impressed me one
bit."

"Angie," Severo says softly, but instead of meeting
his glance, I simply raise a hand to keep him in place.

"No. This guy, Detective? He thinks he's smarter
than us. He thinks he can prove how crafty he is by replicating the deaths of the apostles. Well, you know
what I say? He's a copycat. And if he couldn't come up
with something original, it doesn't impress me. Not one
bit."

"I'm sorry you feel that way, Agent David." Jude's

rasp interrupts my rant. There's no change in his calm, confident demeanor. "Perhaps you and I got off to a bad start. It'd be such a shame if we couldn't put aside our differences. After all, we have so much in common."

"I highly doubt that."

"I overheard that you spoke with my dear friend Philip Martin. How is he, by the way?"

Glancing at Severo, and then through the mirror to the officers on the other side, I take the bait. "Fine. Considering he only has a few more days left."

"Mmm. Such a sad story, isn't it? I'll assume he told you all about the Apostles of Peace."

"He did."

"Then you know I've always had the best of intentions."

"I beg to differ."

"That's a shame. Because, Miss David, if you could only find it in your heart to understand me better, your problems might suddenly seem less difficult to deal with."

"What problems are those, Judas?"

The ticking of the clock sounds in the background, like a time bomb keeping pace with our chat.

"Oh, there are several. Where do I start…. Well," he says, angling in his chair to position himself closer to me. "Both you and I have been betrayed by those whom we grew to trust."

I try not to let my emotions show, even though I'm not certain what he means. I cannot let him get the better of me, so I keep a straight face.

"Those men who you believe betrayed you were only looking out for themselves," I state, remembering how Philip Martin did, in fact, have good intentions at one point in his life. "You were the one to abuse their trust, Judas."

"Is that what you think this is about?"

For the first time since he was escorted into this room, Jude's pitch changes, causing me to react to the difference. My eyes focus on his as I try to read what set off the change.

He leans back in his chair, as though he is amused by this situation, and both the detective and I keep watch on his actions.

"Agent David, you honestly believe this was about them? About those men who scattered themselves silly, running away from me with their tails between their legs? Don't get me wrong, Angela. It hurt. I won't lie. It pained me to see them abandon the brotherhood."

His tone has returned to its steady rasp again, as he leans forward to stare me down. Fluorescent lighting from above creates a wash over his face, turning his skin an opaque, pale yellow. His dark eyes shine like black marbles. "Though if you think I have done all this to seek revenge on their actions, you are not who I thought you were, Agent David."

"Then why, Judas. Tell me your deep, dark secrets. I want to understand. I just don't want to play your games anymore."

Severo looks to me, measuring my attitude, but I

shake my head, letting him know I am fine, under control and handling this situation.

"I would have thought you already understood me, Agent David," Judas drawls slowly, as though with every word he is piercing my flesh. "After all, it didn't take your father nearly as long to figure it out."

The detective pushes out of his chair, quickly coming to my side before I have a chance to react. He pulls me to a corner of the interrogation room and whispers tersely into my ear. "Angie, this is enough. He's just trying to get under your skin. Don't let him do this."

My eyes focus on Carson's and my words are sincere when I tell him, "I'm fine, Severo. Whatever he has to say, I want to know what it is. Honest, I'm fine."

Frustrated with my plea, Severo twists to peer through the mirror, and I wonder briefly if Cain has joined the captain. But I return to the table to meet my match, as I am currently more interested in Jude Barnaby.

"Figure what out?"

A smile creeps across his lips as he turns his head slightly on an angle. "I told you in the crematorium, Angie. I told you I was seeking revenge."

"Yeah, and my father's dead, so you got your way."

"Tsk, tsk. If you would only pay attention, Agent David, and stop thinking of yourself, you might somehow realize this isn't about you. But perhaps I have wasted my time. Perhaps you are nothing like your father at all."

"My father was the best damn fed out there. He

died protecting innocent people from assholes like you. Do me a favor, Jude. Don't waste my time talking about something you don't understand. Either get to the point or get your sorry ass out of my face."

Judas sinks deep into his chair, mocking my plea with an infuriating stuttered chuckle. "My apologies for upsetting you. I only had the best of intentions," he says seriously now, and I exhale deeply as we head down this path again. "I just thought you might want to know what really happened to him. Because if you knew that, Agent David, you wouldn't be wasting your time sitting here talking with me."

Severo slams a palm to the table. "Enough with the bullshit, Jude. Tell us how you got hold of her father's blood. Do you have something more to confess?"

The detective's sudden forceful attitude surprises me, but I'm not going to interrupt. Jude seems content to be dragging this out all he can, so maybe this change of approach will work for us.

Jude's nostrils close in against the cartilage of his pale nose as he breathes before saying, "I took it from his bleeding neck the day he died."

Chapter 18

"You killed him. You killed my father?"

A tapping on the mirror glass distracts Severo, who looks at me. "Stop right there."

He exits the room, keeping the door open a notch as Captain Delaney speaks to him in private. I pay no attention to them, as I am fully concentrated on what Jude Barnaby wants to tell me. "I asked you if you killed my father."

"I'm hurt you would suggest such a thing."

"You wanted revenge. You said so yourself," I say, trying to keep my heated emotions under control. With the closed space sucking oxygen from my every breath, the pale aqua walls making me less than lucid, I pace myself, careful of what's to come. "So you went after the man who put you behind bars the first time. Well, I hate to tell you, Judas, but I'm putting you behind bars this time. And for killing my father? You can expect many years of privacy."

"I'm going to give you the benefit of the doubt, Agent." Judas adjusts his position, but keeps his eyes on me as Severo closes the door, returning to our meeting. "Because you weren't here to understand the relationship I had with your father."

"No. Nuh-uh. I will not for one second believe he took up a deal with you," I say, recalling what Philip said about how Jude was paying someone off to keep quiet. Cain had warned me Judas would try to turn this around on me by making it even more personal. But I won't buy it. "Not my father."

"No. Not your father."

"Then what? What is it, Judas?"

Severo slides me a note, and I read it. "Captain says proceed with caution." I look at him, then toward the double-sided mirror, like those are the stupidest words I have ever laid eyes on.

"Your father knew who had made arrangements with me, I won't keep that a secret. But it wasn't me, Angela," Jude says, his voice firm, as though he wants me to find reason within his words. "It was not I who killed your father. Though I was there all right, to witness the event where both you and I were betrayed by the same man."

"You want me to believe that? You're telling me you want revenge, yet you're also saying you didn't kill my father. Who, Jude? Who is it, exactly, you want to extend revenge to? Me?"

"Were that the case, Agent, I would not have bothered with creating such a display, now would I? It was necessary, of course, to go to so much trouble. I knew you would have a hard time believing me, had I simply told you the truth. One cannot just walk up to another, with a personal history such as we have, and tell you the facts."

His voice is picking up enthusiasm as he explains his motives for killing the apostles. It's exactly like Cain said. Judas wants me to be impressed with his methodology.

"I knew you would not believe it to be true, and thus I had to show you. It took time to carefully plan who would be first, and in what order they would fall victim to this revelation," he says, his breathing intense as he urges me to realize his puppet mastery. "It was quite necessary to proceed with precision, you must know, for me to understand what it was you would see within each of their lifeless bodies. I needed to be exacting in my work, so you would be led to find out for yourself what unfortunate things have occurred."

My mouth clenches, keeping my tongue steady. My spine is rigid as I stare back at this man, and all my muscles are flexed, instinctively, as I confront my opponent. "So you seek no revenge against my father. None against me. And if not against your former partners, Judas, why the charade? Did you simply want to tease me, taunt me with your pathetic copycat abilities?"

"No. You are, despite my earlier statement, not a disappointment at all. I can see how well your father trained you in his image. And I suppose you may have even learned a thing or two from Agent Cain."

"What's your point," I demand, rather than ask.

"He, too, was a fine agent in his day. Perhaps now that your father is no longer with us, he is at the top of the list once again. I'm sure the two of you work well together, Angela, though I don't know I'd go so far as to say he's a suitable mentor for you."

"What about my father?"

"Again, Miss David, I'm going to suggest you work on your ability to pay attention." His tongue darts out the corner of his mouth as though he were a frog, trapping flies in slow motion. "You think it was an accident Cain chose to work with you? You think it was pure coincidence he chose to work with the daughter of the ever-respected Joshua David?"

"Angie," Severo pleads, placing a hand around my arm.

"What is it, Judas. What are you trying to say?"

My heart is thumping against my rib cage, swelling as I listen to this madman reel me in. I'm not the only one to respond to this revelation. The door to our interrogation room swings open and a guard begins to remove Judas, as Captain Delaney calls attention to Severo.

While he is being guided from the room, Judas looks back to me. "Perhaps you should ask your mentor. You ask him what he would do to cover his own sins, Angie.

He went back on his word," Judas is saying, his voice now loud in the hallway. "He and I had an arrangement! He made a promise, to keep his mouth shut and me free. But when he got scared of getting caught, you ask him what he did."

Struggling against Severo's hold, I follow Judas and the officers down the hall, just far enough so I can hear the rest of his speech.

"You ask him, Agent David. Ask Cain how it felt to stand face-to-face with your father and shoot a fellow agent straight through the throat."

"Give me your keys."

"Angie, I don't think you should drive."

"Severo, give me the damn keys!"

He hands them over to me, which in my opinion is the right thing to do, although I can see he obviously doesn't agree, and I hop in the driver's seat of the Jeep.

If Judas is telling the truth, and right now I don't know who or what to believe in this spiderweb of activity, Cain was the one who accepted a bribe to keep quiet about the criminal activity of the Apostles of Peace.

And if that fact can be proved, Judas is telling the whole truth. About everything. Which would mean Cain was the one who shot my father and left him to die.

"Angie, we cannot take this guy's words at face value," Severo says, but I lower my foot to the gas, speeding toward Gramercy Park. "If what Jude says is right, we have to go in easy, you hear? If Cain is guilty of…hell, if Cain is guilty, he's not going to be waiting patiently for us to get there. I can honestly say I don't know what to expect from him."

My voice rises above the squealing tires as I round a corner with speed. "How the hell did this happen?" I glance quickly at the detective, looking for answers. "How the hell did Cain get away with this?"

"I don't know. Right now we cannot leap to any conclusions. And if this is what really happened," he says, shaking his head in disbelief and uncertainty, "he fooled us. He fooled all of us. Angie, listen to me. If Cain killed your father, his bringing you to New York to be your mentor was no accident. Like Judas said, as much as I hate to admit."

The shocks from the Jeep bouncing over bumps in the road hardly register as I keep my focus ahead of me. Though it's late in the evening, holiday traffic is still dense and I have to be watchful of civilians on the streets. Severo's rooftop siren is screaming out to the masses, warning them to keep clear of our path, but I'm careful not to cause any further disruption as we make our way to my uncle's church. We have to get there before Cain does anything stupid.

"But why! Why would he do this? Why would he kill my dad?"

"From what Jude said, Cain knew your father had info on their financial arrangement. Jesus, who knows what he's been up to, if this is what he's made of." Raising his hands to rub his face, the detective groans into his palms. "I hate to say it, but it adds up, Angie. God, I hung out with him, for crying out loud. He was like a friend. I trusted him."

Those words sting and I control my emotions, not letting that phrase eat away at my insides. A friend. Hell, even I took to Cain right away, what with his reputation and all that friggin' praise he had regarding my father's position with the Bureau. Cain took me in, under the guise of mentor, and lied to me every single chance he had.

I just can't believe—or want to believe—this is it. That I once thought Marcus Cain was kind enough to pick me as a mentoring partner, after seeing that I was the daughter of a fed who'd died in the line of duty, brings tears to my eyes. Judas made the point that Cain chose me for a reason. Yeah, he chose me knowing damn well my father died at his hands.

I lower my foot, pushing the speedometer to its limit, as the reason for my return to New York becomes more clear. I wanted to be closer to my family after my father's death, while training under the guidance of a respected mentor. For Cain, it meant keeping an eye on the one person who would find out the truth of his wrongdoings. I will not let this be put to rest easily.

Accompanying squad cars slide in behind me as I park the Jeep on the grass of my uncle's church. I can see Cain's car off to the side of the entrance, where he left it after coming here to tell my family of Jude's intentions. Only it keeps getting worse, and I cannot believe I convinced Severo to leave Cain here, with my family, as a precaution against Judas. How could we have known the real reason they need protection is because of the man who spoke so damn pleasantly to my grandmother?

"Cain!" I yell, rushing through the nave of the church, winding my way past empty pews and prayer rooms. "You better get your ass out here, you son of a bitch. I think you have some explaining to do!"

Safeties being clicked off weapons fill the space with a domino sound, as Captain Delaney, Severo and practically the entire squad scour the vicinity for signs of movement.

"Marcus Cain, this is Detective Severo of the NYPD. I suggest you come out with your hands where I can see them."

My feet carry me quickly to my uncle's rectory, where we'd left my family watching evening game shows. As I enter the room, though, only the television makes a sound, as highlights for the upcoming evening news broadcast the day's events. Whatever has happened in this city today, I can bet it pales in comparison to what is about to go down in this church.

With no one in sight, and Severo now at my side, our eyes meet briefly as we gauge one another's intent to pursue the deceit of my former mentor. The detective nods, moving to the south side of the residence, and I proceed north, heading toward the church office.

I step lightly but swiftly to slide my hand over the doorknob and creak it open. A slight woof alerts me of

Muddy's presence, and as I enter the room I see he is on his own.

"Hey, baby," I whisper, kneeling to pat his back, still keeping aware of who else may be near. "Shh, Mama will be right back, okay?" I give him a good rub, relieved he is safe on his own with full dishes of water and food beside him, before closing the door behind me as I head back down the hall to seek out Cain.

"Agent David," Captain Delaney says, approaching me with another officer. His voice is firm but quiet, so only I can hear his words. "It might be best if you step outside."

"No, Captain. If he killed my father, and lied to my face the whole time, I will not sit quietly and wait outside. This is my time now. This is my time to prove I am my father's daughter," I say, seeing the captain understands my determination.

"I respect that," he whispers. "Just watch your back, Agent. We are here with you."

I nod, acknowledging thanks to the squad, then head down the hallway leading back to the nave of the church.

When we first came in, marching up the middle aisle surrounded by rows of pews, it occurred to me Cain could be watching us, as Judas did at the other scenes. There has to be somewhere, someplace, this man has found sanctuary, and I aim to find him. My family's safety depends on it.

Armed officers search hallways and prayer rooms, determined to seek out the man who may have the only first-person account of what happened to my father the day he died. As I watch their precise movements, it occurs to me there may be one unique place Cain has found solace.

My hand alerts a few officers, and Severo also sees my wave in the direction of the altar. Stepping into the room behind the focal point of my uncle's church, we move cautiously toward the entryway to the catacomb.

Uncle Simon taught me of the ancient burial room, hidden underground, where bodies of the church's original founders lie at rest, forever paying respect for their development of this place of worship. As I lead the way to this sacred and private area, the squad following, I see a shadow dart past the far wall and out to a hallway.

"Cain, you bastard!" I yell, but my nose picks up a familiar and disturbing smell. The Captain, Severo and fellow officers rush to track the burning scent as I chase after the man who owes me one hell of an explanation.

"They're down here!" Severo yells to me, letting me know he has found my uncle, grandmother and Denise.

"Are they hurt?" I ask, desperate to hear a favorable response. My gut wrenches at the possibility….

The detective's coughing alarms me, but I am placated when I hear his follow-up. "They're fine, they're all okay."

Officers beat at the growing flames, and though I am pained to see some of my uncle's church begin to melt at the hands of Cain, it is that man I choose to focus my attention on.

Knowing my family is safe, out of harm's way and being attended to by the detective, I run through the hallway behind the catacomb entranceway, desperate to find Cain and settle this score once and for all.

Chapter 19

My blood heats as I run through the back door, exiting to the churchyard and into the downpour of the night's rainstorm. I spy Cain hopping in that old clunker of his, but to hell if he's getting away so easy.

Officers run behind me as I make my way to Severo's Jeep. Sirens begin to wail, but I press my weight on the gas pedal as I screech off the wet grass and follow this murderer. His fleeing admits his guilt, and he will soon pay for his deceit.

Trailing behind Cain's aged sedan, I stay close to him, and when he turns left, I turn left. He pulls a right, I follow. From the silhouette in his car as he checks the rearview mirror, I know he sees me behind him. I wonder now if he realizes the extent of what he's done.

Regardless of what he has gotten away with in the past, there is no way he could possibly have believed he would get away with this today. With half the Fifth Precinct as witnesses to his actions, there is no way Cain will flee from anything, anymore.

Racing through the streets toward the outskirts of Manhattan, I pull the seat belt over my chest with one arm, chasing after him as he makes a speedy transition onto the Brooklyn Bridge.

My cell phone sounds and I answer quickly, wondering if he's going to make a statement now to set his name free.

"David," I say, gripping the wheel with one hand.

"Angie, it's Carson. Where are you?"

My voice is solid and determined, and my vision remains planted on the car in front of me. I can't lose him.

"Heading over the Brooklyn Bridge, but I can't talk now, Severo." I close my phone as I bypass some slow movers to catch up to Cain, who is weaving in and out of cars ahead of him, trying to lose me in the late night traffic.

I press my foot on the gas, climbing the ramp to the bridge, with Cain a few cars ahead of me.

Despite the reality of this situation, I cannot help feeling daft and confused. Cain was supposed to be my mentor. He was supposed to be the one person who would teach me the tricks of the trade, prepping me for getting into NCAVC. Well, he's shown me a few tricks, all right. But right now, my only determination is nailing his ass for what he's done to my family, both in the past and in the present.

I lay on the horn as I follow him onto the Brooklyn Queens Expressway, looping the outskirts of Cadman Plaza. There are too many cars to get a leg up on him.

Now that we're trailing the border of Brooklyn Heights, I realize Cain knows this area like his own soul. It's home-advantage territory for him, with his bachelor pad somewhere in this vicinity. Hell if I'll let that small detail slow me.

To my right, the Statue of Liberty is lit up in full glory, as the vision of Liberty Island set amid the Upper New York Bay is clear from this expressway. It's a sign of freedom and honor, and I plan on upholding my commitment to these things by making Cain pay for his crimes.

With one hand reaching down my side, I let the safety off my handgun, preparing in advance for the worst. My head is throbbing, just thinking about this. But there is no other possible explanation.

Jude Barnaby killed those four men, and was all too eager to keep up his pace, there is no doubt about that. But his explanation as to why he chose to murder those men in the manner he did—to lead me to the truth about my father's death—is too fantastical to make up.

Why would he? Why would Judas bother fabricating that story? It would only put him in further distress with the law, and something tells me Judas is tired of being dealt a poor hand from the powers that be.

I take no pity on that killer. But Judas claimed both he and I were betrayed by the same man, and if this is

how he had to make it clear to me, I can at least be
thankful for knowing the truth. A truth I had no idea to
seek.

We pass over Cowanus Canal, then head eastbound
to the Belt Parkway, skimming the island shore, and
Cain drives steadily, keeping one at a distance. There
has to be a way to close the gap and lose the cars between us. With darkness upon us and the rain not at all
letting up, it'll be too easy to lose sight of my prey. The
piercing lights towering over the expressway send pe-
riodic flashes, interrupting my vision.

I extend my fingers to the middle console, fumbling
for the appropriate control to set off Severo's rooftop
siren. It takes a second to figure out how to awaken
both the sound and the flashing lights, and I want to
kick myself for not noticing before.

With this vehicular ammunition on my side now,
cars slow to the shoulder, leaving me an open trail behind Cain. I gain momentum on him as he darts along,
passing Fort Hamilton. As we sail over the edge of
Dreier Offerman Park, Cain swerves off on Exit 6
heading to Coney Island, and I have to cross several
lanes to make the merge myself.

He soon takes a left onto the Shore Parkway and I
swerve in his tracks, the Jeep absorbing the shocks as
I hit hard against the road beneath me. I follow along
as he slams through to Bay 52nd Street. We're in the
land of historical lighthouses, tourist beaches and a
world-famous amusement zone. From this entry point,
we could be heading anywhere. He's not slowing down

for anything and there's only one way to put a stop to this.

As he takes a right on Cropsey Avenue, crossing over to Coney Island, I angle my left arm out the window, aiming my gun at his tires.

Checking briefly into my rearview mirror, I see the numerous squad cars following behind. But with no one in front, I lean out the window in an uncomfortable pose, take aim and fire.

My shots don't appear to hit Cain's car. I try again as our vehicles approach an intersection, this time striking his rear fender as he slows to take the corner.

He speeds into the left turn, and I hit the gas, not slowing for the curve. The Jeep screeches along, tires clinging to the road, mud spewing up behind. I lean out and aim again at Cain's car, hoping this shot is a success.

He slides into the north side of the Coney Island Complex of the NYC Transit, his car slowing in gaseous fumes, but I'm not stopping. When he exits the car and starts out on foot, I continue my chase from within the vehicle, barreling over muddy bumps in the landscape, battling my way into the transit yard, breaking through a flimsy fence.

When my vision picks up the rugged collection of silent train tracks and their protruding mile gauges, I slam on my brakes and take a sharp left, aiming to miss their metal bite.

As the Jeep slides into a dip, though, I feel a heavy drop in the car, and as the driver's-side air bag forcefully punches into my chest, I know it's not a clear landing. The tires have been punctured.

Recovering from the blow, I keep my sights on Cain as I rush out after him, into the stormy night, carrying only my weapon with me.

"Cain, you bastard! You can't run from me!"

As I leap over several metal rails, sprinting after him, he has little reaction.

He's heading south now, and his voice is trailing in the wintery wind, almost lost beneath the noisy commotion of aboveground trains in the distance. "It didn't have to be this way, kiddo."

"You son of a bitch!" My voice is raspy from the pounding chase. Though I can hear sirens wailing in the background, closing in, I keep my bloodlust for Cain focused and straight.

This wasn't the ending I had imagined. Through my panting breath, I think back on when I arrived in the city just last week, back to my native ground, with the high hopes of someday working my way to the top of the NCAVC intake pile.

I had determination to find out what it takes to work in the field. This? This was not what I had in mind. But there's only one way to turn the tables in my direction.

I lift the Bauer .25 into my sight line, and when I see Cain running to the east side of the yard's command center, just a hundred feet in front of me, I stop, focus on my target and shoot with tenacity.

He stumbles along, and I know I hit something, but I can't tell what, or if it was even one of his limbs. I pick up the pace again and run after him, though he has taken to hiding behind an abandoned grounds building.

Beating after him, I try to estimate which direction he'll come from, but when I do see him pop out a bit to the side, he takes a shot at me and misses.

"You can't mess with an old pro, kiddo!"

"Then get your ass out here, Cain. I'm not done with you!" I sneak to the opposite side of the building, keeping my breath low and steady as I anticipate his movements.

"I gotta hand it to ya, kiddo. I picked you 'cause you were the best. Second best, that is."

I don't want to play this game. I just want to get Cain and put his words to rest. I'm tired of his useless commentary.

Maybe I'm not ready for profiling. If I couldn't pick up on Cain's reality while working side by side with him, how the hell will I ever understand the mind of a killer?

"The best, of course, being your father."

I slide along the exterior of the building, and Cain is waiting for me, so I take aim and shoot, but my bullet spins into the night air.

"When I saw your name in the files, I knew I had to work with you. If you were anything like your dear old dad was, I knew you'd be a fighter."

"Why didn't you just kill me, Cain? If you wanted to make sure I didn't find out the truth about all this, why did you have to drag it out and let innocent people die!"

"Innocent?" Cain's throaty chuckle interrupts his speech for only a moment. "Oh, kiddo, have I taught you nothing? And damned if I knew Judas was going to get all fancy like that," he shouts. I listen to his words as he tries to explain his inexcusable actions.

"Sure, I knew Judas was fresh out on the streets again. Me, I just wanted to keep an eye on you. As a reminder of what your father was like, that nosy son of a bitch. But when we came onto that first body—that Killarney fellow—I knew I was in for a fight. It became obvious to me right then and there I'd have to play it cool, watch my ass and go through the motions. I had no idea it would go this far, but it's been a good lesson for you, hasn't it? Didn't you learn a thing or two along the way?"

My beating heart is the only sound I can hear other than Cain's diatribe. I slide along the wall, taking a different approach to nabbing my former mentor.

My curiosity is intensifying, though. I can't understand how Cain could ever think he would get away with this. "So why not just kill Judas? Get it over with?"

He carries on in a piercing chuckle, amused by my interest. "I would have, but I couldn't be raising any red flags, you know. I was just hoping we would find him, and put a bullet through his heart before he had a chance to open his mouth. Just hoped for the best, kiddo."

More sirens wail into the area, and I hear muffled sounds of officers trekking through the train yard, though I know I can't wait for their help. This is my deal. This is when everything my father taught me has to come into play.

"Too bad it has to end like this. Like with your father. Good guy, mind you, but he was too righteous for his own welfare. You know I offered him a take on the dough, but he wouldn't budge?"

The words sink into my heart and I can't help but hurt for my father. He was a good man. He didn't deserve to die. Especially not at the hands of slime like Cain.

"Not that I could afford to share any of it, mind you. I got me an ex-wife who lives like friggin' royalty with that new guy of hers, and two kids in private school. I don't get paid enough to cover all that, even with Jude's contributions. But I was willing to share it with your father if he'd keep his mouth shut. That's how much I cared."

I think of Cain's family, and wonder how much of his lifestyle his wife knew about. Maybe that's the real reason she left him. Maybe she knew he was benefiting from someone else's crimes. Regardless, I have no soft spot left for him.

"So when he thought he was top shit for uncovering what Jude was up to, well, I had to step in, ya see. You gotta understand that, Angie. I have a family to take care of. I didn't have a choice."

"Like hell you didn't!" I yell, and my voice carries across the backdrop of the building's metal frame. Distant from this ironclad yard, I hear the familiar gust of a subway train rattling on its rails, coming closer to our location.

"Course I didn't. He knew I was turning an eye to Judas and what those twits were up to, ya see. If I'd a let him, your father would have nailed my ass, too. And, eh, I couldn't let that happen."

I scuttle across the corner to make it to the next side of the building, edging my way to Cain. I'll have to keep my mouth shut now, or he'll expect me to come from this angle.

I keep my breath quiet as I think of the many times Cain said great things about my father, encouraging me to find my place in the field. All along, this past week, I believed every word he said, and valued him as a mentor. Right before my eyes, this man I trusted and grew to appreciate was guilty of taking my father's life.

Between all his words of bullshit, with all his false pleasantries as he acted suitably as a mentor, he was watching his own back, ensuring that whatever I learned on this case would not break his silence.

If Severo couldn't see behind Cain's well-dressed facade all these years, after working with him on the Violent Crime Task Force and spending social time with this two-faced man, how was I ever supposed to uncover the truth when I didn't even know what to look for?

Moving cautiously across the rain-slicked ground, I take a few steps closer to where Cain is hiding.

"Kiddo, I'm sorry you had to find out about this. I fully intended to keep this a secret. Hell, my freedom depended on it. Such a shame we couldn't shut Judas up before he blabbered to you. That bastard was never much good for anything. Still, I'm sorry for your loss. I'm sure you'll understand I had no choice in the matter."

The lights from surrounding cruisers sprinkle the transit yard's outer limits, filtering past idle train cars and metal wreckage.

"Angie? I'm sorry, kiddo. If it means anything to you, your father put up a good fight."

This statement ignites my blood as I flip my body around to face the side of the building where Cain is leaning. I aim, and when my trigger is set, he faces me, looking proud and pleased with himself.

"You're a good kid, Angie. Put your gun down."

My eyes zero in on Cain, my hands centered in front of me as I grip the trigger. "You lied to me about knowing my father, Cain. All week you lied about everything. I don't like liars. Not one bit."

He steps in front of me, and as I steady my grip, I aim my gun, but he begins to run back across the tracks, knees high in the air as he leaps through the metal traps. I chase after him, firing as he runs from me, but he pivots and returns the gesture tenfold.

I feel a sting of heat burn through my flesh, and from the blood below my right knee, I know I've been hit.

"You're a bad shot, Cain," I say, steadying my balance onto my left leg. I step forward, my right muscles burning, as I make it closer to the foul agent.

"You're not so bad." He grasps his left arm, his handgun still intact.

A gust of wind raises debris from the yard, and beneath my feet, the earthquake of vibrations pose an interesting option for my punishment of Cain. But I leap across a set of tracks, hurtling myself onto him as I roll us out of the way while a subway train barrels past at top speed.

"Angie!" Severo's familiar voice skips to me between the cars, and though I don't turn to locate him, I flinch at the sound. Cain takes this opportunity to roll away from me and knock my weapon from my grasp.

"Angie, kiddo, it's so sweet that you care," he says, dusting himself off after the save I made on his life.

"I wasn't about to let a train take all the fun out of my job, Cain."

As he fumbles to grasp on to me and aim his gun, I leap and roll him to his back, then deliver a forceful uppercut to his cheek. There is something bittersweet in this moment as I fight back against the one human being I thought would boost my career since my father's death. Man, did I have it wrong.

Cain shoots but doesn't hit me as I straddle him and roll backward, onto my spine, and peel him along, with my knees braced around his neck.

"This is nice," Cain mocks, and I squeeze my knees together despite the pain coming from my lower limb. With this motion, I bring his face closer to my abdomen and I send a fierce jab to his head, knocking him hard enough to draw blood.

I wriggle from under him, stepping on his gun and

kicking it to the right, where Severo and the approaching squad officers run to meet us.

"That's my girl, Angie," Cain mutters despite the discomfort. "You sure have it. Your father would be so proud."

"Cain, you are one sick bastard," I say, my left foot propped on his stomach, pressing into the wound I see my gun has made.

"Angie, kiddo. Don't blame me. Blame your father. That son of a bitch should have kept his eyes closed and his mouth shut. Just the way I left him and his bleeding throat. Silent."

With my weight balanced on my right leg, pressing into his wound, Cain arches his neck up to stare me down. I focus my eyes on my prey and say, "That's precisely how I'm leaving you, Cain. Say good night." Shifting my weight to my injured right foot, I send a powerful kick into Cain's temple.

"Holy shit, Angie," Severo says breathlessly, sliding up to me. The squad is right behind him, and they soon center in on Cain and me.

"It's true, Carson. He killed my father."

The detective peels me away from Cain, who is covered in blood and mud, though I know he'll survive. I wouldn't have it any other way. They'll pile on enough lengthy sentences that he'll never see the light of day again.

"You okay?" Severo asks, lending an arm for me to balance my walk while keeping the pressure off my wounded leg.

Not knowing what words there are to express this release of tension, this discovery of truth, or the reality that my father died trying to set right the wrongs of this pathetic, lying agent, I do nothing but shake my head as the tears well in my eyes. For the first time since my return to New York, I weep in memory of my father.

Severo removes his coat and places it on a wooden rail post, urging me to sit. His face is flushed, no doubt from running after me.

My head, feeling swollen with tension, lifts enough for me to look him in the eyes. "Are they okay?" I ask, wanting to know how my family is doing.

"They're fine. We got them out and they're doing fine." The detective rubs my knee, as though the pressure will wipe away this moment of distress. "And the church is okay, too. There's some damage, of course, but not enough to worry about. Your family will be just fine, Angie."

This news is a relief to hear. I don't know how I would endure it if something awful had happened to any one of them, including Denise, who has proved to be so much part of our family. With the newly acquired knowledge pertaining to my father's death, there will be more healing for us all to embrace, but this time around, I will not shut out my father's significant other.

Severo reaches to brush my messy hair away from my face, and I look into his caring eyes, thankful he has been a great support this week. "Sorry about the Jeep."

"What about it?"

I shrug and offer a weak grin, figuring whatever damage has been done can always be fixed. "Let's just say you won't be giving me your keys again anytime soon."

"I don't know about that," he says, wrapping a portion of his jacket up around my legs, keeping me steady as he blots at the blood. "Captain says you're a pretty slick driver, the way you tailed after Cain."

"What can I say?" I look into his eyes, a grim smile creeping across my face. "My father taught me."

Chapter 20

"*Mi porti del vino!*" Severo's mother calls out, following after Antonio to bring wine to the table, as we settle in for a small gathering in the comfortable atmosphere of La Costa.

The Closed sign is hanging from the doorknob, as the family wanted a private affair on this quiet night. December has officially kicked in, and as though the weather needed to enforce that notion, snow is silently sprinkling down, making a very pretty sight against the vibrant patio lanterns decorating the café exterior.

"It's just so lovely to meet you all," Maria says, peering around the dining room as she addresses my entire family.

Uncle Simon and my grandmother sit across from

me, beside Antonio and Maria, and even Denise is here, placed next to Severo's sister Frances as we mingle in this quaint situation. All the members of Severo's family I met at his niece's birthday are gathered around the table, and between his relatives and mine this has to be the largest, most pleasant social event I have been to in years.

"Thanks very much for inviting us," I say, passing the tossed salad to the detective. "I think, finally, things are starting to settle down."

"Then what now?" Maria hands a platter of baked ziti toward her mother, who gleefully digs in to fill her plate.

"Now I go back to working on getting field experience. With this piece of the puzzle put behind me, knowing the strange truth of what really happened to my father, I can seriously focus on my career."

My grandmother reaches a hand across the table and I accept her soft squeeze as she looks over the surrounding family. "My Angela already has focus on the future. She's such a sweet dear, and I always knew she'd be just like her father. Joshua was a good man, and he did a stunning job of raising this girl."

"She certainly knows how to kick some butt out there," Severo says, and I elbow him in the ribs as he leans in closer to me, from his chair beside mine. "It's true. Cain obviously didn't know who he was up against."

Antonio passes a bottle of red in my direction and asks, "What's going to happen to him?"

I fill my glass and then Severo's, while relaying the best news I've heard all week. "He's being shipped off and will likely do more than one life sentence, I'm happy to report. Same goes for Judas, though I doubt the system will buddy them up in the same facility. There's too much history with those two to let them be cellmates."

The detective offers me a cheer, so we clink glasses politely and then I gently swirl the crimson liquid in its glass. Raising it to my lips, I let the nutty undertone slide across my taste buds.

There's no denying it's been hard to take in all that's occurred since I returned to New York. Uncovering what happened to my father, and coping with the recent revelation of my mentor's true intentions, I've had more emotions running through me than I know what to do with. Now that I have a clean slate, though, I am able to start anew and embrace my time and purpose back in my hometown.

Uncle Simon dons a wide smile as he leans toward one of the Severos sitting beside him. "My Angie is going to do what her papa did, and she will make us all so proud."

Maria and Antonio look to me for an explanation, so I fill them in. "Even after this, it's still my intention to work toward profiling with the National Center for Analysis of Violent Crime. Virginia won't wait for me forever."

Maria's eyes move to Severo, and I watch his reaction as he meets her subtle glance. "Hey, it's where she belongs. She's got the right mind for it. Trust me on that." He focuses his eyes toward me, and they soften a little in the ambient light. "The center will snap you up in a heartbeat. If they know what's good for them."

Admittedly, I have considered the weight of my decision to keep on track with the profiling program. Things between the detective and me may be heating up, but I can't lose sight of my career ambitions.

Besides, I still have years of work to do before NCAVC will even look at my application. Who knows? It could be a decade before I leave New York. If Severo is still in the picture when that time comes, we'll figure out the destination together.

"For now I'm more focused on what's going to happen for me in this city." I look to Severo's mother, who is wide-eyed and attentive, hanging on to the English words with intensity. "They need to find me a mentor replacement. Plus, I have to fill in the blanks for Internal Affairs with the whole Cain episode, not to mention see to it that kid who was originally and wrongfully charged with my father's death gets his leave and proper apologies. That'll be fun."

"The worst is over." Severo raises a glass in salute, and his family follows suit.

"Amen to that," I say, mimicking his movement. His cell phone drills and on the second ring he retrieves it, so I turn my attention back to Maria.

"Thanks again for the dinner invitation. It's really nice to get our families together and have you get to know one another. It almost feels like the holidays."

With a giggle, she raises a serviette to dab her lips before speaking. "My brother says you very rarely sit down for a proper meal. I thought it'd be nice for your family, too, now that you're all in the city. You know we'll have to do it often. Family is very important to us, and to you, I see."

"Maybe someday we can do it at my place," I offer, as my grandmother makes a surprised face. She knows me and my cooking skills too well. "Once I finish unpacking, that is."

"What makes you think you've got time to unpack?" Severo asks, dropping back into the conversation. He slides his phone into his jacket pocket as he stands up from the table. "You're still looking to get some field experience, aren't you, Agent?"

I feel my brows instinctively arch as I hear these words. "You know I am. Anything interesting?"

As I pull away from the table to join the detective in another night of unknown action, his lips curl and his teasingly smug expression fuels my adrenaline. "Let's just say I hope you're full," he says, holding the door open for me as we wave good-night to our families. "You won't have much of an appetite after we get through with this one."

Maybe not, but my curiosity is certainly hungry for more.

* * * * *

*Ready for more excitement, action, danger, and
thrilling romance from Silhouette Bombshell?*

*Turn the page for a sneak peek at one of next
month's gripping reads
MEDUSA RISING
by Cindy Dees*

*Available in September 2005
at your favorite retail outlet.*

To hell with the training exercise.

The SEAL divers needed help. Now.

Aleesha Gautier kicked into trauma surgeon mode instantly. Possible crushed ribs. Punctured lungs. Contused heart. Inability to breathe. And blood. *Oh, God. Blood.* There were sharks in these waters.

One of the other men reached for the injured diver, and she lifted his well-meaning hands out of the way. Fortunately, these guys knew she was a Harvard-educated trauma surgeon, and would let her take charge of their buddy's care. And the first order of business was to reestablish breathing. She inhaled a mouthful of oxygen from her own regulator, holding it in her cheeks. She blew into the injured man's mouth forcefully to clear it of water. Quickly, she placed the victim's oxygen regulator back in his mouth. She grabbed one of the other SEAL's hands and put it over the regulator to hold it in place. He nodded his understanding of what to do.

They had to immobilize the man's chest cavity as best they could while they surfaced. She lid her hands behind him, grabbing his armpits from underneath. Bracing her elbows on either side of his head, she used her forearms as a makeshift backboard and then nodded to the other men. *Now* it was time to go.

They were deep enough that a rapid ascent put them all at risk of getting the bends, that bane of divers where nitrogen bubbles formed in the blood, causing great pain and possible death. She controlled her breathing carefully so as not to rupture a lung of her own as they shot upward toward the light as fast as they could go.

She spared a glance downward and saw an ominous smudge of brown trailing in the water behind them. Dammit. Sharks could smell a few drops of blood at distances of a mile or more. The long, swirling trail of it behind them was more than enough to attract any sharks in the vicinity. That was the last complication they needed right now.

She fished around with her fingers, searching for a pulse in the guy's armpit. It was faint and thready, but she felt a throb of circulation beneath one finger. Thank God. Maybe this guy stood a chance of pulling through, after all. But every second without air was costly. Too many seconds and brain cells would start to die.

They burst to the surface of the ocean. She tore off her mask and immediately put her mouth on the injured man's. In-the-water resuscitation was Diving 101. She felt a distinctive gurgle in the exhaled air against her lips. Damn. Collapsed lung. Nothing she could do about that at the moment.

"Take over this mouth-to-mouth," she ordered one of the other divers. He nodded and glided into her place, treading water and breathing into his comrade's mouth.

The second diver commented dryly, "Glad you could join us, Doc."

She glanced up as she traced the victim's rib cage with her fingers. "You looked like you could use a little help."

"Save him, eh?" the guy grunted back.

"I'll do my best. Wrap a couple buoyancy belts around his hips, will you? It's damn hard to triage a patient who keeps trying to sink."

The second SEAL complied rapidly. Meanwhile, the first SEAL lifted his head and announced, "He's breathing again."

She glanced at her watch. One minute and fourteen seconds after the torpedo had landed on his chest. Not bad. In fact, it was amazing, given the situation. If he lived, the guy probably wouldn't suffer any brain damage.

She announced, "I'm going underneath him to see

where he's bleeding. Either of you got a med kit on you?"

The resuscitator shook his head. "Got a crash kit on the Zodiac, but that's it. I already hit the panic button. Boat should be here in ten to fifteen minutes."

Crap. That was a long time to keep this guy alive until she could render proper medical treatment. She nodded grimly, pulled her mask over her face and quickly submerged. A long, ragged tear in the back of her patient's wet suit marked the source of the blood seeping steadily into the water. Arterial bleeding. Not good.

Swishing bloody water away from the wound, she slapped her finger on top of the lacerated artery and pressed as hard as she could. Using her fin, she kicked one of the guys above in the leg to get his attention. Quickly, he submerged beside her. She gestured for him to take over the pressure.

Then she did a quick inspection of the rest of the victim's underside. Some scrapes and cuts, but nothing else life threatening. Something hard smacked her in the side of the head. She lurched and saw a swim fin headed directly at her face again. She dodged out of the way, popping back up to the surface.

The guy up top didn't need to explain why he'd kicked her. The rattling, rasping gasps from her patient were self-explanatory. He was in huge respiratory distress. As she repositioned herself to have another look at his chest, he went into a seizure. His back arched and his face dipped below the water. Any buoyancy he'd had was completely lost. She and the other topside diver muscled his rigid body higher in the water. She kicked for all she was worth, her legs burning like fire. C'mon, c'mon. Relax already, she begged him.

And then a movement in her peripheral vision caught her attention. Dorsal fin. Big one. Shark. What else could go wrong?

"Shark," she grunted.

"*Shit.* Back in a sec."

She made out a harpoon in the submerged diver's hand. He had the sharks handled, then.

The second diver surfaced just as the seizure began to ease. The rigidity left the victim's body, leaving behind an ominous stillness.

"His heart's failing on me." She reached for the carotid artery in the patient's neck. Yup. Pulse uneven and fading fast. "Here's the thing," she told the other diver. "His sternum may be fractured. If we do CPR on him, we run the risk of puncturing his heart. If we don't do CPR, we risk brain damage and possibly not getting his heart going again once I get access to a defibrillator."

"You're the doctor. You make the call," the SEAL replied.

She wasn't a top-notch emergency physician for nothing. She faced these life-and-death decisions all the time. And she had complete faith in her skills. "I'll do the CPR myself. My malpractice insurance is still paid up."

She could only pray her current patient didn't have a lacerated aorta on top of his other injuries.

"Incoming," the other diver murmured.

Incoming?

A dorsal fin maybe fifty yards away headed straight at them and was, indeed, coming in fast. It dipped below the surface of the water about thirty yards out. The shark would come up from below, striking his victim in the soft underbelly.

A metallic, hissing noise from below startled her and then a mighty thrashing erupted in the water about twenty yards away. The gray, sinuous body of a shark breached the surface of the water, writhing violently. A flash of steel was embedded in its belly. It seemed like only seconds until a second dorsal fin appeared, slamming into the wounded shark like a sledgehammer. The water around the twisting beasts frothed red and angry. Oh, Lord. She got to do meatball medicine on a gravely injured man mere yards from a full-blown shark feeding frenzy? Uncle Sam wasn't paying her enough for the day's work.

Well, she'd signed on with the Medusas because she craved adventure. She had to give Uncle Sam credit for delivering, because this was one hell of a challenge. It made practicing trauma medicine in an actual hospital seem downright tame by comparison.

How long she carefully compressed Smitty's chest, stopping every so often to breathe into his mouth, she had no idea. But she was light-headed from the exertion of forcing air into his dying lungs; she was cramping, hips to toes, from keeping both him and herself afloat; and in another minute or so, she was going to puke from all the seawater she'd swallowed.

Finally, a new noise intruded upon the thrashing and splashing behind her as the sharks made lunch out of their wounded companion. An engine. Running at high rpms and coming fast. As she moved from Smitty's mouth back to his chest, she saw a black Zodiac flying across the water. *Praise the Lord.*

In a matter of seconds, many strong hands were reaching down, lifting Smitty gently into the vessel and hoisting her unceremoniously in afterward. Without ado, she leaned over the side of the boat and barfed up the entire seawater contents of her stomach. No time to feel sorry for herself, though. She had a patient to take care of.

After using the mobile defibrillator, setting up a breathing bag and applying an internal pressure bandage to the damaged artery, she continued to monitor his vital signs on the ride back to shore. An ambulance met them at the dock, and she rode to the hospital with Smitty. Only when she'd assured herself that the waiting trauma team knew its stuff did she relinquish control of her patient.

And then it was over.

"You did good, Doc."

Praise? From a SEAL team captain? Wow. Her insides warmed with the compliment. "Thanks," she replied, pleased.

"Let me give you a ride back to your quarters. I expect you're ready to clean up and get out of that wet suit. Next training evolution begins at midnight, tonight. We'll be swimming, so bring your dive gear."

Right. One of their men had just escaped death by a whisker, but training went on. How harsh was that? But then Special Ops was a callous world that had no time for the weak.

So what was she doing in it, then?

She'd asked herself that question many times since she'd joined the Medusa Project. She was a doctor. A healer. But ever since her first mission in the field a few months back, where she'd been ordered to shoot to kill—and had—this dilemma had been building.

How in the hell was she supposed to work and live among people who held life so cheaply, to become one of them herself, when she'd dedicated her entire life to saving lives, not taking them?

Houston, we have a problem.

If you enjoyed what you just read,
then we've got an offer you can't resist!

Take 2 bestselling love stories FREE!

Plus get a FREE surprise gift!

Clip this page and mail it to Silhouette Reader Service®

IN U.S.A.	IN CANADA
3010 Walden Ave.	P.O. Box 609
P.O. Box 1867	Fort Erie, Ontario
Buffalo, N.Y. 14240-1867	L2A 5X3

YES! Please send me 2 free Silhouette Bombshell™ novels and my free surprise gift. After receiving them, if I don't wish to receive any more, I can return the shipping statement marked cancel. If I don't cancel, I will receive 4 brand-new novels every month, before they're available in stores! In the U.S.A., bill me at the bargain price of $4.69 plus 25¢ shipping & handling per book and applicable sales tax, if any*. In Canada, bill me at the bargain price of $5.24 plus 25¢ shipping & handling per book and applicable taxes**. That's the complete price and a savings of 10% off the cover prices—what a great deal! I understand that accepting the 2 free books and gift places me under no obligation ever to buy any books. I can always return a shipment and cancel at any time. Even if I never buy another book from Silhouettte, the 2 free books and gift are mine to keep forever.

200 HDN D34H
300 HDN D34J

Name	(PLEASE PRINT)	
Address	Apt.#	
City	State/Prov.	Zip/Postal Code

Not valid to current Silhouette Bombshell™ subscribers.

Want to try another series?
Call 1-800-873-8635 or visit www.morefreebooks.com.

* Terms and prices subject to change without notice. Sales tax applicable in N.Y.
** Canadian residents will be charged applicable provincial taxes and GST.
 All orders subject to approval. Offer limited to one per household.
 ® and ™ are registered trademarks owned and used by the trademark owner and
 or its licensee.

BOMB04   ©2004 Harlequin Enterprises Limited

Silhouette®
BOMBSHELL™

COMING NEXT MONTH

#57 TOUCH OF THE WHITE TIGER by Julie Beard
An Angel Baker Novel

Times were tough in Chicago in the year 2104. As a Certified Retribution Specialist, Angel Baker had the responsibility of making criminals pay for their crimes. But now she and her fellow specialists were the targets—of smear campaigns, lies, even assassination. Not even her cop boyfriend trusted her. Only Angel could bring the mastermind of this twisted plot to justice before she became the next victim.

#58 THE GOLDEN GIRL by Erica Orloff
The It Girls

Real-estate heiress Madison Taylor-Pruitt had it all—money in the bank, the looks and labels to die for and her pick of eligible bachelors. But when her own father was named prime suspect in her coworker's murder, Madison's reversal of fortune seemed like a done deal—until the elite Gotham Rose spy ring asked her to find the real killer. Could the savvy socialite stay on the A-list *and* keep her father off the Most-Wanted list?

#59 BEYOND THE RULES by Doranna Durgin

For once in Kimmer Reed's life, all the pieces were falling into place. She had a dream job with the Hunter Agency, and a man she actually trusted at her back. Then her deadbeat brother showed up on her doorstep with a sob story and gunmen in hot pursuit. Now a major crime organization had Kimmer in its sights and her love life was on the rocks. It was enough to make this undercover gal bend the rules one more time....

#60 MEDUSA RISING by Cindy Dees
The Medusa Project

When terrorists hijacked the *Grand Adventure* cruise ship and took all the women and children on board hostage, the all-female Medusa Special Forces team quickly infiltrated and made plans to take back the ship. But Medusa medic Aleesha Gautier soon found out that one of the hijackers wasn't who he seemed to be. Could she trust his offer of help, or was she bringing a viper into their midst before the final showdown?

SBCNM0805